I0831325

THE FORSAKEN HOUSE AT MISTY VALE

THE FORSAKEN HOUSE AT MISTY VALE

MARY L. PENDERED

Edited and with an introduction by
Gina R. Collia

Published by Nezu Press
Queensgate House,
48 Queen Street,
Exeter, Devon,
EX4 3SR,
United Kingdom.

This edition published 2024

The Forsaken House at Misty Vale first published by Heath Cranton. Ltd., 1932.

ISBN-13: 978-1-917113-02-1

In the interest of preservation, the punctuation and spelling of the original first edition text have been maintained, and the original formatting has been used wherever possible. Only minor publisher errors and spelling inconsistencies have been silently corrected.

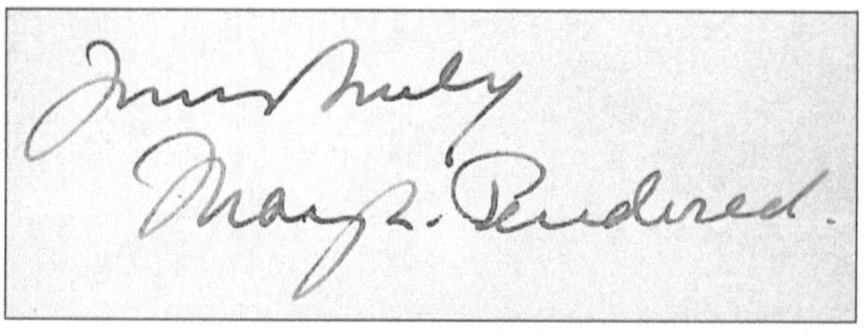

Above: From *The Idler*, 1894.

Below: From a letter dated 1937, collection of Gina R. Collia.

Mary L. Pendered

Author, Suffragist, Pacifist, & Thoroughly Good Woman

by Gina R. Collia

Mary Lucy Pendered was born on 9 October 1858 at 4 Trafalgar Road (now Avenue), in the handsome, middle-class suburb of Peckham, to Thomas Pendered (1834-1906) and his wife, Elizabeth (née Hill, 1829-1885),[1] who had married the previous year.[2] Mary was the eldest of four children; John was born on 1 July 1861, Ellen Sophia followed on 2 June 1862, and William Hill arrived on 15 May 1863,[3] by which time the family had moved to 9 Gloucester Cottages, Park Road (now Parkfield Road).[4]

Elizabeth Pendered was the daughter of William Hill (1789-1870) and his wife, Mary (née Elliot c. 1798-1832).[5] William, one of the most important organ-builders in the country, was one half of Elliot and Hill of Tottenham Court Road, the other half being his father-in-law, Thomas Elliot (1758-1832), from whom he inherited the firm in 1832.[6] The two men built a number of famous organs; Thomas Elliot constructed a 'new magnificent organ' over the altar of Westminster Abbey for the coronation of King George IV in 1821, and in the 1830s the firm of Elliot and Hill built organs at York Minster, Ely Cathedral, King's College Chapel, and the newly-built Town Hall in Birmingham.[7]

Thomas Pendered, who was working as a merchant's clerk and living in London at the time of his marriage to Elizabeth, was born in Wellingborough, Northamptonshire.[8] His father, Joseph Pendered (1799-1872), started out as a cabinet, chair and sofa manufacturer in Northampton, offering 'good fashionable furniture, at a moderate price'.[9] In 1822, Joseph relocated his business to Market Square,

Wellingborough, where he operated as an 'Auctioneer, Upholsterer, and Paper Hanger'.[10] In 1854, he went into partnership with his eldest son, William, and Pendered & Son added 'Estate Agent' and 'Pianoforte Dealer' to its list of services.[11] By the early 1860s, William had taken on sole management of the furniture manufacturing side of the business, while his father acted as auctioneer, valuer and estate agent, and in April 1865, with the aim of giving each area 'undivided attention', the partnership was dissolved and the firm was split in two.[12] William, under the name of W. Pendered & Co., continued as a cabinet maker, upholsterer, and pianoforte dealer. Joseph Pendered went into partnership with his second son, Thomas, who by then had moved back to Wellingborough with his family; they formed J. Pendered & Son, 'Auctioneers, Valuers, Estate Agents, and Accountants'.[13]

When Mary's family first moved to Wellingborough from London, they lived at 38 Cambridge Street.[14] By 1881, they had moved to 'Redwell', Hatton Park, which remained in the Pendered family's possession for the next hundred years.[15] Mary was educated in Wellingborough, attended university extension courses, and studied for the Higher Local Examination, 'of which she passed one group (English Language and Literature)'.[16] Mary's family was a musical one, and she began her career as a vocalist. She studied for three years with a view to the light opera stage, receiving many offers of engagements,[17] but her passion for the stage was 'firmly discountenanced' by her family.[18]

Her family did not, however, object to her performing at various social and charitable events. She composed her own songs, and she regularly received encores and loud applause.[19] She was a favourite at the Temperance Choral Society's concerts, and she performed at and organised musical entertainments laid on at the dahlia flower shows which took place in Wellingborough.[20] For many years she organised an annual *café chantant* in aid of the Amalgamated Society of Railway Servants' Orphan Fund;[21] this particular entertainment had been Mary's idea, and the society's committee left everything in her hands, satisfied that she would always do her best. As a result, each year the event was more and more successful.

Mary first appeared in print as an author in 1886, at the age of twenty-seven. Her first published story, 'Chobertstein', appeared in the *Magazine of Music* in the August of that year, for which she received a cheque for two and a half guineas.[22] The same magazine published 'That Haunting Minor Strain' (1886), 'A Baneful Banjo' (1888), some poems and a short piece on 'Amateur Singing' (1887). In July 1889, her short story 'His Model' appeared in *Belgravia*.[23] In December 1890, 'Attraction!: A Melody in Two Keys' was published in the *Girl's Own Paper*, and the following year 'In Cowslip Time' appeared in the same periodical.

Mary's parents don't appear to have objected to her trying her hand at writing, but when she expressed a desire to move to London to become a journalist they were very much opposed to her doing so. They decreed that, should she choose to pursue such a career, she would have to 'earn her bed and board without financial assistance from home.'[24] Nonetheless, during the first half of 1892, she went ahead with her move to London,[25] took up residence in a single room in Kensington, and for a year 'battled for a place in the literary scheme of things', against her family's wishes and 'undaunted by the starvation wage of £1 a week.'[26] Her first employment was with a society weekly called *Life*, where she wrote a column called 'Twitters, by Tom Tit'; she 'attended weddings, described trousseaux, canvassed for advertisements, corrected proofs, harried the printers, corresponded with all and sundry for the paper, was art critic,' and did 'everything except sweep out the office.'[27] From there, she went on to work as sub-editor for the London edition of the *Detroit Free Press*, where she met Hall Caine and George Bernard Shaw and became 'well known to the denizens of Bohemia'.[28] According to the *Aberdeen Evening Express*, at the age of thirty-five she was 'tall and stately, brown-haired, blue-eyed, of the proverbial English type', and she could 'handle a racquet and a pair of reins better than most women.'[29]

Mary's short story 'Mademoiselle Guarier' appeared in *Christmas Arrows*, the *Quiver* Christmas annual for 1892, and 'A Swerve Aside' was published in the *Quiver* in May 1893. A few weeks later, Griffith, Farran and Co. published her first novel, *Dust and Laurels: A Study in Nineteenth Century Womanhood*, the story of modern woman Vera Grace and her various romantic entanglements. It was dedicated 'to that hybrid complication, the woman of to-day, whose food is fruit of the tree of knowledge of good and evil, and whose drink is the intoxicating ether of freedom and independence'. Described by the *Aberdeen Evening Express* as 'one of the most adventurous books of the season',[30] nearly every English reviewer flattered the author and abused her heroine.[31] 'Despite the undoubted ability of the authoress,' wrote the reviewer for the *Gentlewoman*, 'the heroine of "Dust and Laurels" is distinctly vulgar, which is worse than being "frightfully thrilling".'[32] According to the reviewer for *The Bookseller*, if Vera really was a type of nineteenth-century woman it would be 'so much the worse for the century'.[33] *Black & White* found her 'detestable', and the *Daily Telegraph & Courier* found the novel 'clever but disagreeable'.[34] The lesson to be learned from reading about Vera's entanglements, according to the critic for the *Manchester Chronicle*, was 'that a woman ought to marry young, otherwise she becomes incapable of her mission on earth.'[35]

When *Dust and Laurels* came out, Mary was still doing what she called 'literary hack work'.[36] A year later, after completing her novel *A Pastoral Played Out*, and having 'made her mark as a novelist of power', Mary gave up journalism and returned to her family home.[37] Much later in life, at the age of seventy-five, she confessed that she hadn't liked working as a journalist.[38] Newspaper hack work involved working at 'top speed' to meet deadlines, without time for revision, and it was a marvel to her that any journalist could turn in well-written 'copy' in the short time available.[39] 'I need time to think about what I write,' she explained, 'and I like to revise my work.'[40] At the beginning of her career, the creative part of her work was done at night because she found 'the imaginative faculties are more active and less illusive.' Revision was done in the mornings, when the 'critical and practical side of the mind is most alert and assertive.'[41]

Mary began contributing to Jerome K. Jerome's *Idler* in 1894, when, within The Idler's Club column, she was one of an all-female group of respondents to the question of 'How to Court the Advanced Woman'.[42] Under the heading 'Deferential Domination Required', she suggested that the advanced woman—the new, independent woman as opposed to the 'traditional' one—'does not so much require to be courted as convinced'. The new woman, she explained, would be quite willing to marry if her suitor could 'command her respect, attract her senses, and assure her of his right to her'; she was to be wooed by means of 'a kind of deferential domination, a peremptory homage', by a man whose character 'does not wither under her criticism'.

In 1897, within the same column and on the subject of 'Early Marriages', Mary wrote that it was a very good thing for a man to marry early, as he was 'sure to fall into bad habits' if he failed to do so.[43] But women, she suggested, needed to be 'out' long enough—well into their twenties—to discover who they were. As a result, she supported 'compulsory marriage for men before the age of twenty-five and prohibition of it for women under that age'. She admitted that the former group may feel hard done to, as many women 'lose their charm with their teens', and most men prefer charm to all other things, but she pointed out 'what a good time girls would have before the prime business of life had to be considered!' Early marriage for women, she concluded, could not be abolished entirely without the total abolition of man, and she was not prepared to advocate that… 'at present.'

During the next few years, a number of Mary's short stories were published in various periodicals, including the *Idler*, *New Century Review*, *Longman's Magazine*, *Belgravia*, and *Cassell's Family Magazine*. *To Luniland with a Moon Goblin*, an illustrated fairytale for children, was published in 1897, and Mary's third novel, *An Englishmen*, a tale of class distinction in which the hero is a handsome middle-class tradesman, followed in 1899.[44] *An Englishman* received positive reviews, and William Leonard Courtney thought it to be one of the best books of 1899; he described it as 'a thoroughly wholesome, sympathetic, effective story…handled with considerable adroitness and manifesting no inconsiderable originality of characterisation'.[45] The book sold very well and a new edition was issued by Mills & Boon in 1912.

The Truth about Man by 'A Spinster' was published by Hutchinson and Co., in 1905.[46] It was written as a witty response to T. W. H. Crossland's *Lovely Woman*, in which he insulted women, claiming that only kings and coal porters kept their wives in their proper place; to 'bring the enemy to whatever small sense she possesses', he recommended that ladies should make fewer appearances in public places, have less freedom, and receive fewer compliments.[47] In *The Truth about Man*, Mary claimed that wives are generally content with Man 'as a husband and breadwinner', whereas the variety of spinster who regards marriage as a snare—who avoids it 'while she sports round the rim of it'—has more time and opportunity and is best placed to probe Man as 'a problem', which is what she, as the type of spinster described, then proceeded to do. She based her analysis upon personal experience, having 'been loved by three Americans, two Frenchmen, one German, one Irishman, one Swiss, three Scotsmen, and two or three Colonials'. She did not, she explained, intend her remarks as an attack; no indeed, for 'dear Man himself' is 'certainly most estimable and delightful—till you know him!'

Woman, she argued, was learning from experience that it was perfectly possible to be happy without being married. Marriage was a lottery, and, while there were prizes to be had, women embarked upon the career of a wife knowing that they stood a good chance of experiencing suffering 'and even death'.

> 'Give a woman certain interests in life, something to love and to be absorbed in; insure her a safe income, good friends, enough amusement and variety to spice existence, and see whether she cannot have a real good time without a husband.'

The Truth about Man sold very well indeed and was widely reviewed.[48] The *Review of Reviews* called it 'both amusing and provocative';[49] 'it puts pepper in the eyes and it wakes one up'.[50] The *Northampton Herald* thought it a 'seriously amusing shillingsworth'.[51] 'Her standpoint is distinctly original,' wrote the reviewer for *The Era*, 'and the results are exquisitely piquant'.[52] The *Yorkshire Post*, on the other hand, 'soundly trounced it, spreading themselves in a scathing review', and called Mary 'a minx', which very much amused her.[53]

At some time during 1907, Mary moved to The Fold, Beltinge, in Herne Bay, Kent. In December 1907, when the Railway Servants' Orphan Fund held its annual fundraiser in Wellingborough, the *café chantant* took place without Mary's presence for the first time in seventeen years.[54] Though unable to be present, she continued to write to the *Wellingborough News*, urging support for the fund, in which she still held 'the deepest interest'.[55]

Mary was 'much charmed by the air and surroundings of Beltinge' and advised several of her friends to take houses in the area.[56] She was not, however, much charmed by her neighbours' 'obnoxious and destructive' poultry. In a letter of complaint to the Blean Rural District Council, that was published in the *Herne Bay Press* on 18 January 1908, she complained that her neighbours, for the sake of a few cheap eggs, let their 'irrepressible poultry' run wild in other people's gardens, including her own, scratching up and destroying peas, beans and cabbages.[57]

In June 1908, Mary wrote a long letter to the editor of the *Wellingborough News* on the subject of women's suffrage.[58] The paper printed her letter, which included extracts from a speech made by Israel Zangwill the previous year, but its 'printing wags' included a number of errors that left her open to looking foolish as a woman and less than competent as a writer. In her follow-up letter, she corrected the errors and added:

> 'I have long had the presumption to believe myself capable of using a vote usefully, [at] least as capable as many of the male voters who nightly roll home from their pubs to their long-suffering wives. And I don't believe a vote

would hurt me a bit. If I left my home once in three years to inscribe a cross upon a card at a polling station, I feel sure it would not unsex me in the least, nor rub the bloom off either my modesty or my domestic virtues.'[59]

In February 1909, Mary wrote a letter to the editor of the *Herne Bay Press* on the subject of the newly-formed Women's National Anti-Suffrage League. Was there not, she asked, something extremely ignoble, even cruel, about the actions of women who, on the basis that they were happy with their lot, fought tooth and nail to deprive other women, unhappy with theirs, of the right to improve their condition. The 'so-called sex war', she suggested, threatened to become a war of woman v. woman rather than man v. woman, of 'the idle and happy women v. the hard-working and unhappy'.[60] She urged sympathisers to aid in halting the spread of 'ignorance and uncharity' and suggested that there did not exist 'a single "Anti" earnest enough to go to prison for her faith'.[61] Her letter received a response from Edith Somervell,[62] Honorary Secretary of the Anti-Suffrage League, who explained that women's suffrage—which 'would inevitably increase largely the ignorant vote'—had never been tried in a country which could 'be compared with Imperial Britain' and posed a 'profound danger to the Empire and the race'.[63] Mary's response was to point out the fact that 'Anti' arguments were 'practically the same as those brought forward by Southern Americans in defence of slavery', by people 'afraid of a leap in the dark' and 'satisfied with things as they ought *not* to have been.'[64]

In 1912 and 1913, Mary produced what *The Bookman* called 'her three most characteristic novels of country life in Northamptonshire': *At Lavender Cottage*, *Phyllida Flouts Me*, and *Lily Magic*.[65] Whilst some of Mary's earlier work had attracted criticism for being 'immoral and too daring', these three novels received praise for being wholesome and pretty.[66] Reviewers described *At Lavender Cottage* as a 'fresh, sweet, natural book',[67] thought *Phyllida Flouts Me* 'an uncommonly pretty story',[68] and found *Lily Magic* 'wholesomely fresh and stimulating'.[69]

Mary 'ever declined to write in a groove'.[70] On the subject of the variety in her work, she said:

> 'I cannot and don't want to write two books alike. I cannot make a name for a certain type of book, because my fancy pulls in so many directions. At one moment I long to write, like Herrick, "of books, of blossoms, birds and flowers, of April, May, of June and July flowers." At another time I feel impelled to write of poor, frail, fallen humankind. At another I write of naughty people and their passions. Or again I have a sudden desire to recreate a once living man or woman in biography. Or I feel sententious and wish to spend myself in essays. Or a dramatic inspiration seizes me and I turn to write a play.'[71]

Mary had begun attending, and speaking at, suffragist meetings in Herne Bay in 1909;[72] by the following year, she was presiding over them.[73] In June 1913, 'law-abiding suffragists' held an open-air meeting, 'of a most orderly description', at the top of Beacon Hill, on Herne Bay Downs, and, despite the fact that a cold, north-westerly wind was blowing, a considerable crowd gathered to hear the speeches.[74] Further open-air meetings took place the following month, and by August the ranks of the Herne Bay society had swollen enough for it to become affiliated with the National Union of Women's Suffrage Societies. In October, a committee, president, treasurer, secretary, and chairman were elected, and by the middle of November a social evening was organised, at which the membership rose from thirty-five to forty-nine.[75] The society was renamed The Herne Bay Society for Women's Suffrage, and Mary, the society's president, took on the role of press secretary.[76]

At the outbreak of war in 1914, the Herne Bay suffragists ceased political activity and devoted themselves to war work, with the understanding that their fight for the vote would resume 'with doubly increased vigour' at the cessation of hostilities.[77] Mary registered as a voluntary worker, and she and her sister Ellen instigated the opening of The Soldiers' Club at Mr Mitchell's garage, Beltinge, for 'music, reading and writing', for which a call was immediately sent out for donations of magazines, writing paper, pens, pencils, and 'anyone able to play and sing'.[78] In 1915, the club moved to a large bungalow, which had been lent for the purpose, and wounded soldiers from the Military Hospital found it 'very cosy and homelike'; Mary became chairman of the committee and entertainment organiser, and she took on 'her fair share in the general housework and canteen management.'[79]

A number of years later, at the beginning of the Second World War, Mary wrote of her experiences during the First World War. She was present for the first air raid warning that went out over Herne Bay; it turned out to be the last. It went off at about 11:30 at night, when the first Zeppelin came over, and the whole town turned out into the streets to watch the skies. Mary was in bed and got up to find all of her neighbours in the road. The police could not cope with the crowds, and the warnings were discontinued.[80] The 'continued and violent practising of the big guns' at Sheerness 'made writing a misery to her', and she found the noise so intolerable that eventually, in order to complete the novel she was working on, she was forced to leave her seaside home.[81]

In the spring of 1917, Mary resigned from her position as president of The Herne Bay Society for Women's Suffrage, left Beltinge, and returned to her family's home in Northamptonshire, where she lived with her widowed brother, John, and took on the role of president of the Wellingborough branch of the National Union of Women's Suffrage Societies.[82] Of Mary and her home, Redwell, H. E. Bates wrote:

> 'Wellingborough is to be congratulated in having so charming a novelist as Miss Mary L. Pendered in its midst. One wonders if any of her charm is due to environment, for she lives in a beautiful house, set in gardens that Rupert Brooke would have loved for their beauty and colour and scent. One hardly knows whom to envy most—Miss Pendered or Wellingborough.'[83]

Throughout the war years, Mary continued to write. Chapman and Hall published *Plain Jill* in 1915, followed by *The Secret Sympathy* in 1916, and in the same year J. M. Dent published *The Book of Common Joys*. The latter is a collection of essays, skilfully woven together to form 'a series of reflections which alike soothe and stimulate', 'Written in Autumn Sunshine for those who have left Summer behind', on the simple joys of being alive, reading, country life, gardens, etc.[84] Mary loved the countryside and was a keen gardener, and, though she did not like complete isolation from human contact, she found that 'Silence and leisure are the sweetest things on earth'.[85] She loved 'the joy of morning, and the cool, calm peace of evening' and found both in her garden.[86]

Mary was an active, productive person throughout her life. She was also an extremely clever and amusing one; she had an excellent sense of humour, and she loved to laugh and to make other people laugh with her.

> 'For the sense of humour may we be truly thankful! It is the *sauce piquant* at the daily fare of life, and those who are blessed with it in the smallest degree may feel a deep compassion for those who lack it; though, fortunately for the latter, they are unaware of their deprivation.'[87]

On 11 November 1918, after more than four years of conflict and the horrendous loss of millions of lives, the First World War came to an end. A month earlier, the League of Nations Union, the most influential organisation in the British peace movement, was formed.[88] Its goal was to secure justice, peace and security for all nations based on the ideals of The League of Nations.[89] On 5 September 1920, under the auspices of the League of Nations Union, and under Mary's direction, a pageant and play entitled *The Crowning of Peace* was performed to a large audience at the Wellingborough Palace. Mary said that her reason for producing the pageant 'was her passionate burning zeal for the League of Nations'.[90] It was not only the thought of men lying in agony on the field of battle that moved her to action, for there were worse things than that; men who went to war were changed by the experience and 'had to become no longer human, but wild beasts, before they could do the sanguinary work they were called on to do.'[91] If only people would think about this, she explained, they would come to realise that 'anything to stop war should at least be tried'.[92]

Mary addressed meetings of 'co-operators' in Wellingborough and took every opportunity to voice her support for the League of Nations Union.[93] In April 1924, a *café chantant* took place for the benefit of Greek refugees, in league with the Wellingborough branch of the union, and Mary, its instigator, presided over what turned out to be a very successful event.[94] In November 1924, the Northamptonshire Council for the League of Nations Union was formed; the Bishop of Peterborough was elected as president, and Mary was chosen as one of its vice presidents.[95] She took a great deal of interest in local and national politics; she was a member of the Fabian Society for more than forty years and was present at the victory celebrations when W. G. Cove was re-elected as Labour MP for Wellingborough.[96] Mary cared about the wellbeing of those within and outside of her community, supported equality, and continued to call for peace until the day she died.

Peace was the subject of Mary's four-act play *The Quaker*, first performed in Rushden on 18 March 1926, where it received an enthusiastic reception. In the play, the hero, Nathanael Harlock, is involved in a duel, contrary to the faith in which he has been raised. On the point of victory over his opponent, he lays down his sword and refuses further combat. As she explained to her audience in Rushden, Mary had devoted her life to the cause of peace, and she wrote the play with a distinct purpose: 'to instil a dislike for war', and to force home the principles of which she was so stalwart a supporter.[97] The proceeds from performances of the play were divided between the League of Nations Union and a local cause.[98] *The Quaker* was put on at various locations during the next few years; it was performed at the Royalty in London in November 1930.[99]

The Uncanny House was published by Hutchinson & Co. Ltd. in 1927. It is the story of Peggy and Percy Dacre who, having bought The Beeches—commonly referred to as 'Hell Corner' by the locals—for an absurdly cheap price, move into their new home with their four young children only to discover that it is haunted. The previous owner, old Mr Barker, was a curmudgeon who underfed his dogs to make them vicious and kept his low-paid staff loyal with promises of legacies that never materialised. But, though its owner acquired something of a reputation, the house itself, a villa located on the outskirts of a country town, is an ordinary sort of place; the only unusual thing about it is its lack of electricity. Peggy describes it as 'about as commonplace as they make 'em.'[100]

> 'It was all nonsense, she told herself, about the house being haunted. It was a nice, homely, commonplace sort of house; not a bit the kind in which any ghost would disport itself. Like most of us, she visualized the haunted house as of the Moated Grange type—a place where awful crimes had been committed.'[101]

When strange things begin to happen in the Dacres' perfectly normal home, Percy, a firm unbeliever when it comes to all things ghostly, goes to great lengths to explain the unexplainable. Peggy, on the other hand, is 'sensitive' and becomes increasingly frustrated by her husband's willingness to believe the ridiculous rather than give credence to anything supernatural; 'such a form of scepticism, dependent on believing absurdities, was beyond her ken.'[102]

In comparison with Mary's previous novels, *The Uncanny House* received relatively little attention from reviewers. The *Northern Whig* described it as 'a simple, unpretentious tale, the characters of which are all very natural, likeable people'.[103] 'Mary L. Pendered', wrote the *Dundee Courier*, 'gets the creepy atmosphere of a house in which strange things happen… the dramatic situations are well handled and the eerie feeling maintained'.[104] And the reviewer for *The Bookman* thought that 'those who like to indulge their eerie fancies and give their imagination a little exercise' would enjoy 'participating in the weird experiences' of Peggy and her sceptical, matter-of-fact husband.[105]

Mary had more than a passing interest in the paranormal. It is obvious from her characters' comments in *The Uncanny House* that she had read Frederic W. H. Myers' *Human Personality and its Survival of Bodily Death*, published in 1903, which presented an overview of his pioneering research into the unconscious mind, the nature of human personality, and the possibility of the continued existence of human consciousness after death of the physical body. Myers proposed a theory that explained ghost-seeing as the result of telepathy and the projection of a 'phantasm', whether on the part of a living person—a 'phantasm of the living'—or a dead one. On the subject of ghost stories, Mary wrote:

> 'Whether we believe in the tales or not, whether we are born sceptics or put some faith in psychic phenomena, there are few of us who cannot enjoy a ghost yarn round a Christmas fire. And at this period we have come to prefer the unexplained, the "authenticated" ghost story. Once it was the fashion to account for every occult experience by some absurd anti-climax; but it is not so to-day. We don't like our ghost to be explained away, though he may have a moral reason for his appearance.'[106]

The Forsaken House at Misty Vale was published in the autumn of 1932 by Heath Cranton. 'Written in that delightful style which is so peculiarly Miss Pendered's own', it tells the story of Celia Grey, a fifty-year-old, unmarried writer who, having longed for a home of her own for decades, thinks all her prayers have been answered when she inherits her uncle's house.[107] But Clew Lodge is a property with an uncanny reputation. It is a 'grim and daunting' place, desolate and derelict, having been 'left to the forces of corruption' since Uncle Jerrold abandoned it—because he 'could not stand the whispering'—a decade prior to his death. When Celia begins to hear those whispers too, she feels unable to go on sleeping in it alone; she has 'the horrors' when she tries. Like Peggy Dacre in

The Uncanny House, Celia doesn't have a lot of options when is comes to where she lives; she can't afford to give up her house. But unlike Peggy, Celia *wants* a matter-of-fact sceptic to scoff at her when she senses the presence of something supernatural. So, she invites plain, sensible, no-nonsense Miss Flack to live with her, whose scorn gives her 'a sense of security and support'. 'There is nothing gruesome or repellent' about the book, wrote the reviewer for the *Northampton Mercury*; though 'gripping it certainly is', and its author 'who knows well how to create atmosphere, sustains the suspense admirably'.[108] 'The strangeness of the forsaken house is convincing,' wrote another critic, 'but no one need be afraid to read it before turning off the light.'[109]

During the last years of Mary's life, she devoted only two hours of each day to her writing; 'I am on lots of committees in Wellingborough', she explained to a reporter for the *Northampton Mercury*, 'and I am running this big family here.'[110] She did not work in a study or at a table, preferring to sit in 'a big, deep armchair by the corner of the fireside, her feet on a stool and a board on her knee.'[111] She wrote quickly, as she always had, and thoroughly revised the first manuscript before typing up a second one and revising that. Unlike the early days of her career, she preferred to write during the morning, finding that, though she still considered herself a 'young thing',[112] she was tired in the evening and 'glad to get to bed.'[113] Her favourite authors were Charles Dickens—she was vice president of the Wellingborough branch of the Dickens Fellowship—and Sir Walter Scott; amongst modern writers, she liked Francis Brett Young.[114]

Some time between the autumn of 1935 and the spring of 1936, Mary moved to The Spinney, Great Addington, where she lived alone, with the help of her housekeeper, for the remainder of her life.[115] She remained active in every respect; she was an indefatigable writer and a tireless campaigner for peace and equality. She gave talks to, and produced plays for, the Overstone and Sywell branch of the Women's Institute, and she continued to pen letters to the local newspapers on a regular basis. And, still a practising vocalist and musician at the age of seventy-seven, after hearing all about 'the principles of pianoforte technique as expounded by that incomparable master, Tobias Matthay', she 'resolutely attempted to reorganise her considerable pianistic gifts upon entirely new lines'.[116]

In April 1939, though still recovering from influenza, Mary gave a talk at the Wellingborough Co-operative Old Folk's Party, at which she entertained six hundred or so elderly people. A report of the event appeared in the *Northamptonshire Evening Telegraph* under the headline 'Authoress Attacks the "Mike".'[117] At eighty years of age, she had so clear a voice that she had no need of a microphone, and she made that fact clear; 'Take away that bauble!' she declared, very much to the amusement of her audience. She then proceeded to recite a number of verses, declaring the whole thing 'a great lark'.

Mary was taken ill on 15 December 1940. She was transferred by ambulance to the home of her niece, Mary Stephens, and she died four days later. She was eighty-two years old.[118] Her funeral service, which was 'of simple character' in accordance with her wishes, was held in the old parish church of Great Addington on Monday 23 December.[119] There was no music; the rector, Rev. D. H. Meggy, read the hymn 'Now the Labourer's Task Is O'er' while the congregation stood in silence.[120] Following her cremation at Kettering Crematorium, her ashes were scattered in the consecrated portion of the Garden of Remembrance.[121]

In her will, Mary left all copies of her peace plays—*William Penn*, *The Quaker*, and *Banish the Bogie*—and all proceeds and royalties derived from them to the League of Nations Union. She left various bequests to good causes, including the Society of Authors, for its pension fund, Wellingborough Cottage Hospital, the juvenile branch of Wellingborough Labour Institute, and the Committee of Wellingborough Free Library. She left £50 each to her maid and housekeeper, and '£1,000 upon trust for her former companion, Marta Davies, for life'.[122]

Mary left behind at least three completed manuscripts, 'two novels and a pastoral', which remained unpublished following the outbreak of war in 1939. Two of her books were being translated into Danish at the time of her death, and she was eager to see how they would turn out. And she had also begun writing her memoirs, which, had they been completed and published, would have proved immensely interesting to those who knew her when she was alive and those who have discovered her work since her death.[123]

Mary L. Pendered,
Northampton Mercury, 1933.

In his intimate tribute to his dear old friend, the author Reginald Underwood described his old friend as 'a fine personality... incapable of a mean word or action' and 'utterly honest'; 'There was in her make-up no taint of snobbery... She was, in short, an essentially and thoroughly good woman.[124] Though she was drawn to

Quakerism, Mary found the various religious beliefs and doctrines too limiting and 'maintained a tolerant agnosticism' throughout her life.[125]

> 'She has gone forth into the Great Unknown with her colours flying, bravely prepared to meet the all or the nothing that may be in store.'[126]

Notes

1 *London, England, Church of England Births and Baptisms, 1813-1923.* Peckham was in the parish of Camberwell, London.

2 *London, England, Church of England Marriages and Banns, 1754-1938.*

3 *London, England, Church of England Births and Baptisms, 1813-1923.*

4 Their home on Park Road in Peckham was a couple of miles or so from Trafalgar Road.

5 *London, England, Church of England Births and Baptisms, 1813-1923.*

6 12 Tottenham Court Road, London. *London, England, City Directories, 1736-1943*, 1840, p. 171.

7 *Morning Post*, 2 July 1821, p. 3.

8 Thomas Pendered was living on New Kent Road, Surrey (which now falls within the London borough of Southwark) at the time of his marriage. *1871 England Census* and *London, England, Church of England Births and Baptisms, 1813-1923.*

9 *Northampton Mercury*, 9 March 1822, p. 3.

10 Ibid., and 7 March 1835, p. 2. Wellingborough is a market town in the civil parish of North Northamptonshire.

11 *Northampton Mercury*, 2 September, 1854, p. 2, and 8 April 1865, p. 4.

12 *Northampton Mercury*, 8 April 1865, p. 4.

13 Ibid.

14 *1871 England Census.*

15 *1881 England Census* and *England & Wales, National Probate Calendar (Index of Wills and Administrations), 1858-1995.* Redwell remained in the family until the death of Richard Dudley Pendered, Mary's nephew (son of her brother John), in 1979.

16 *Morning Leader*, 31 July 1893, p. 3. Extension lectures prepared candidates for the Higher Local Examination. The examinations, open to female students over the age of eighteen, were designed to enable women to

demonstrate academic ability in order to apply to study at university.

17 *Morning Leader*, 31 July 1893, p. 3.

18 *Northampton Mercury*, 24 March 1933, p. 12.

19 *Northampton Mercury*, 15 December 1899, p. 7.

20 *Northampton Mercury*, 30 October 1889, p. 10, and 17 September 1897, p. 7.

21 *Café chantant:* Café concert. *Northampton Mercury*, 1 January 1904, p. 5.

22 *Morning Leader*, 31 July 1893, p. 3, and *Herne Bay Press*, 15 April 1911, p. 1.

23 Several poems by Mary were published in the *Magazine of Music*: 'I Love Thee So' (1886), 'The Lady is so Sweet' (1887), 'When Kissing is in Fashion' (1888), and 'A Little Bird Told Me' (1888).

24 *Northampton Mercury*, 24 August 1934, p. 6.

25 *Morning Leader*, 31 July 1893, p. 3.

26 *Northampton Mercury*, 24 August 1934, p. 6, and *Herne Bay Press*, 15 April 1911, p. 1.

27 Ibid.

28 *Northampton Mercury*, 24 August 1934, p. 6, and *Aberdeen Evening Express*, 15 July 1893, p. 2.

29 *Aberdeen Evening Express*, 15 July 1893, p. 2.

30 Ibid.

31 Note to the American edition, published D. Appleton and Company in 1894.

32 *Gentlewoman*, 5 August 1893, p. 20.

33 *The Bookseller*, 5 August 1893, p. 14.

34 *Black & White*, 15 July 1893, p. 20, and *Daily Telegraph & Courier*, 24 July 1893, p. 7.

35 *Manchester Courier*, 18 November 1893, p. 10.

36 *Northampton Mercury*, 24 March 1933, p. 12.

37 *Morning Leader*, 19 March 1894, p. 1. *A Pastoral Played Out*, originally intended as a three-volume novel, was completed in the spring of 1894 and published by Heinemann one year later.

38 *Northampton Mercury*, 24 August 1934, p. 6.

39 Ibid.

40 Ibid.

41 *Northampton Mercury*, 24 March 1933, p. 12.

42 *Idler*, vol. VI, August 1894 to January 1895, pp. 204-206.

43 *Idler*, vol. XII, August 1897 to January 1898, p. 425.

44 *To Luniland with a Moon Goblin* was published by Sanders, Bellamy and Sons of Wellingborough. The illustrations were provided by Dorothy Hope, a child of ten. *An Englishman* was published by Methuen and Co.

45 *The Bookman*, October 1919, p. 6.

46 Previously published by the *Lady's Realm* as a 'series of fearless and trenchant papers', beginning in the November 1904 issue.

47 *Morpeth Herald*, 20 June 1903, p. 7.

48 *Northampton Mercury*, 24 August 1934, p. 6.

49 *Review of Reviews*, August 1805, p. 204.

50 Ibid.

51 *Northampton Herald*, 11 October 1912, p. 13, in response to the publication of a new cheap edition.

52 *The Era*, 21 September 1912, p. 27.

53 *Northampton Mercury*, 24 August 1934, p. 6.

54 *Wellingborough News*, 3 January 1908, p. 6.

55 *Wellingborough News*, 25 December 1908, p. 5.

56 *Herne Bay Press*, 18 January 1908, p. 2.

57 Ibid.

58 *Wellingborough News*, 19 June 1908, p. 5.

59 *Wellingborough News*, 26 June 1908, p. 5.

60 *Herne Bay Press*, 20 February 1909, p. 6.

61 Ibid.

62 Wife of the composer Arthur Somervell and grandmother of the novelist Elizabeth Jane Howard.

63 *Herne Bay Press*, 6 March 1909, p. 6.

64 *Herne Bay Press*, 13 March 1909, p. 6.

65 Published by Mills & Boon. *The Bookman*, October 1919, p. 6.

66 Ibid.

67 *Bedfordshire Times and Independent*, 27 December 1912, p. 5.

68 *Dundee Courier*, 20 February 1913, p. 7.

69 *Northampton Mercury*, 17 October 1913, p. 5.

70 *The Bookman*, October 1919, p. 6.

71 Ibid.

72 *Votes for Women*, 5 November 1909, p. 93.

73 *Herne Bay Press*, 19 March 1910, p. 8.

74 *Herne Bay Press*, 28 June 1913, p. 1.

75 *Herne Bay Press*, 7 February 1914, p. 1.

76 Ibid.

77 *Herne Bay Press*, 13 November 1915, p. 1.

78 *The Bookman*, August 1916, p. 118, and *Herne Bay Press*, 21 November 1914, p. 8. Ellen Pendered, then Mrs Harley, was by then living at The Sheeling, Beltinge.

79 *Herne Bay Press*, 6 November 1915, p. 1, and *The Bookman*, August 1916, p. 118.

80 *Northamptonshire Evening Telegraph*, 12 December 1939, p. 6.

81 The Bookman, August 1916, p. 118.

82 *Herne Bay Press*, 1 December 1917, p. 1, and *The Common Cause*, 7 December 1917, p. 435.

83 Dean R. Baldwin, *H. E. Bates: A Literary Life*. Susquehanna University Press, 1987, p. 55.

84 *The Sphere*, 13 May 1916, p. 30.

85 *Northampton Mercury*, 24 August 1934, p. 6. She wrote, in *The Book of Common Joys*, 'my own ideal of the country does not figure complete solitude', that 'would not spell happiness for me' (p. 221).

86 *Northampton Mercury*, 24 August 1934, p. 6.

87 *The Book of Common Joys*, J. M. Dent, 1916, p. 189.

88 The League of Nations Union was formed by the merger of two older organisations: the League of Free Nations Association and the League

of Nations Society. The new union's first president was Viscount Grey (*Daily News*, 25 October 1918, p. 3).

89 The League of Nations, founded on 10 January 1920, was the first worldwide organisation dedicated to securing world peace and security via international cooperation.

90 *Midland Mail*, 10 September 1920, p. 2.

91 Ibid.

92 Ibid.

93 *Northampton Mercury*, 18 February 1921, p. 10.

94 *Northampton Chronicle and Echo*, 5 April 1924, p. 7.

95 *Peterborough Standard*, 28 November 1924, p. 10.

96 *Herne Bay Press*, 15 April 1911, p. 1, and *Northampton Chronicle and Echo*, 19 January 1925, p. 8.

97 *Northampton Mercury*, 26 March 1926, p. 5.

98 Ibid.

99 J. P. Wearing, *The London Stage 1930-1939: A Calendar of Productions, Performers, and Personnel*. Plymouth: Rowman & Littlefield, 2014, p. 66.

100 Nezu Press edition (2024), p. 3.

101 Ibid. p. 35.

102 Ibid. p. 92

103 *Northern Whig*, 22 October 1927, p. 9.

104 *Dundee Courier*, 29 November 1927, p. 5.

105 *The Bookman*, January 1928, p. 236.

106 Light, 28 December 1912, p. 618, quoting an article from the Daily Chronicle.

107 *Northampton Mercury*, 7 October 1932, p. 9.

108 Ibid.

109 *The Spectator*, 1 October 1932, p. 40.

110 *Northampton Mercury*, 24 August 1934, p. 6.

111 Ibid.

112 *Northampton Mercury*, 27 December 1940, p. 8.

113 *Northampton Mercury*, 24 August 1934, p. 6.

114 Ibid. She contributed may articles to *The Dickensian*, see vols 37-38, 1941, p. 163.

115 Mary moved to Great Addington, about seven or eight miles from Redwell, when she was seventy-seven years old, some time after 9 October 1935, see *Market Harborough Advertiser and Midland Mail*, 27 December 1940, p. 5. In April 1936, she placed an advertisement for a housekeeper in the *Peterborough Standard* (17 April 1936), by which time she was living in Great Addington. So, she moved some time between October 1935 and April 1936.

116 *Market Harborough Advertiser and Midland Mail*, 27 December 1940, p. 5.

117 *Northamptonshire Evening Telegraph*, 17 April 1939, p. 3.

118 *Northampton Mercury*, 20 December 1940, p. 10. Mary died at Beechwood, Overstone Park, the home of her niece Mary Stephens, née Mary Elizabeth Pendered, daughter of John Pendered.

119 *Market Harborough Advertiser and Midland Mail*, 27 December 1940, p. 1, and *Register of Cremations*, Crematorium at Rothwell Road Cemetery, Kettering.

120 *Market Harborough Advertiser and Midland Mail*, 27 December 1940, p. 1.

121 Ibid.

122 *Northampton Mercury*, 28 February 1941, p. 3.

123 *Market Harborough Advertiser and Midland Mail*, 27 December 1940, p. 5.

124 Ibid. Reginald Underwood was an author and musician, known for Bachelor's Hall (1934), Flame of Freedom (1936), Hidden Lights (1937), etc. He lived in Finedon, a few miles from Mary's home in Great Addington.

125 Ibid.

126 Ibid.

"Oe'r all there hung the shadow of a fear,
A sense of mystery the spirit daunted,
And said, as plain as whisper in the ear,
'The place is haunted.' "

TO
ALL LOVERS OF THINGS PAST AND
PITIFUL, HIDDEN AND MYSTERIOUS

CHAPTER ONE

THE forlorn old house stood half-way down a flinty by-road between tall Sussex hedges set above a deep cutting in the rock, through which the way had been hewn. There was no other habitation near, and it lay far back from the high wall of local stone that concealed its pitiful garden. The land dipped a little so that the house seemed to squat there, as if crushed by its dolour, and from the wrought-iron gate in the wall only its roof and tall chimneys, with those windows that frowned just under the eaves, could be seen. On the north side a row of aspens guarded it, severe-looking sentinels now, in their naked sharpness: on the south a row of Lombardy poplars, pointing skyward as severely, suggested a heavenly aspiration. The walls enclosed house and garden on three sides, but on the fourth, at the back, a thick hedge of unkempt yew stood between them and a dense wood, of which it seemed a part.

The visible roof told the story of the mansion's age in its uneven lines and the size of its greenish-grey stone slates. They hung over the ivy-clad walls of the house, forming a long scowling eyebrow to the narrow, diamond-paned windows of the second storey. One small dormer window above them looked like the single eye of a Cyclops, and two great chimney-stacks rose from the roof at either end of the house; while a third, set below the ridge behind, showed only its pots, whitened, as the rest of them, by the excretions of many jackdaws.

The square stone porch did not come into sight until one had reached half-way down the paved way to the door, a pavement so choked with grass and weeds that its slabs were to be felt rather than seen. Like the house, this porch was clothed in thick ivy. Here Celia Grey paused to survey her property, with a pang of dismay that had a sharp edge of fear.

For it looked desolate and derelict, this ancient house, as if, deserted by man, it had been left to the forces of corruption; the birds about its chimneys seemed waiting to pick its bones. The garden appeared, if possible, even more wretched than the house. It had the forlorn and pitiful aspect worn by all things, human or inanimate, that man has ceased to tend and care for, the thing dishonoured and forgotten. The sorrow of it sent a throb of pity through Celia's heart, tincturing all selfish concern. Her first thought had been: "How shall I ever bring order into this chaos?" Her second, "How shall I ever dare to live in so lonely and gruesome a place?" But now this wave of compassion flushed away all other feeling, and she thought how dreadful it was to be left like this, unloved, neglected, forsaken; and in its old age, when it most needed care and affection! To her the old house had taken on the personality of a sentient being. She thought of its past, when it had been young and beautiful, with happy people laughing within its walls. A sudden yearning came over her to comfort and restore. It was hers now, and she would love and cherish it as long as she lived.

She noted how the front garden still struggled against its hard fate, its overwhelming battalions of weed and coarse grass. A little clump of daffodils by the path had sent up a sheaf of green spears with a couple of buds just beginning to duck before breaking into gold. From under a straggling lilac-bush there came a sweet breath of violets.

Celia felt the hope and promise of spring, and it revived her spirits. It was good to be reminded that the long days and short nights were on their way hither; not the melancholy autumn with its mists and dripping rain, ushering in the darkness and cold of winter.

For, there could be no denying, the old house was grim and daunting. It gave her no cheery welcome, appealing only to pity. As she approached it Celia felt the chill of a strange dread. If ever a house looked haunted, this one did. She was not superstitious and had never dabbled in the occult, but a sentence spoken by her uncle the last time she had visited him, nearly a year before his death, had clung to her mind, and came forward now as she looked up at the hooded eyes of the windows.

"I could not stand the whispering."

She had smiled at the words then, and he, too, had smiled as he uttered them, adding: "The aspens, you know. In summer time they keep up a continual sound like whispering, and it seemed to get into the house."

Celia had no idea, then, that he had left Clew Lodge and its small estate to her, his only brother's child. There was no reason why he should do so, since he had not lived on friendly terms with his brother, or offered his niece any help when she had been forced to earn her living. While her mother lived Celia had felt bitter towards him, and it was only within the last few years that she had gone, at his request, to see him. She had always been fond of Aunt Emily, his wife, who was kind and affectionate, giving Celia small presents when she could; but for Uncle Jerrold it had seemed that no creature could feel affection, not even his own children.

He had lived at Clew Lodge for some years, having bought it, Celia believed, because it was cheap. But when his wife died, nearly ten years ago, he had left it suddenly and gone to live in Surrey, in a new house, with a new housekeeper and new servants. Why he had done so nobody knew. Celia thought it was because he could not bear the house that reminded him of his lost wife. She gave him credit for, at least, so much feeling and affection, unlovable and selfish as she knew him to be. And she would fain give him credit, also, for some remorse over his treatment of her father, accepting her legacy as a reparation.

At first the news of it had given her a sense of discomfort. He had two children, a son and a daughter, who, she felt, ought to have inherited his property, although she knew they were estranged from him. They had both married against his wishes, and he had refused to see them again. Their mother visited them surreptitiously, and it was probably her unhappiness over his unnatural conduct that finally caused her death. He had isolated her in Clew Lodge, and she had pined there. But Celia had no idea how deep the antagonism between father and children had been until she wrote to her cousin Charles, offering to give up the legacy, to which she felt no right, and received his reply:

> "Neither my sister nor I want to own the house that killed our mother, and that she died in. I am thankful to say, we are both independent of our father's whims. He did not act as a father to us, and we do not want his property. It is very considerate of you to offer to make it over to us, and we appreciate your generosity. But, in any case, it would only be a white elephant, since neither of us could live in it, and it is extremely unlikely that it will ever find either a tenant or a purchaser. We hope, however, you may be lucky enough to find one or the other."

The doubt implied here had not struck her as sinister at the time, but it did now that she looked up at the house. Assuredly it did not look a house to let easily, even in these days when antiquity counts for so much and the country is ransacked for old dwelling-places. There was something rankly forbidding about it, suggesting ugly, hidden things: skeletons in cupboards; rats and mice and death-watches in the wainscoting; deadly fungus in the cellars; disease germs in unclean corners. It was off the main road, too, and its drainage was worse than doubtful. She was still ignorant of its material qualities, good or bad. All she knew about it was that it was old; that her uncle had lived and her aunt had died in it; that it had not been inhabited for nearly ten years. Whether Uncle Jerrold had tried to let or sell it, she had no idea. But she had a very definite idea of what she meant to do with it, now that it was hers. She meant to live in it.

"Sell it! Sell my house, the only home possible to me after twenty-five years without one!" she had cried to herself. "Never! It shall be my own dear home, and I will live in it till I die. No more lodgings for me."

The letter from Charles had brought a great relief to her mind. For a few days she had feared that her offer would be accepted and had groaned over the troublesome conscience that had obliged her to make it. When his refusal arrived she had danced for joy.

Twenty-five years in the homes of other people had brought her the full significance of that sacred English word. Two rooms had seemed but an apology for the lack of a home, and only a shade better than a room in a boarding-house. She had tried herding with a number of other women in a 'Ladies' Residential Club,' and the experience had left a distasteful memory behind. It had taught her to realise that she was one of the old-fashioned women who yearn for a home of their own. The word 'home' set a chime ringing in her heart and made pictures in her fancy. She had not yet had an opportunity of learning that it must be shared to yield its full essence and quality; that, with one person alone in it, home is not much more than a warm cushion is to a cat. The name enthralled and hypnotised her. Over and over she had said to herself: "My home—my own home," and it was not until she stood in this forlorn garden, looking at the forlorn house, with its air of ghostly possession, its pitiful aspect of decay, that her rosy dream began to dissolve in a mist of doubt, her fire of joy to die down in ashes.

As she went up to the door and inserted her key in the keyhole a shudder went through her. She thought of her uncle's words: "I could not stand the whispering," and her cousin's grim suggestion that no one would ever live in the house. A sudden inclination to turn back on it and flee held her for a moment, irresolute. But pride of possession came to her aid. It is an instinct we all share, and the thought of entering her own house sustained Celia in her instant of panic. It gave her a thrill of excitement that banished all fear. And when she looked round on the hall she had entered, Celia felt that here was, if not exactly the realisation of her dreams, a home to be proud of.

The low square hall, stone-paved and wainscoted in oak, had a ceiling supported by huge rough-hewn beams, from one of which hung a big brass lamp hung on chains, all coated with dust and verdigris. To the left ascended a really beautiful carved oak staircase which turned sharply about half-way up, as if to avoid the next floor into which it had been cut, and not quite succeeding, since anyone going up had to duck the head to avoid it. The only light in the hall entered from a dim and dirty fanlight over the front door and a window upstairs.

The sudden change from bright daylight to this twilight gloom was somewhat depressing, but she was subtly cheered by the beauty of the staircase, the old-world charm of the hanging lamp and a moulded arch over a passage-way to the right, leading to the back of the house. For Celia was one of those fortunate mortals who can be exhilarated by the sight of beauty or by the suggestion of romance. And when she found, at the end of this passage, a long panelled room with a narrow latticed window and an ingle-nook, her spirits rose absurdly. She decided at once that it must be her sitting room.

The window, which had a deep, low seat and shutters to fold back, showed the great thickness of the wall in which it was set. It looked out upon a courtyard fringed with old trees. The fireplace that crouched back under the arch of the ingle-nook was of old-fashioned, but not ancient, design, with bars in front and a hob on either side. It lay between two low cupboards, under tiny windows fixed in the wall. Celia concluded that the room had probably been once the housekeeper's sanctum, as it was almost surrounded by cupboards, and had a door in the wainscoting that opened on to a narrow staircase, leading to two small rooms above. Another door led into a dark passage and the kitchens, with butler's pantry, larder and lamp-room. In the further kitchen there was a huge open fireplace with a cauldron, hanging by a chain over the hearth, and a copper in one corner; while in the other corner by the hearth a big, rounded oven was built half in and half out of the wall. The remains of a wood fire still lay on the stones of the wide chimney-place, indicating how hastily the house had been left. From a door at the back Celia went out into the courtyard, wherein she found dairy, laundry, brew-house, stables and other offices. All three places, and the kitchens, were stone-paved like the hall, and a large stone mounting-block stood outside the stables.

At the far side of the court wide wooden gates, in a sad state of disrepair, led out upon a carriage track that ran beside the house, under the aspens, to the road. It had been cobbled, but grass and moss had so obliterated the stones that it showed but a green way. Through a wooden door in the wall, overshadowed by an ancient chestnut tree, just beginning to show a delicate fretwork of red buds, she reached the garden beyond; but one glance was enough to send her back, shuddering, to the house. The awful jungle that met her eyes appalled her.

Inside the house the air was stifling with the odours of Time's diseases—decay, woodworm, maggot, mice, moth—all the corrupting creatures of the lower world. She tried to open the windows, but most of them had been warped by damp, and stuck fast to their casements. The only thing to do, therefore, was to set all the doors open, and this she promptly did. The fresh wind of March, with its reviving tang of late winter frost, winged its way through room and passage like a laughing spirit, a purifying angel, and Celia followed it.

She found four reception-rooms on the ground floor, all facing the eastern front of the house. The two on either side of the wide hall opened into each other, and one, on the south side, had great folding doors leading to another room. When these were laid back, the two formed a spacious apartment; but none of the rooms were very large, and one at the back, with a long narrow window, she surmised had once been a powder closet. Another, with empty book-shelves, had obviously been used as a library, and one as an office or gun-room.

The floors were of oak and had probably once been polished. They were now thick with dust. From all the corners long cobwebs hung, and the wide hearths were a litter of dirt and small twigs from nests in the chimney. There were shutters to all the windows, but even when these were thrown open but little light shone in, so covered up were they by the rank ivy growth outside; so crusted were their lozenge panes with the dirt of years. They were, however, more easily opened than others Celia had tried to unfasten. A few odd pieces of furniture had been left by her uncle here and in other rooms, and for these, although of little intrinsic value, she was thankful. Having to furnish the house with but little money to spare, she welcomed any old chair or table that, through haste, carelessness or intention had been left behind in her uncle's flitting. He had left the place to her "with all its contents and appurtenances," so said his will, so she might conclude there had been intention; although, in such a singular man, it was impossible for anyone to know the springs of his actions.

In one of the reception-rooms she found an old sofa upholstered in faded damask: one of those sofas that graced Victorian parlours, with a scrolled headpiece, a hard back, high legs and a narrow seat, unsprung and comfortless. This Celia hailed with joy as a welcome contribution to her sitting-room. She would have the legs shortened, and thought that, with a mattress and cushions, it could be made sufferable. An armchair to match was equally uncomfortable, having lost its springs, but they could be put right; and a small, low chair, with a high back worked in faded wools, delighted her. She fancied poor Aunt Emily had worked it in her girlhood. In one of the cupboards she found a roll of carpet and her expectations rose; only to sink again as she saw that it was a mass of moth-maggots and falling to pieces.

As she was crossing the passage between two of her rooms there came a crack and her foot sank into dust. The wood-beetle had eaten through a board, and again she realised how time and decay were devouring slowly the ancient neglected house. She thought of Hood's "Haunted House," with its meretricious description of the ravages made by moth and maggot.[1] Stray lines of the gruesome poem floated through her mind: "All ruined, desolate, forlorn and savage"... "the cobweb hung across in mazy tangle"... "the subtle spider hung—like a spy on human guilt"... she could only remember fragments and the recurring stanza:

"O'er all there hung the shadow of a fear,
A sense of mystery the spirit daunted,
And said, as plain as whisper in the ear,
'The place is haunted.' "

It was horrible to think of all the greedy forms of life that were eating away the poor old house as disease eats away the human organism. She visualised the slow work of corruption, and shuddered to think how it was still going on, as it had gone on for ages. The house was haunted—yes, it was undoubtedly haunted by invisible and yet material agents of destruction, tiny creatures that gnaw and pierce and feast on decay. The 'death-watch' beetle was no doubt under her feet where she stood, undermining the strong timber set to the building of the house hundreds of years ago. How was she to fight it? How save her precious house from crumbling to dust? Her affection grew with every moment in these drear rooms, fed by a deep well of compassion.

Upstairs she found unexpected treasures. The bedrooms on the first floor were delightfully quaint. She stepped down into them, and, at the next step the floor seemed to rise up beneath her feet, so uneven were the oaken boards. The largest room at the top of the staircase she decided should be hers. It faced the east, looking over a great stretch of country to the sea. Celia loved an

[1] Thomas Hood, *The Haunted House.* London: Lawrence and Bullen, 1896. A ghost story told in verse.

east room to sleep in, where the sun smiled on the opening hours. And in this one she found, to her delight, an enchanting old four-post bedstead hung with chintz of a Jacobean pattern, birds with long tails in a flowery setting—"dirty but delicious," she said to herself rapturously. Moreover, in the dark corner she found a still greater treasure, an ancient tall-boy. It gave her startled surprise. She could understand her uncle leaving a four-poster in the house, but not so valuable an 'antique' as a tall-boy. Surely he could not be unaware of its value. But, since she could never find out why he had done so, she dismissed the problem as enigmatical and referable only to her uncle's unaccountability.

Besides the long, low window in front, the bedroom had a small one on the south side, looking out over what had once been a small sunken lawn with a sundial in its midst. Beyond it were trees, and she recognised, for the first time, that long rank of aspens to which her uncle had alluded. They were naked now and silent, grimly stark in their winter beauty of reticulated branch and twig, exquisite form without colour. Celia began to wonder whether the room she had chosen for her own was the one her uncle had slept in, her aunt had died in. He had spoken of being disturbed by the whispering of the aspens, but she seemed to remember that he had added: "One hears them everywhere, even through the walls." She thrust out of her mind the suggestion that had risen there, resolving to think no more of it.

"And, after all," she told herself, "if I do hear them whispering, why should it trouble me? Would it not be summer music, sweetly reminiscent of lovely things—hamadryads dancing in sylvan scenes, of nature's ever-springing sap and fertility? There would be birds in the branches, nests perhaps, full of little chirping babes to chime with the aspens' gentle rustling." She smiled at the thought and at the poet's image of woman "variable as the shade by the light quivering aspen made."[2] Yes, certainly, the aspen was a poet's tree. It looked poetic even now, in its dainty nudity, with the last rays of the setting sun gilding some of its branches.

This room led into another and that, again, had a door leading to a back room. Celia found that the passage outside from north to south of the house had only a door here and there in it. She found, to her dismay, there was no bathroom, although a small room had been set aside as one, with a tap in the wall for cold water, which, she found, had first to be pumped up to a cistern in the roof from a well in the courtyard. As she had surmised, there was but primitive drainage, and she wondered, not for the first time, that her uncle had ever been content to live there under such conditions. She could only account for his doing so by a general acceptance of his queerness; the oddness of his temper, his avarice and love of solitude.

She went back to her chosen bedroom to think out her problems and, sitting on the low window-seat that was a feature in all the rooms, set in the windows' deep embrasure, she took out notebook and pencil from her bag. What was to be done first was the main consideration. She could not possibly live in the house until it had been made habitable, as it was not at present. What *must* be done and what could be left, she had now to decide. With the limited income of not much more than a hundred a year, which was all she could command when she resigned her present situation, Celia knew that only the most absolutely necessary work could be done. And how to pay for repairs and improvements she hardly knew. It would certainly involve a drain on her slender capital. If only Uncle Jarrold

---

[2] From the poem 'Marmion: A Tale of Flodden Field' by Sir Walter Scott.

had left her a little money with the house! she thought, and then frowned at herself. 'Much wants more.' She ought to be grateful for a home, and she was. But the sanitation must be made safe—she was sufficiently endowed with the perceptions of her time to know that—and goodness only knew what that would cost! Decay must be arrested, the water tested and the garden cleared, at least near the house. She could do a good deal herself at week-ends, if she could find a cottage in Misty Vale to take her in cheaply while she worked. And perhaps a village man and wife could be found to help her, at a moderate charge. The village was not near. She had been told it was a mile and a half from it to Clew Lodge, but it had seemed a good deal further. To a London woman, used to omnibuses and pavements, the hard road, up and downhill, had been fatiguing. But she would soon get used to that.

As she sat, absorbed in her notebook and plans, a sudden loud crack disturbed her reflections, and she had a shiver of the nerves. Sometime in her life she had been told that cracking furniture is ominous, either of death or disaster. But she knew that wood was apt to expand or contract under changes of atmosphere, and concluded that the ancient tall-boy felt the change of air from the window, which she had succeeded in opening. Nevertheless, she thought it was time to depart. The light was beginning to wane, and she did not desire to remain after dusk had fallen. Rising, she stood to look once more round the room, at the quaint bedstead and chest of drawers, the littered hearth with its rusty fender, the uneven boards and open door into the next apartment. She must shut that door. As she crossed the room to do so, she noticed for the first time that, set on each side of the fireplace, were two doors, evidently opening into cupboards or closets, and she went to open them. They were locked, and the first one she opened was empty.

She rejoiced in it, as every natural woman rejoices in finding a good, serviceable cupboard with shelves and hooks. The further one, however, that standing further from the window and in darker shadow, was not empty. As she opened the door, something fell out of it at her feet.

It gave her a shock, and she uttered a little cry, shivering with uncontrollable fear. A moment later she was ready to laugh at herself, for she saw on inspection that there was nothing to be alarmed at. It was only an old garment that had fallen off its hook. And yet, as she took it up, gingerly, to examine it, the tight clasp of her scalp did not immediately lessen. She felt a vague, mysterious terror.

A faint perfume lingered about it. Was it of lavender, bergamot or ambergris? From the open cupboard, too, it was wafted, mingling with the smell of dust and decay that pervaded the house. It seemed to create a mystical atmosphere in the dim room, as if invisible forms were softly moving and breathing about it.

Who could have left this old silken robe in the cupboard? From its fashion Celia knew that it could not have been one of her aunt's dresses. She laid its period to the eighteenth century, the day of full skirts and pointed stomachers, of frilled elbow-sleeves and much exquisite embroidery. There was something almost indecent to her in the leaving of so dainty a garment to rot in a musty closet. It was like leaving a beautiful dead creature unburied. At least it should have been laid in lavender and enclosed in a drawer or chest, as it certainly should be now. The mystery of its sudden appearance perturbed her. She could in no way conceive how it came to be left there, in a house that had been unoccupied for ten years; and before then occupied by a plain, matter-of-fact couple, the last persons in the world, she reflected, to have acquired a fancy dress, or to have kept one from a day long past.

No, she decided, the gown had never belonged to her middle-class family. At the time it had been made no woman of the middle classes would have possessed such an elegant garment, and—she smiled to herself—her ancestry had no records. She scarcely knew the status of her great-grandfather, although she remembered hearing that he was a man of some culture who collected books. She had some of his books now. But he was certainly humble and obscure; he had not even made money. That this embroidered damask gown, so perfectly cut and shaped, could ever have belonged to one of her ancestresses, Celia concluded, was unthinkable. To whom, then, could it have belonged? Surely it had not remained there during the years of her uncle's tenancy, carelessly hung on a peg near the door, not even hidden away in the depths of the big closet.

Taking it to the window, to get the last of the waning light, she turned it over and over with her hands that shook a little. The colour was barely discernible—a lavender-grey broidered with flowers of a deeper shade. The lace about the shoulders was yellow with age and dropping to pieces. As she handled it something fell from its folds, a wisp of white, and she stooped to pick up a small handkerchief, bordered with exquisite lace. In one corner there was fine embroidery, a monogram twined by tiny flowers. The wan light made it hard to decipher, but Celia thought it looked like L.S.

The room had taken on a ghostly look and seemed colder. Celia hastily folded the dress and laid it, reverently, in the bottom drawer of the tall-boy. Then she left the room and went downstairs quickly. A sense of impalpable presences set her nerves quivering again, and she had but one desire—to find herself in outer air.

Once there she breathed more easily. It was still quite light outside, deliciously fresh and invigorating. She began to feel hungry and thought she would just have time to eat something from a village shop before catching the omnibus that was to take her back to the nearest town, where she had to catch a train a little later. There was plenty of time before that train went, and the omnibus was not due for an hour at least. So she walked once round the house to take a last look at it before starting—*her* house, the home she had so long yearned for.

At the back she noted its formation, as she had not done when examining the courtyard and its premises. It seemed to her more beautiful than the front, with its huddle of penthouse roofs, its queer stone slates and tile-hung gables, its enormously tall chimneys. As she wandered round it a great curiosity possessed her as to its history, of which she had heard no word. And it must have a history. Standing there in its jungle of monstrous vegetation, with its mournful air of brooding over the past, its shrouded and relinquished beauty, she felt that it knew something she did not know—something nobody knew: that it guarded a secret of its own. Would she ever discern it?

But dusk was falling, with its soft, slow swoop of grey wings, and soon dark night must follow, to blot out the beauty and disorder of the old house, and leave but the outlines of its roof and tall chimneys against the purple sky. Celia turned reluctantly from it and went through the iron gate to the road, abandoning it to its solitude and silence.

What would happen there, when night reigned and no living creature was nigh to see? Would the old habitation wake up as soon as her back was turned, and live a queer, ghostly life of its own? As she turned to close and padlock the gate, she raised her eyes to the roof, with its row of narrow windows just visible beneath, and started violently. For it seemed to her that a strange luminosity shone from the small panes of those windows, as if they caught some light from a sky in which there was no light. Was there a moon rising somewhere behind the trees, or was there indeed, as her fancy had suggested, Something walking in those still, deserted rooms she had recently quitted? With a slight shiver she turned to look up behind her. And yes, there was a moon—a young moon sailing up, like a little silver boat, in the watchet blue of the March sky. She felt a sense of relief as she turned back for one more glance at her house. In the pearly light the great chimney stacks, under their cloak of ivy, looked like hovering genii. Two jackdaws were perched on one of them, and said "Jack" very loudly two or three times. She could not remember whether two jackdaws boded good or ill, but had a lurking fear it was ill. She started up the road quickly, breathing the callow air with enjoyment, and soon found herself in the village of Misty Vale, where the ground sloped upward steeply in its one long street.

CHAPTER TWO

SHE walked along it till she reached a somewhat new red-brick building with "Co-operative Stores" over its doors. Therein she found a buxom woman and a lean man serving customers. The woman came towards her, and Celia asked for something to eat—cake, biscuits, anything they had. Her smile made a friend at once, and she was served with tea as well as cakes. Then she asked the woman whether there was anyone in the village who would take her in for week-ends and help put the house in order; adding that she was coming to live at Clew Lodge.

The man drew near, interested. Both he and his wife remained strangely silent for a few moments. Then he said in a hesitating voice:

"Did I really understand you to say, ma'am, that you are coming to *live* at Clew Lodge?"

The slight emphasis on the word 'live' struck significantly on Celia's ear.

"Yes, certainly," she said. "It is my house now, having been left to me by my uncle, Mr. Jerrold Grey. But I find it in a terrible state of dirt and dilapidation. It will need a great deal doing to it before I can go in."

"You really mean to live there?"

The note of astonishment in the woman's tone was matched by the wonder in her wide eyes as she asked this question. It was so obviously a question.

"I certainly am. Is there any reason why I should not?" demanded Celia.

Again there was a silent pause. The man moved away and pulled out a drawer. After a few moments his wife said, hesitatingly: "It's got a bad name."

"Why has it a bad name?"

Celia spoke a little tartly. Were these people trying to set her against her house?

"I can't tell you exactly, ma'am. But nobody in this village would live in it for gold untold. I wouldn't myself. But maybe it's all fancy."

"Oh, you mean a superstitious reason." Celia smiled. "I think I can live that down. I am not superstitious."

"That is a good thing, ma'am. And I'm sure I hope you will never have cause to be," the woman said, with significance.

Celia made no further remark till she had paid for her tea and thanked the worthy couple for their civility. She asked again about a lodging, and they promised to make enquiries for her. Leaving her address she went out, feeling as if the gloss had been rubbed off the shining pride she had felt in her house. She had persuaded herself, on her way to the village, that the eeriness of Clew Lodge had existed solely in her own imagination; she had actually seen nothing in it to evoke a fear of the supernatural. But when the Store manager and his wife looked at each other in that queer way, and the woman declared she would not live in it for 'gold untold,' all the perturbation of spirit Celia had felt in the house returned with doubled force.

"It's got a bad name"—the words recurred to her many times as the omnibus rumbled its noisy way along the tarred road; and the more she thought about it, the more Celia wondered if she would ever dare to live in Clew Lodge. She imagined herself alone there at night and shuddered. But her commonsense determined her to cast aside vain imaginings. Was she going to lose her longed-for home and live for the rest of her life in lodgings because of foolish talk by the ignorant and her own unbridled fancies? No. Celia was resolved on a wiser course. She would make her home there and snap her fingers at superstition, either in herself or others.

She found, during the next few days, however, that, whether the old lodge was haunted or not, it haunted her: rising before her mind's eye day and night. She saw its tall chimneys, its windows like dark, lidless eyes, its heavy mantle of dull green and jumble of uneven, grey-slated roofs, all the time she was showing off expensive gowns to preposterously over-dressed women in the show-room where she was a saleswoman. And at night the vision became even clearer; so clear, indeed, that she seemed to be moving about the deserted rooms and opening the deep cupboard wherein lay strange raiment. In her dreams she found herself struggling to open windows that some unknown force held against her, and unlocking closets full of queer clothes and uncanny secrets. In one of these dreams a skeleton fell out, and her shriek of horror awoke her. She found her skin clammy with fear.

The Stores manager, whose name she learnt was Moore, sent her the address of a couple who would lodge and board her for week-ends, if she would be content with cottage fare. So the next week Celia went to Misty Vale again, with a suitcase, and arranged with them to go there. The man was, luckily for her, the village jack-of-all-trades, able to turn his hand to carpentering or plumbing or gardening. His name was Coles, and his wife was a clean, tidy woman with energetic tongue and hands. She helped Celia turn out two rooms, scrubbed their floors and washed their windows, talking all the time in her genial Sussex brogue, which Celia found delightful. She enjoyed her week-end with this decent couple, and slept well in their tiny room under a thatched roof. She was unused to housework, and found it, with the mile and half walk to and from the village, very fatiguing.

It was necessary to call in expert help from Millborough for overhauling her drains and water-supply, both clogged up and not in working order. But all the rest of the work was done during the next six weeks, by the Coles pair and herself. She made up many yards of rose-coloured casement cloth into curtains for her windows; thinking, by its brightness, to symbolise her hopes and give the old house a look of renewed youth. This occupied her evenings during the week, and thrilled her with joy when they were finished and hung, those in her sitting-room and bedroom first. Coles cleaned all the nests and rubbish out of the chimneys, mended broken floors, loosed the windows from their moorings, and cleared away immense heaps of rubbish from the garden. The acrid scent of bonfires filled the air of the house and was pleasant to Celia; a wholesome country smell she had almost forgotten.

Mrs. Coles had not worked many hours with Celia before she diffused the information, accepted in good faith, but without any sign of fear, that Clew Lodge was haunted. With a smile of happy credulity on her round face, she added an observation of her own to the effect that she would liefer have ghostes in a house than mice and spiders and beetles. It was plain that, although she credited the uncanny belief shared with the rest of the village, it did not scare her in the least; for when Celia asked if she would mind sleeping in the house alone, Mrs. Coles replied with a jolly laugh: "Not me! I'd sleep anywhere and shouldn't see nor 'ear nothink. It 'ud take more than a ghost to wake me up when once I'm asleep."

She was a rare comfort to Celia, and her husband was a marvel. He seemed able to do everything about a house, in his own time and in his own way. He brooked no interference.

One day, when they were hanging the rosy curtains in Celia's room, she told Mrs. Coles about the silken robe she had found in the closet, and received some light on the subject. The woman, it appeared, had been called in to help with the removal of her uncle's chattels from the house, and it was she who had hung up the dress there. When she, with Mr. Grey's servants, had been clearing the rooms ready for the removal-men, they had wanted boxes which they found in the attics above; and in one old wooden trunk they had discovered this beautiful old garment. What to do with it they did not know, and when they appealed to the master he told them to hang it in a cupboard and leave it there. He was not going to be bothered with it.

"I thought he looked a bit queer when I mentioned it to him," Mrs. Coles added, "and he muttered something to 'isself about 'letting 'em have it and welcome.' I've thought since he must have meant the ghostes. It may have belonged to one of 'em. *He'd seen summat*, had the master. We was sure of that. He went so sudden and seemed so funny."

So that part of the mystery was solved. The gown had lain there, in its coffer under the roof, before her uncle took the house, perhaps for centuries. And still the other questions remained unanswered: to whom had it belonged and why was it there? This last query was destined to have no immediate reply.

Celia was getting used to the uneven floors and the jerk of finding a short step down into her bedroom from the passage outside. She no longer received a slight shock and gave a trip. And when the chimney was cleared of rubbish and a fire of longs sent its ruddy glow over the four-post bedstead and polished oak boards, it looked a lovely and lovable apartment to couch in. A few cheap mats relieved its austerity, and she found, in one of London's many second-hand shops, the necessary furniture.

When the room was prepared, swept and garnished for her body to repose in, and the room downstairs at the back made into a comfortable sitting-room, Celia began to feel that, at last, she had really a home. It had seemed like a dream at first: one of those cloud-capped towers that dissolve into mist, so impossibly ideal as to challenge belief. And then, only then, a hope, once cherished and long since thrust aside, began to revive in her heart. The hope of again writing a book.

Between her twentieth and thirtieth birthdays Celia had written two novels, in a glow of joy and faith. The first was crudely written and constructed, but vivid. It arrested a passing attention, was well noticed and moderately well read, fluttered in the air for a year or two and then fell to earth, as autumn leaves fall, to die forgotten. The second was not crude, nor was it vivid. She had matured in thought, and was full of ideas that jostled and obscured her drama. Whether it be that the public loves drama better than ideas, or whether her ideas were presented ineffectually, who shall say? But this second book did not flutter its wings in bright air, to fall naturally as the autumn leaves fall. It dropped to earth straightway and its publishers lost heavily by it. Perhaps one cause of its failure may have been Celia's dreadful earnestness. He first novel had humour and gay life in it. When she was writing the second the shadows of sorrow and dread had closed about her. She lost both parents and her home. Fear of the future weighed her soul and clogged her mind. She had but a tiny income, her father's life insurance to live on, and the problem was how to increase it. She could not, under these circumstances, write lightly or brightly; too much depended on the book. A success would have solved her problem. Failure crushed her almost to despair. And never since then had she found courage, or time, to write another novel. She tried to use her pen in journalism, but failed there dismally. Her brain did not move quickly enough. She earned next to nothing, and wearied in the attempt. As she told herself, her springs were broken, her elasticity gone with her hopes. For 'your sad heart tires in a mile-O!' and Celia's body suffered from her heart's lassitude.[3] After teaching for a few years in private families, for she had no scholastic qualifications, she had decided that this was no life for her and had sought a situation in a shop, so that she could, at least, call her time and two rooms her own. Tall, graceful and of gracious manner, she had soon found a post as a show-woman in one of the larger London shops, and there she had remained to this day; living in fair comfort on her increased income, and able, also, to put by a little money.

Had it not been that her springs were broken, Celia might have found time in the evenings to take up the creative work she had laid down; but, although she wrote an occasional article—chiefly on dress or shopping—for one of the women's magazines, the wings of her fancy would soar no further. A sure sign that she lacked the divine fire, since genius is unquenchable. Her gift was a lesser one, and it was wrapped in a napkin of distrust and humility; she had no faith in her own power, and needed stimulus to evoke inspiration. That stimulus had been withheld up to now, and she was like to carry her gift in its napkin to the grave.

But now the creative impulse stirred again, and she felt the sudden *élan* which is like nothing else on earth.[4] It was as if she

---

[3] Based on the lines 'A merry heart goes all the day,/Your sad tires in a mile-a.' William Shakespeare, *The Winter's Tale*, Act 4 Scene 3.

[4] Élan: vigorous spirit, enthusiasm.

became alive after being dead and buried; a resurrection of the spirit set free from trammels; no longer earthbound to the body's needs only but reacting to the stimulus of a house, leisure, silence and solitude, conditions dear to the artist, in which the mind can work freely and meditation can take its tranquil way.

There would still be work to do, earthly claims to be met, as she was well aware. Half the hours of her working day would, probably, have to be spent on keeping her home clean and satisfying the demands of her body. But it would leave her mind free, and she would be her own mistress. Even her duties would be self-imposed. There was manna in that thought, and sparkling wine. She had liberty of action, her time was now her own, and the precious boon of silence. All these last years in London had taught her how to value that 'vanishing lady,' sweet, soft, winged Silence; only to be found now in far corners, in bye-lanes and backwaters of our land. It would always be still, and for that stillness she had long yearned. "Only to be quiet—able to hear my own thoughts!" she had prayed; and now that prayer was answered. How she blessed the churlish old uncle who had bestowed upon her this precious jewel of silence! In her gratitude she could have offered masses for the repose of his soul.

In the village she began to know a few people. Besides Mr. and Mrs. Moore of the Stores there was Mrs. Cobb, a widow, who kept the Post Office and a sweet-stuff shop combined. She was a gentle, melancholy soul of decorous mien, and a fondness for dwelling on the war as a topic of conversation. There was Job Johnson, host of the Packhorse Inn, and his buxom spouse, always ready to provide her with a meal and let her sit by their own fire to enjoy it. Always ready, moreover, to provide polite conversation with the meal, and tell her all she wished to know about Misty Vale and its inhabitants.

She observed in all these good folk a lively curiosity about her and her house, though they exhibited less frankness than Mrs. Coles, and did not inform her that Clew Lodge was haunted. She felt this implied, however, when they spoke of it, which they very often did.

"Your uncle went away rather sudden, miss, didn't he?" one would say, with a furtive glance at her face as she replied; and another would observe, significantly, that it was best not to believe all that you hear. Or that it was strange how houses, like people, got bad names. She knew that these remarks were directed towards one end—that of luring her to ask questions; but she studiously refrained from doing so. She had heard enough to know what they were thinking.

One day she ventured to ask Mrs. Coles whether it would be possible to induce one of the village girls to live with her. The reply was not encouraging.

"I'm afraid not, miss," the good woman said, apologetically. "You see, gals don't like sleeping in, anyhow, and it's not very likely one would care to sleep in an 'ouse what was said to be 'aunted. They're a pack of silly cuckoos."

This was, for so unpretentious a person, delicately put. If Mrs. Coles had spoken exactly what was in her mind, Celia would have been told that no girl in Misty Vale would sleep in Clew Lodge for love or money, and no parent would wish her to do so. But the kindly soul had by now grown anxious that this gentle maiden lady, who was so nice and friendly, and who worked so hard beside her, was beginning to dread sleeping alone in her house, however stoutly she affected to despise the ill rumours about it. The next time Celia came down, Mrs. Coles offered to spend the first few nights with her and 'settle her in' when she came for good; an offer Celia was sorely tempted to accept. But she had resolved to conquer all foolish fears, and it seemed to her that if she dared not sleep alone the first nights she would be letting fear conquer her. So she thanked the good soul for her friendly offer and declined it.

She made no pretence, however, of not feeling nervous. "I've never slept in a house alone before," she told Mrs. Coles, "and I expect it will be a nerve-racking experience. But I must begin as I intend to go on. There is one thing, however, I should like, and that is your little black kitten, the one you say is such a sportsman. He will be company for me and chase the mice away, if there are any. I am more frightened of mice and rats than of any ghosts. Or, at least, I dislike them more."

This, of course, was mere bravado; but a cat was almost a necessity in this house, where the rodent tribe had evidently once swarmed, and might do so again. The black kitten, a chubby eunuch of six months or so, was the son of a hunting mother of no particular breed, and reported by Mrs. Coles to be 'death on rats' even at that early age. She made Celia a present of him forthwith, and he was promptly christened Lob-lie-by-the-fire, a name accurately appropriate, as he promptly showed.[5]

March had come in like a lion and his exit was by no means lamb-like. But his keen airs, laden with the scent of burning wood and weeds aforesaid, and with a sweeter whiff of violet and pine, seemed to aerate the old house and drive out its ill odours. In the wood beyond her hedge of yew Celia snuffed up the delicious fragrance that belongs to woods only and can be found nowhere else: the very breath of Maia, goddess of growth, from her green living fire and peaty earth. Celia thought of Shelley's lines:

---

[5] Lob-lie-by-the-fire: a kind of brownie or house elf. A rough, hairy, good-natured goblin of the hearth (see *The Devil and His Imps: An Etymological Inquisition* by Charles P. G. Scott, 1895, p. 118).

"And each flower and herb on earth's dark breast
Rose from the dreams of its wintry rest . . .
"And their breath was mixed with fresh odour sent
From the turf, like the voice and the instrument."[6]

The image pleased her, the flower voice, the accompaniment of earth, and she asked herself how she could so long have remained in a city when all this ineffable beauty and sweetness was calling for her. "I could have been a dairymaid," she thought, "or even have taken service in a garden."

It was her last week-end in the Misty Vale cottage. Next week her term at the shop expired, and she had given up her London rooms. April would see her established in her own house. She walked round it till she was tired and the dusk fell. Some order had been restored in the chaos, although much remained to be done. She picked a twig of aspen, its budding leaves all crinkled like a baby's hand, with a couple of daffodils, just breaking, and a tiny bunch of short-stemmed violets, 'sweet as Cytherea's breath,' to take back with her to town.[7]

Waking in the night she caught a faint whiff of that sweet breath and was back in her garden, to dream there again.

---

[6] Percy Bysshe Shelley, 'The Sensitive Plant'.

[7] Based on the lines 'But sweeter than the lids of Juno's eyes/Or Cytherea's breath', William Shakespeare, *The Winter's Tale*, Act 4 Scene 4.

CHAPTER THREE

WHEN the ramshackle car of the Packhorse Inn had discharged her with her luggage at Clew Lodge, and Job Johnson had carried her heaviest boxes upstairs, Celia felt an exultant thrill such as she had not experienced since the day, thirty years or so before, when she believed love had come to crown her life with fulfilment. This new thrill was different, of course, not so ecstatic and overwhelming; but a very joyous one, none the less. She felt as if she had entered into a little kingdom of the blest "whose right there was none to dispute."[8]

Mrs. Coles had greeted her with a beaming smile of welcome, and the little black kitten had run to meet her, which made the home-coming all the more ideal. In her sitting-room a log fire blazed, with aromatic odour, and a kettle sang on the hob. In the ingle-nook a small table stood, white-clothed and covered with cheap china of a pretty yellow hue. The room had a western aspect, and a sinking sun cast red shafts through the small panes of the window. It was a dark room, for the window was a narrow one, and the wainscoted walls were almost black with age. But with fire and sunlight combined at this hour it looked very cheerful. Looking upon it Celia felt a glow of sweet content.

A small square of carpet occupied the middle of the polished floor; two armchairs were set on each side of the hearth—one she had found in the house, the other a low wicker-chair she had

[8] Based on 'I am monarch of all I survey,/My right there is none to dispute,' from 'The Solitude of Alexander Selkirk' by William Cowper.

bought cheaply and fitted with cushions. A round rosewood table she had picked up at a sale stood in the darker shadow of the room, and her little tea-table by the fire. There were a few other articles of furniture, odd chairs, a desk, several bookcases, filled with her precious books, and, between the window and the door to the kitchen passage, the old sofa she had brought from one of the reception-rooms and made comfortable with a mattress and cushions. It had quite an imposing air of elegance now, and seemed to look down upon the humbler furniture of the room.

In the ingle-nook lay a mat supplied by Mrs. Coles and made by that lady's own hands. It was composed of scarlet and black snippets of cloth, knitted together in a diamond pattern, and taken, as she informed Celia, from old soldiers' and gentlemen's coats. Since the khaki had come in for soldiers, it was easy to get hold of cast-off red coats, and she had made many of these mats, of which she was extremely proud. The one in front of Celia's hearth had been intended to replace one in her own kitchen that had become rather the worse for wear; but as it was just what Miss Grey wanted, nice and cosy to the feet, Miss Grey must have it, and she would make herself another. She would not take any payment for it, but Celia had presented her with a photogravure and an old black cloth coat to cut up for another mat, with which Mrs. Coles had appeared delighted. She loved the picture of a child caressing a dog, and thought it was 'sweet.' There was no such beautiful picture in her house, she said, and it would be a treasure.

A tight posy of spring flowers was stuffed into a gaudy vase and occupied the middle of the small table by the fire, with a large fruit cake. To the cake were added a plate of hot buttered toast and two boiled eggs, a pot of jam and a solid chunk of cold boiled bacon: every inch of the table was covered. Celia laughed at the sumptuous spread, and begged Mrs. Coles to partake of it with her. They sat eating and talking till the light failed and the lamp had to be lighted. It was a new one, bought from the Stores, with a painted china body and a pink frosted bowl. There was no gas in the village, and none in Millborough either, Mrs. Coles said. They still had oil-lamps in the streets, as their forefathers had. But there were incandescent mantles now, and new kinds of lamps, besides wonderful cooking stoves that used scarce any oil and were cheaper than coal fires.[9] Celia realised that she had still much to learn, for she did not yet even know how to light, or put out, a lamp: still less how to clean the wick and fill one. Mrs. Coles would come and teach her that in the morning.

She enjoyed the woman's genial talk; her Sussex brogue, her rather cracked voice, her eager interest in everything, her homely knowledge of useful things, her bits of news and gossip. After so many years among sophisticated people, especially after those *blasé* and languid women who were her employers' principal customer at the shop, she could appreciate to the full this alert and simple creature whose eyes shone as she talked about the new omnibus that was coming to run through the village to the sea, ten miles off, as soon as the seaside season began, and who was counting already on pleasures to come, in visits to the shore, paddling, shrimping, listening to bands. Celia had never seen such shining light in the eyes of those who had bought gowns in the show-room, wisps of silken fabric, exquisitely broidered, for thirty, forty, fifty guineas, or more. Her own eyes had often gloated on the beauties she had displayed, but her customers showed little enthusiasm, even if they

[9] The incandescent mantle was placed over an Aladdin lamp burner and produced a much brighter light than a bare flame.

felt it. Mrs. Coles expressed far more over the picture Celia had given her. And when she left it was as if some light had gone from the room.

Twilight had fallen outside, and to catch the day's last glimmer Celia went into her garden with the black kitten. He was a very friendly kitten with an abnormally loud purr, a wide face and a thick tail. He followed her like a dog and kept rolling over on his back at her feet, as if to arrest her steps and claim her attention. She felt that his blithe spirit would help her to banish any vapours that solitude might evoke. Her nerves and imagination would, she knew, play tricks with her; every creak of the old woodwork, or gust of wind through a keyhole, would have its terrors. But with Lob-lie-by-the-fire purring by her side she could laugh at them.

Half-way up the garden she paused to adore her property. "My house—my very own house!" she murmured sentimentally. There is a sweet joy in feeling thoroughly sentimental. And as her eyes rested on the long slope of a penthouse roof, the odd tiled gables, the roofed well, with its bucket, in the courtyard, she added, "My lovely old house," for its beauty of line and colour was undeniable. And beauty was a great refreshment to her spirit.

Along the flagged path that wound about the garden, thyme was beginning to spring between the blocks. When Coles had cleared them of weeds and made a way for her feet, Celia had commanded certain roots to be left. In the borders the pink and blue stars of hepatica were till shining, with here and there a belated crocus, snowdrop and scilla; but these were giving place to primrose and forget-me-not. The trees and hedges were just clothing their exquisite naked branches in a veil of green lace. There was still much hard work to be done in the garden, but the thought of that did not intimidate Celia. Rather it exhilarated her.

She would not, for worlds, have found it all neat and trim, requiring no further effort on her part.

The south-east wind sighing through her trees changed suddenly to an icy blast, swooped over the yew hedge by which she was standing and caught her unprepared. She shivered and ran down the path to the house. It had grown quite dark, and she was glad of the lamplight from her room to guide her back to the house.

What a delicious soft light it was, she thought, so full of romance, so different from the searching cold light of electricity. A tender mystery lurked in its yellow beams; the very shadows cast by it were full of poetic suggestion. There was a time to come when she would long for the power to flood a room with silver light at the touch of a button in the wall; but at this moment Celia felt nothing but the charm of old association, the lamp's sweet evocation.

In her bedroom Mrs. Coles had lighted a fire; by its rays, and two glimmering candles, Celia unpacked her boxes. This done she made up her two fires, drew her curtains and wrote letters to old friends. They were full of joyous description, and as she wrote, she thought "I can describe things again, make pictures in words as I could long years ago. My gift has come back." She found herself longing to go on expressing what she saw and what was in her mind. Images rose vividly, ideas crowded. It was past nine o'clock when she shook herself free from this glamour and finished her last letter, becoming aware that she was hungry and also tired. She made herself a bowl of bread and milk, gave some to the black kitten and, after raking out her fire, lighted her bedroom candle.

As she lowered the lamp and watched it die slowly a slight tremor shook her. Up to that moment she had not felt nervous at all, but the slow flickering out of the friendly light seemed to call up powers of darkness and she felt suddenly afraid. Vexed with herself at this weakness she muttered, "You fool!" and took up her candle in one hand, her kitten with the other. A gust of wind moaned through the keyhole at the front door as she passed it, and blew her skirts softly as she mounted the staircase. Who does not know that curious sensation of a grisly something behind which is apt to assail us in the dark? Celia felt it now, and it caught her breath, but the purring kitten in her arms comforted her with living warmth and friendliness. At the top of the stairs her candle fluttered and caused her a horrid dread lest it should go out, leaving her in darkness; but it rose again and, once in her room, the firelight cheered her. She lighted two more candles on her dressing-table and, to save them from the draught from the open windows, closed the lower parts of the casements. All the vague rumours she had heard about the old house drifted into her mind, and she found it no easy matter to shake them out of it. The queer shadows thrown by fire and candle-light helped to maintain them.

She was glad to get into bed, after throwing a fresh log on the fire and setting a match to a night-light by her bed. In her London lodging, Celia's room had always been lighted by a street-lamp outside, and by the passing flares of motor vehicles. Now the blackness of her windows and the dead silence were terrifying, and she was glad of the little fairy-lamp Mrs. Coles had bought for her, with its box of waxen tablets. With Lob lying warmly at her feet, purring and washing, and with the night-light shining "like a good deed in a naughty world" beside her, Celia grew happily drowsy and lost her fears.[10] she thought of the old rhyme that had comforted her in darkness when she was a child:

---

[10] Based on the lines 'How far that little candle throws his beams!/So shines a good deed in a naughty world.' William Shakespeare, *The Merchant of Venice*, Act 5 Scene 1.

"There are four angels round my bed:
Two at my feet, two at my head."

and smiled at the lovely fancy. She had always loved the conception of angels—exquisite spiritual messengers, all white, with soft, long-plumed wings—and the four pillars supporting the roof of her great square bed, their curtains moving slightly in the draught from the top of a window, suggested those shadowy forms. She sank to sleep in the soft feather bed, lulled by the silence, for she was very tired.

But her rest was fitful and disturbed. She began to dream at once, and her dreams were strange. In them she saw people moving about her room, in attire like to that she had found in the closet, moving and whispering. She could not hear what they were saying, though sometimes they came quite near to her bed. And, although she felt no definite fear, she was worried because they did not speak to her and because she could not speak to them. She could not be sure, moreover, whether they were many or only one, and this, again, worried her. The queer, indefinite trouble of nightmare oppressed her till she suddenly threw out her arms and awoke. The whispering was still in her ears. It was like the singing of the sea to its shingles and, for one moment, she wondered whether the wind might have carried that sound from ten or twelve miles off. But no. It must have been in her ears only, for as she regained full consciousness the sound died away and the abysmal silence of the country night fell again, smothering her with its heavy mantle. Celia turned over on her pillow and, concluding that she had dreamed a dream compounded of her own fancy and the uncanny suggestions she had heard, set herself resolutely to sleep again. She had other dreams and wakings in a fright, but finally she slept peacefully till broad daylight, when the chorus of birds outside her windows awoke her.

CHAPTER FOUR

IN the amber light and spicy air of an April morn Celia felt blithe as a lark and free from all care. The night's strange dreams and tremors seemed but a foolish memory for which she took herself to task. At her age, she told herself, one should not be so easily influenced by outside suggestion. No doubt the words of her uncle, "I could not stand the whispering," recurring again and again in her mind, had bred a microbe of fancy there which rumour, aided by loneliness and silence, had nourished into a chimæra. There had been nothing really to disturb her; no sight or sound, except in her dreams. She laughed at herself and spent a happy, busy day in her house and garden. Nobody, seeing her there, in a pretty, flowered print overall, like a graceful frock, with her crisp and wavy russet hair hardly touched with silver, her fair skin pink with exercise, and showing but a few wrinkles round her shining eyes, would have taken her for an elderly woman. She had a girl's face, full of eagerness and expectation; her teeth had remained sound and white; she had the spring and elasticity of youth still in her muscles, and her slender figure had poise and grace. Women who do nothing but lounge do not preserve their shapes as those who are active, either through choice or necessity. Celia had not found time to indulge in those health-giving sports which the modern woman enjoys, but she had been obliged to exercise her muscles in other ways, and had not been able to spend much time sitting or lounging. She had been a healthy pretty girl and was a healthy pretty woman. Only when she was very weary, discouraged or unhappy, did her eyes lose their greenish sparkle and her skin its youthful glow.

Perhaps it was in her eyes that youth lurked longest. These were of that curious grey-green so often found with auburn hair, long in shape and shaded with burnished lashes, which gave them a starry look. They were always full of light, even when half-closed in laughter, shining like a running brook in a dark wood. And when those eyes laughed people had to laugh with them, just as they have to laugh with a child, however naughty it is. Eternal youth danced there.

She worked all day in the garden, cutting away ragged growths, tearing up weeds, making a bonfire. There is no greater fun than making a bonfire. No one disturbed her. Few persons passed her house, and when any did so the high walls and hedges made them invisible to her, and she to them. That was in front. In the back garden no one could see her at all. The black kitten gambolled about her, caught a young bird, for which he was reprimanded, and a mouse for which he was praised. How is a baby cat to understand such ethics of right and wrong? Lob was perfectly satisfied in both instances, of course, and probably congratulated himself most on catching the bird, as the bigger feat. Celia cooked two large potatoes in her bonfire and ate them for dinner, with an inch of butter, pepper and salt. Potatoes have a heavenly taste when cooked in a bonfire and eaten after strong exercise.

But gardening is tiring, and when one has chopped and hoed and wheeled a barrow and forked up a fire for three or four hours, one is very glad, if a woman of fifty, to go indoors, sink into a chair and rest. Celia dozed by her fire after tea, and felt almost too tired to rouse herself at 8 o'clock and get her supper. The fire she had neglected sank low. She decided to go to bed and save fuel.

The wind had fallen and a deep silence lay over the house. It was an eerie silence, like the dead pause before a storm. Suddenly, for no accountable reason, Celia began to tremble. A great horror came over her and was quite uncontrollable. She was just about to put out the lamp when this spasm took her. Turning up the lamp again she threw a fresh log on the fire and sat down by it. Her legs simply refused to carry her upstairs.

"This is ridiculous—this is madness," she muttered. "If I give way to it, I must surrender all I have gained—my home, my freedom, my leisure—and go back to London, to a shop and two rooms!"

She bit her lip and tears sprang to her eyes. Was it not a wretched thing to be dominated and mastered by a senseless fear that had its rise purely in superstition—the silly superstition of ignorant people? She got up again from her chair, kicked the log off the fire and stamped upon the floor.

"I will not give way to it—*I will not*," she swore to herself, and stalked away upstairs, her kitten under her arm, with the air of a soldier going into the front line of battle.

All night she lay and trembled, asleep or awake. Awake she was able to control her fear, to some extent; asleep it controlled her—and her dreams. Every time she woke up it was to find her skin wet and cold, as with the dews of death. It was not until dawn made her flickering nightlight effete that she was able to shake off the nightmare and take command of herself. With the coming of full day she slept dreamlessly until Lob waked her with piteous cries to go out.

Celia dressed and went downstairs feeling as if all the starch had been taken out of her; as tired as when she had gone up the night before. In the glass, as she coiled her thick hair, she saw a face with little youth left in it, pinched and pallid, whose reddish eyelids lay heavily over dull eyes. Her very hair seemed to have lost its crispness and colour, showing grey threads that had not been visible in it before.

At breakfast she pondered over the night's experience and came to a decision. She could not go through such a night again: she could not pass another alone in the house. Her nerves had given way, she told herself, bitterly. She had heard of people having 'the horrors'—dipsomaniacs who fancied they saw demons, or crawling things about their bed. That might be the next stage of her diseased imagination; she would be fancying she saw things! Certainly that sudden spasm which had come over her last night was very like 'the horrors' she had heard described. She could not face that mental condition again. What, then, was she to do?

Like a flash of light on dark waters a name floated into her consciousness.

Miss Flack.

She had no idea why Miss Flack entered her mind. She had not seen her, nor thought of her, for a very long while. It must be years since she had said to herself: "How I should love to rescue that poor soul from bondage and give her a better time!" Never dreaming then that she might ever be in a position to fulfil her desire in this respect. Now she remembered that desire.

In all her life Celia had never felt more sorry for anyone than she had felt for Miss Flack. In the first place, Miss Flack was plain, to ugliness. In the first bloom of her youth she could never have been anything but plain, and now she was over middle age, probably older than Celia, as she certainly appeared. She had a flat face, small eyes, absurd nose, like a dab of putty, thin, straight, dull hair, muddy skin, stumpy figure. Only when a smile lighted Miss Flack's face did she look even moderately prepossessing; and that was very seldom, as she rarely smiled. Indeed, what had she to smile about?

Celia asked herself, for the dreariest of lots had fallen to Miss Flack, and the only joy that she could ever have known was that vaunted (but somewhat over-estimated) one which comes from doing one's duty.

Celia, like most pretty women, felt an intense compassion for plain women, especially when she was a girl. It seemed to her then that plainness must mean despair and misery. Now she was older, this view was moderated. She had seen many ugly women married, and unmarried ones leading jolly, independent lives. But her pity for Miss Flack had not been entirely based on the little woman's plainness. Like Celia, she was impecunious, and the only way she had been able to earn a living was by taking a post as companion. By ill chance she had lighted on a selfish, garrulous invalid named Crump, and had lived with her for many years, fearful to change her place lest she might not easily get another. Her employer never spared her in any way: demanded her constant attention; gave her as little time off as Miss Flack would be content with; expected her to be always sympathetic and to manage a large house and servants on the least possible expenditure of money. This lady saw to it that she was personally supplied with every luxury; Miss Flack was allowed none. She had to shiver in cold rooms while Mrs. Crump lay in a bedroom with a warm fire; and only when she fancied herself well enough to get up were fires lighted downstairs.

Celia had not seen Miss Flack for several years, but had a very distinct recollection of the last time she had called upon her, when she realised, with a sharp pang of compassion, what it must be like to occupy such a position as hers, subordinate to a thoroughly peevish and selfish woman; how it must feel never to hear one's Christian name spoken, but always to be Miss Flack, or Flacky, week after week, month after month, year after year. To live with a querulous invalid, unloved and unconsidered—what a fate!

Perhaps one reason why the name of Miss Flack had suddenly come to her mind was the fact that, before she left London, Celia had heard from an old friend that Mrs. Crump was very seriously ill and might not need a companion-housekeeper much longer. She had thought then: "Whatever will poor Miss Flack do if Mrs. Crump dies? She is too old to find another post easily." It occurred to her now that Miss Flack might, at this very moment, be free and glad to come to her at Clew Lodge, if not permanently, at least for a time.

When, therefore, she had eaten her breakfast and set her rooms in order, Celia walked down to the post-office and sent the following telegram to Miss Flack, with a prepaid answer:

"Can I see you if I call to-day?

Celia Grey: Clew Lodge, Misty Vale, Sussex."

She would not risk a train journey to call on Miss Flack without this assurance of finding her. But she was resolved either to go and see her that day, and, if possible, to bring her back here; or to make a clean breast of her fears to Mrs. Coles and ask her to sleep in the next room to hers (as she had offered to do) until she, Celia, could find someone to live with her.

Her hopes were, however, centred now on getting Miss Flack to come to her. No one could be a more suitable companion, she reflected, than this lady: a dry, matter-of-fact, undeflected little person, with no tiresome nerves or fancies to trouble her. Celia smiled to herself, as she imagined how Miss Flack would flout the idea of ghosts in a house, and scoff at Celia for indulgence in such nonsense. Living, as she had for years, with a hypochondriac, nursing doubt and scorn of her fancied complaints, she would not have much sympathy with superstitious fears. And Celia felt that she wanted someone to scoff at her.

The answer to her telegram came at 2 o'clock: "Yes, pleased to see you." At three Celia raked out her fire, locked up her house and went to catch the omnibus to Millborough, leaving Lob with Mrs. Coles, to whom she said that she was called away for a night or two. Her destination was Guildford, near where her old home had been, in the heart of Surrey loveliness, and it gave her a pang of nostalgia to walk in the long hilly street she had once known so well. What ages ago it seemed since she had gone shopping with her mother in that street; strolled with friends in that town; danced, a very happy girl, in a hall she passed on her way.

When she was shown by a prim maid into Mrs. Crump's chilly drawing-room, Celia began to feel a sense of awkwardness she had not felt before. She had planned what she meant to say to Miss Flack, but now it seemed hard to say it. She wanted Miss Flack to come and stay with her, with a view to remaining permanently, but how explain why she had thought of this? When the little woman came into the room, looking plain to grimness and rather forbidding, Celia had to swallow her first words and repeat them. Miss Flack's face was white and pinched; the tip of her short nose was red, and her hands, half encased in mittens, still redder. She was pathetic and yet rather intimidating. Celia felt tongue-tied.

"You are surprised to see me Miss Flack," she managed to say, when she had shaken the cold hand stretched out to her; "but not so surprised as you will be when I've told you why I am here. Indeed, I am surprised at myself."

She laughed nervously.

But Miss Flack did not laugh. She made a kind of grimace, probably intended for a smile, and said nothing.

"I wondered . . ." Celia stammered on . . . "I heard incidentally that Mrs. Crump was ill. Marian Christie told me . . . you remember Marian? She said she had seen you . . . it was some weeks ago, about a month, I think. She thought you might be leaving here . . . giving up your post to a trained nurse. She had heard . . ."

"I am leaving. I've left," was the astonishing reply.

"You've left!" echoed Celia. "Then why . . ."

"Why am I here now? I come in every afternoon while the nurse rests. I expect it won't be for long, as the doctor is getting another for day duty."

"But why are you not living here?"

Miss Flack shrugged her thin shoulders.

"Oh, well . . . Mrs. Crump thought she could not afford to keep me and a nurse too. I have left her and got a bed-sitting-room near, for the present; so that I can come in and help a bit. There was no one else to do it, and after being with her for so many years I couldn't leave her in the lurch."

She screwed up her ugly little face. It was rather like the face of a Chinese idol, Celia thought, and then she realised that Miss Flack was struggling with tears. Did she love the selfish old woman who had been such a tyrant to her all these years? Impossible!

"It is very good of you," Celia muttered: "I hope Mrs. Crump appreciates your kindness."

"I think she does—in her way. She never was one to say much. She is really ill now, after making believe all these years. The doctor thinks her days are numbered."

"Then I suppose you would not like to leave her."

"I should *not*," said Miss Flack decisively. "I couldn't, so long as I can be of any use to her."

Celia looked at the little plain person before her and thought,

"Why aren't people given bodies to match their souls?" She recognised a beautiful soul here. Aloud she said:

"I really cannot see that Mrs. Crump has any claim on your time now that she has discharged you from her service—if that is so?"

Miss Flack nodded.

"She has never treated you well," Celia went on, a rising inflection of anger in her tone.

"She has not. She couldn't think of anyone but herself," observed Miss Flack, dispassionately, "but I've grown used to her and . . . fond of her . . . in a way. You get fond of people you look after—people who lean on you. And she has been kind sometimes. I think she's fond of me—in her way. There's something pathetic about her; there always is about people who love themselves, and nobody else cares for: if you know what I mean. She has relations, but they have no affection for the poor old soul. They're only waiting for her money. I have a sort of fellow-feeling for her, having no one who cares whether I live or die. And perhaps if I had been rich like her I should have grown selfish. As it is," she gave a grim little smile, "I've never had a chance of growing selfish or fancying myself ill. I've had to get up and bustle about however I felt. In that way I'm better off than she is, poor soul!"

Celia looked at her earnestly.

"Miss Flack . . ." she began, paused, went on, "I want you . . . I want you to come and stay with me. That is why I've come here to-day."

Miss Flack gave a slight gasp and said: "You don't mean it. Why?"

Celia tried to explain. Her uncle had left her a great rambling old house. She was lonely in it. She wanted someone to share it with her and thought of Miss Flack.

"That is not it at all. I see through you. You're sorry for me. You want to be kind to me," said Miss Flack, drawing herself up stiffly and frowning.

"No, I want you to be kind to me," declared Celia, smiling.

The responding smile was no longer grudging. It spread over the plain little face like sunlight over a dull landscape.

"I only wish I could be kind to you—or anyone else. But you can't when you're poor. Except in one way, perhaps—looking after an invalid. And you're not an invalid."

"And," she added. "I'm not a trained nurse, worse luck. There's not much chance for anyone who isn't trained to-day. But I did my best, night and day. She would get me up half a dozen times in the night, and if I went to lie down in the day she sent someone to call me up. The doctor said I should break down and she must have another nurse. He thought I should stay on and get a nurse for the night-work. But she wouldn't do it then—said she couldn't afford to pay us both. And now she'll have to pay two nurses—both of them twice as much as she gave me."

Miss Flack smiled, but her smile was sad.

"I thought she was well off," said Celia.

"She is. But she likes to hoard. It's her nature. You can't help your own nature, can you?"

Celia made no reply to that.

"Well, I only hope she has left you a good thumping sum in her will," was her only observation. And Miss Flack answered rather sharply:

"She says she has, but I don't count on that, Miss Grey. If she does, she does, and I shall be grateful for even a ten-pound note. But if she don't, I shall not be surprised or owe her any grudge. She has paid me what I asked for all these years, with board and keep. It hasn't been a lot—it's not her nature to be generous—but I've managed to save a bit, and when she is gone I can look out for another situation."

"If you come to me I couldn't pay you a salary—or very little," Celia said; "but you would share my home, and be doing a good turn to a fellow-creature."

This was a wily speech. Celia knew, by a sudden intuition, that to be of service to a fellow-creature was the strongest desire in the little woman's mind. And then she resolved to tell all her trouble. "I can't sleep in the house another night alone," she declared, and explained why. Or at least, she explained the reason as being due to the fact that solitude and silence gave her 'the horrors.' Of ghost or haunting she made no mention, having a shrewd notion that Miss Flack would turn down such a reason with scorn. She concluded with the words:

"Don't you see the situation? Nothing will induce me to sleep there alone again, and I must either find a companion or give up my house . . . the dear home I've longed for—and love."

Tears sprang into her eyes, and were not without effect on Miss Flack.

"But you don't expect me to come back with you?" she asked. "If you do, I can't."

Celia told her she was prepared to spend the night in Guildford, or more than one night, if only Miss Flack would return with her. "After all," she added, "you say yourself that the doctor has ordered another nurse and you will not then be wanted. Why not tell the doctor you are leaving to-morrow or next day."

"Because I won't—I *can't*," was the quick reply. "My duty lies here—to that poor thing upstairs, so long as she needs me. You're young and healthy—you can look after yourself—she's——"

"Young!" Celia broke in. "I'm not young at all. I'm quite old—fifty this year. I don't suppose Mrs. Crump is much older than I am."

"She's a hundred years older! She has never been young—so far as I can see. I'm not much older than you, though I look it, and she's not much older than me. But we're both children compared with her. Old as Methuselah and helpless as a babe. You'd say so if you saw her. I must stay by her till I'm not wanted—till another nurse comes or . . . then I'll come to you if you really want me."

Celia looked at her with reverence. There was a soul of goodness shining in that plain face. She murmured something appreciative that Miss Flack did not seem to hear. She had moved to a small writing-table in the window, seeking paper and pencil.

"Here's my address," she said, "I believe my landlady can give you a room for to-night. Her daughter is away. Anyhow, you can go and see. It will save hotel expenses."

As she was speaking a bell rang sharply through the house. She jumped and went quickly to the door.

"That's for me," she said, "Mrs. Crump will be thinking I'm a long time away. Good-bye for the present. If you can't have the bedroom you can use my sitting-room till I come, if you like. But I think Mrs. Smith will tuck you in somewhere."

With that she was gone. Celia went out of the house, feeling rather forlorn. The more she had seen of Miss Flack, the more she desired her for a companion, and it was exasperating to think that perhaps Mrs. Crump might not give her up. She had a suspicion that if it came to the question of engaging another nurse at a high fee, the mean woman would beg Miss Flack to return on her old terms; and, if she did, Miss Flack would certainly not refuse. She would consider it her duty to return. Celia felt no compassion for the selfish woman and nothing but vexation with Miss Flack at this moment, in spite of a very deep admiration for her disinterested and unselfish devotion.

She was making her way towards the side-street written down in the address, and consulting the scrap of paper in her hand, when she was pulled up by hearing her name spoken excitedly, and a tall man, coming out of a tobacconist's shop, stood before her.

"Celia!"

She looked up into a pair of very blue eyes in a bronzed handsome face, as their owner grasped her hand and lifted his hat with the other.

"Leslie!"

CHAPTER FIVE

IT was nearly ten years since Celia had seen Leslie Hale, and the swift thought darted through her mind: "Does he find me much altered?" He had altered very little, but then he was ten years younger than she was, and a man of forty is counted young. A woman of fifty is counted old, at least by the next generation. Leslie was as handsome as ever. He had not grown stout and he had not grown bald, as she glimpsed at the lifting of his hat. And he had just the same physical attraction for her as he had twenty years ago, when he made love in the old simple romantic way, vowing he could not live without her and would never marry anyone else.

He had lived without her and he had married another woman, more than ten years ago. But since his marriage, the last time she saw him, he had assured her that she was the only woman he had ever loved. He had said it simply, with no apparent consciousness of infidelity to his wife, and Celia had pretended to take the assertion as jest. But she knew it was true, nevertheless, and she read the same truth in his eyes now. They were the eyes of youth, and Leslie stood in Celia's mind as a symbol of Romance. Just that and nothing more. She had never desired him as a husband, though as a lover he was enchanting, if not ideal. She loved his kisses in the past; she loved the look of him now, and the warm clasp of his muscular hand. The excuse she had made to him for the rejection of his suit had been on the score of age; she could not, dared not, marry a man ten years younger than herself. But it was not the true reason. How could she tell him that he was not her equal and had nothing in common with her; that the amused tolerance she felt for his elementary intelligence would certainly develop into contempt and probably dislike under marriage conditions. She had been thankful, since, that she had not succumbed to his physical and romantic allurement, while conscious of refusing some thrilling moments that life would never offer her again. He was so handsome, so lovable, so perfect as a lover—and yet so stupid!

She found that he could still evoke a thrill of romance when he looked down upon her with the old adoring gaze she remembered so well.

"What are you doing here?" he asked, still gripping her hand firmly. "The last person on earth I expected to meet."

She laughed and drew her hand away. "I'm looking for a night's lodging," she said.

"Come to us. Dora will be delighted."

Celia was not so convinced of that. She had no apprehension of Dora's jealousy, but an unexpected guest, invited by a husband, is rarely welcome to a wife.

"You are very kind, Leslie, and I am sure Dora would be as kind. But I am spending the night with Miss Flack. Do you remember Miss Flack?"

"Rather. She is the old girl who used to play tennis with her racquet held in the middle, and always ran up to the ball. Isn't she living with some rich old bird here? I've seen her about in a victoria."[11]

"The rich old bird is dying, or at least very ill. Miss Flack has left her and has lodgings in King Street."

"Come and dine with me?"

"No, thanks. I shall have supper with Miss Flack."

---

[11] Victoria: a doorless, four-wheeled carriage, based on the phaeton.

"You will not do anything of the kind. You'll have dinner with me at the Crown Restaurant. They give one a topping meal there. It's such ages since I had a word with you, Celia. You can't refuse me."

Celia gave in. The temptation was too strong to be resisted. She was very hungry and Leslie was so nice. A meal in his company would be agreeable, if not stimulating. But she had to find Miss Flack's lodging first, and ascertain whether she could be accommodated there. Fortunately she could. The landlady expressed herself as only too pleased to welcome any friend of Miss Flack's. Celia joined Leslie Hale again, and they proceeded to the restaurant together.

"Lovely! lovely! lovely! You are just as lovely as ever," were his first words, under his breath, when they were seated at a little table in a corner.

She looked at him with eyes in which tenderness and fun sparkled. "Just the same silly old Leslie," she said. "Won't you try to remember that I am an old lady and you are a married man?"

He gazed at her a moment before replying, and Celia blushed under that gaze.

"I'm married right enough; but you're not an old lady and never will be," he declared. "Not that it would make any difference if you were, bless you!"

She knew it would not. In his eyes she was Celia, of no age. He saw her exactly as he had seen her when she was thirty and he was not quite twenty. The loveliness he saw in her had been born in his own mind, had rooted and grown there. Time and age did not affect it. She was Romance to him, as he was to her. And to him something more—an Ideal.

He chose her menu with great care. Celia thought of 'The Eve of St. Agnes' and "lucent syrops, tinct with cinnamon"—all the dainty things with lovely names that Porphyro chose for Madeline.[12] It was long since she had identified herself with a heroine of romance. The glamour floated, like a soft rosy mist, round her: the chattering people at the other tables were only as the murmur of a sea.

When Leslie asked, as he had done at intervals during many years: "Why wouldn't you marry me, Celia?" she experienced quite a youthful thrill, and with it a mild regret for her past youth. She assumed, however, the air of commonsense frankness.

"To tell the truth, Leslie, I've never met the man I wanted to marry. I'm sorry. I wish I had, and that it had been you. Marriage has always seemed to me very desirable. I've longed for my own man, my own home and children. But—well it's no good talking about it. These things are not for me, and what is the good of turning over back numbers? Let us talk of something fresh."

He heaved a tremendous sigh. Regarding it as a stage effort Celia wanted to laugh, but refrained. She knew he was in earnest, and wished not to wound him. But she also knew, or felt sure, that he was not in the least unhappy; being convinced that he had a wife who suited him exactly, and with whom he was much happier than he would have been with herself. Only his vision of romance disturbed him. It disturbed her a little, too. She felt a spasm of rebellion against her own perverseness in cherishing a conviction—a crotchet in her brain, perhaps—that one ought not to marry for any reason but love and spiritual affinity. That people joined as 'one flesh' should also be one mind and heart. But she knew that to talk of that to Leslie would be speaking in a language he could not understand.

---

12 From the poem 'The Eve of St. Agnes' by John Keats.

So she talked about her uncle's will and the house he had left her, describing it and trying to make him realise its charm. She said nothing of its uncanny reputation or her own nervous fears. If she had, it is probable that his interest might not have flagged, as it did when she ceased to speak of drains and drinking-water. He could make practical suggestions there; but when it came to history—the historical associations of the surrounding country, the Blue Idol Meeting House of the Quakers, the out-of-the-world character of Sussex villages—his mind quite plainly wandered and his face wore that 'ginger-bread rabbit' expression she remembered so well in former days, when conversations rose above the level of everyday things.[13]

"How splendidly handsome he is, and how abysmally stupid, the dear fellow!" she said to herself, as she had said many times before, vaguely wishing for a better match between body and mind. Inadvertently, with the coffee and cigarettes, she happened to let fall the fact that she was rather lonely in her new old home and was seeking a companion. It brought the inevitable rejoinder: "It is your own choice—you needn't have been alone, ever, if you had married me. Why wouldn't you, Celia?"

As it was impossible to say: "Because you never had any ideas. I couldn't live with anyone who had no ideas," she simply smiled at his blue eyes and said: "Don't, don't be sentimental, Leslie. You ought to congratulate yourself on your escape from me. I should have been the wrong wife for you."

But it was no good denying to herself that she yearned towards him at that moment. And when he murmured, clasping her hand,

---

[13] The Blue Idol Meeting House, built as a farmhouse c. 1580, bought by William Penn and other Friends, and converted into a permanent Quaker meeting house in 1691.

"My lovely, lovely Celia," she felt the old thrill of romance run all along her nerves and flush colour to her face. From his adoring eyes she was aware of her own beauty at the moment.

The curious part of it all was that neither of them were in the least conscious of unlawful dallying. Maybe if Dora Hale had walked into the restaurant at that moment, they might have felt a slight confusion, but no more. It was just a scene out of a romantic play they were enjoying. They were actors in it, but the play would be over directly and they would go their ways, forgetting it.

When, on the doorstep of Miss Flack's lodging, Leslie whispered, "I want to kiss you, Celia," she felt nothing of that mysterious ignition, half physical, half spiritual, which true lovers feel. With a laugh she told him that the street was hardly the right setting for kisses. She almost wished it had been; that she could experience once more the sensation of girlhood. It was so long since any man had shown a desire to kiss her.

She sat reading *The Church Times* and a book of religious essays, the only literature she could find in Miss Flack's room, till a church clock, not far away, chimed ten. The noises in the street had somewhat diminished, though taxi-cabs still glided by occasionally, with their unearthly hoots and gurgles. When, soon after, Miss Flack came in they had some food and sat talking till midnight, chiefly about old times. Celia told her about having met Leslie Hale and dined with him, at which Miss Flack made a little face, half a smile, and said: "Your old sweetheart. Most improper. Where was his wife?"

"At home. The proper place for wives—or so we are told," relied Celia. "I envy her."

"Then why on earth——"

"One may envy a woman without wanting to be in her place.

I envy her lack of critical faculty, for one thing: to say nothing of her home and children. Though, now I have a home of my own again, I need envy no woman," Celia concluded.

"No indeed; you are a lucky woman," Miss Flack declared positively. Then she gave a little sigh. "And yet you are going to let your nerves upset all the pleasure of your home! I should have given you credit for more sense."

"So should I," Celia agreed. "I never imagined I could be so silly."

Miss Flack gave vent to a little snort of disdain. "Nervous people are the limit!" she said. "I've lived with one for nearly twenty years, so I ought to know. And selfishness is at the bottom of it—thinking and brooding over yourself day in, day out. That's the way to get a fine crop of nerves."

"How can you help being selfish when you've no one to live for but yourself?" Celia demanded.

Miss Flack conceded that point. But there were, she suggested, ways of avoiding a too self-centred existence. She finished the discussion that followed by observing grimly: "I suppose I should have been as selfish as most people if I hadn't had to live with someone who was more so."

It was an idea to ponder a few moments in silence: the culture of unselfishness by outside egoism. It would seem that someone must be selfish for the good of others—an upsetting creed.

"Well, my dear," the plain little woman said at last, "I will give you my advice for what it is worth. You won't take it, of course: nobody ever does. But, if I were you, I'd set my teeth and conquer my nerves. If you give way to them, you'll have no pleasure in your home, or in anything else. It is all nonsense about ghosts and goblins, dreams and whispers. They're things of the past—ignorance and foolishness. Take my word for it. Go back to-morrow and look your fancies in the face. They'll vanish right enough. Let me know if I'm not right."

Before she went to sleep that night Celia had resolved to follow that excellent advice. Her own fears now seemed extremely foolish to her, seeing them with Miss Flack's eyes. Invigorated and fortified by such a counsel of common sense, she returned next morning by the first train to Millborough she could catch, and was at Clew Lodge soon after noon. She found Coles there, weeding and digging, with a huge bonfire burning, like a sacrifice, to the garden gods, and Lob-lie-by-the-fire dancing round him after the robins that followed each scoop of his spade with an eye to worms. Celia put on her working attire and joined him blithely, obeying his orders, wheeling rubbish to the fire and forking it up into flame. A jubilant chorus of birds cheered on their toil, and in the choir from the wood the nightingales shook free from all the rest their thrilling flutes and long wooing notes of sweetness. There was one who sang, in a beech overhanging the garden hedge, from noon each day to sunrise the next. The days were lengthening now, and when her gardener went home and Celia went in to make her tea it was nearly six o'clock. After that the evening passed quickly, and she went early to bed. A sense of security and comfort possessed her, and she was deliciously tired. The dread of invisible things no longer made her tremble as she mounted the staircase with Lob in her arms; the candle's queer shadow-shapes had no terrors. Her mind seemed to have shaken off its nervous fancies. She sank immediately into a pleasant slumber which lasted till the crowing of a distant cock at three o'clock broke into her dreams, and she found herself suddenly wide awake, with her heart beating fast and loud.

For a few minutes she had a strange consciousness of not being alone in her room, and fancied she heard the soft rustling of a silken robe near her bed. The fowl's clarion call from the nearest farm reassured her and she smiled, thinking of Milton's words:

"As when the sun from watery bed,
All curtained with a cloudy red,
Pillows his chin upon an orient wave,
The wandering shadows, ghastly pale,
All troop to their infernal jail,
Each fettered ghost troops to its several grave."[14]

"Curious old notion," she thought dreamily, "that the cock's crow should be the signal for all shadows to depart. Symbolism, of course. The warfare between light and darkness. But the cocks crow long before dawn for most of the year. I wonder why?"

Wondering she fell asleep again, and did not wake till it was full day, when the birds had finished their morning glee and had gone to seek for breakfast. Celia rose and went to her window. Another lovely day was promised by the soft amber haze that lay over the country, shot through with the gold of the rising sun. She stood there some moments, enthralled by the beauty of land and sky—the emerald points on the shrubs and hedges, the dainty filigree of half-clad trees in the misty, translucent air. And as she stood, warm with recent sleep and half dreaming, some words floated through her mind, like the echo of a voice heard in a dream, a plaintive husky voice that seemed to come from far away:

"I had to leave it there—I had to leave my treasure."

And the queer thing about it was that Celia could not remember anything more of her dream but those crying words. She gave herself a little shake and shivered. It was cold by the open window,

[14] Based on 'On the Morning of Christ's Nativity' by John Milton.

and she did not like the way in which that strange lament suddenly obsessed her. What did it mean? Why had it come into her head now? She remembered nothing of the night, no dream or vision with which to connect it; yet she knew she must have heard the voice, half wail, half whisper, as she heard it now, an echo from the night.

"I had to leave it there—I had to leave my treasure."

"Miss Flack would say I am indulging in nerves," Celia said to herself as she bathed and dressed. "It is only one of those vague, disconnected sentences the mind hears and stores up subconsciously from something heard the day before. I may have heard it in the street outside Miss Flack's room, or in the train. Or it may have come into a forgotten dream."

And then the word 'treasure' seized her imagination. "Suppose there is a treasure trove in the old house?" she thought. But swiftly poured scorn on such a supposition. "As if there could be, all these years, and nobody discover it. Absurd!" Resolutely, she put the whole thing out of her mind and went down to get her breakfast.

After a hearty meal and a couple of hours' housework Celia went down to the village shopping. She fancied that Mrs. Moore at the Stores looked a little questioningly at her as she enquired how Miss Grey liked her new home. But Celia was not to be drawn. She replied, very composedly, that she liked it extremely well. Mrs. Moore then observed that she had heard Miss Grey had been away for a night. She hoped nothing had happened to cause her anxiety. Again the piercing look of enquiry. Celia acutely surmised from it, and the question put, that the village was watching her movements, and had drawn conclusions about her leaving home. She smiled:

"Not in the least, Mrs. Moore," she replied. "I had to go to Guildford on business, that was all. I had to sleep that night in a noisy room on a street, and was thankful to get back to my nice quiet home last night."

"It *is* quiet," observed the lady grudgingly; as if one hardly liked to admit even so much about a house with a 'bad name.' But she made no further comment, and Celia, having given her order, walked on up the long village street, to make herself further acquainted with its side-lanes, its church and little chapels, its vicarage, schools, parish hall, and the Squire's stately mansion. The Squire, she had heard, did not live there much, as the winter fogs from the sea did not suit his health. He lived, with his only unmarried daughter, in London, and came to Misty Vale during the summer months.

Half-way up the long, rambling street, where cottages were set at odd angles, some facing the road, others with gables abutting on it, and their door opening into green little courts and alleys, Celia came upon a small open space of grass, where a thatched house sat back from the road with a retired and seclusive air. It was not much bigger than the cottages near it, yet there was a difference between it and every other house in the village which Celia's eyes were quick to note.

It was very clean and well-kept, even grim of aspect, with its dove-coloured curtains, its wide-open casements, and the beau-pots of spring flowers on the sills. The row of geraniums and other pot plants that filled most of the cottage windows were not here. Its front door stood back, showing a little lounge hall, plainly furnished, with a polished floor. It had a homely, gracious look that Celia liked, and she hoped she might know its inhabitants.

Coming back from her walk and picturing the kind of folk she thought might be likely to dwell in the thatched house, Celia heard the loud voices of children quarrelling, and at a turn of the road came upon two small boys fighting like dragons, while a crowd of their schoolfellows looked on, yelling as only children can yell, with a deafening shrillness that tears the air and seems like to split the ears. Celia hurried up to interfere, but halted as she saw, standing by and watching the combatants, a slender man of middle height, with a half-amused, half-pitiful look on his face.

As it struck her that he was the right person to put an end to the fray, she went up to him.

"Won't you, please, stop them?" she asked.

CHAPTER SIX

THE answer startled her.

"Do you think I ought? God doesn't. But I will if you like," he said, turning on her a pair of grey eyes behind glasses. There was a faint twinkle in them in spite of his rueful expression. Celia felt a strange little shock of recognition, as if she had known him all her life and lost sight of him.

"Please."

In a minute he had separated the combatants, very firmly but gently. They were both dirty, dishevelled and howling; one with blood on his face. Each started to defend himself.

"He begun wiv me first," was the reiterated excuse of both. Their umpire stood between them, appearing to listen attentively. When they paused for breath their supporters on either side took up the tale until it was cut short.

"Now, look here, boys," said he to whom they appealed, and they were instantly silent." I will give a penny to the one who can tell me what is the use of fighting."

The silence became even more pronounced.

"Does it do anybody any good? Does it settle which is in the right?"

"Yes, sir," shouted both boys promptly.

"How does it do that?"

Again dead silence.

"Now you go home and think it over," the man with grey eyes said, smiling, "and if one of you can bring me a true answer to that question I'll give—yes—I'll give him twopence. And don't forget that street fighting is against the law of the land. If Mr.

Martin had caught you, he would have clouted both your heads, so you may think yourselves lucky it was only me who happened along. Get your mother to put some butter on your nose, Bobby, though it's a fearful waste of butter to put it on silly boys' noses. You're bleeding like a pig, Ernest. Haven't you a handkerchief? Here, take mine. Wipe it off, boy, before it gets on your collar."

The small crowd dispersed as Celia and her new acquaintance walked on. She remarked that he seemed to know the village boys, and he said that he ran a small library for them. He had lived in the village a good many years, and the schoolmaster was a friend of his.

It did not seem in the least surprising to be walking up the street with this stranger. Indeed, he did not seem to be a stranger to her. She liked his voice and his smile; she liked his slight, upright figure and buoyant carriage; his humorous eyes and mouth; his air of alert interest in everything. Presently she thought of his first words and asked:

"What did you mean by saying God wouldn't interfere?"

"Well. He never does, does He? It appears to be His intention that men should discover for themselves the law that governs cause and effect, the consequences of foolish and evil actions."

Celia pondered over this for a few steps before she observed that surely young things ought to be protected and prevented from wrong action.

"You have sons?" he questioned.

"No such luck. Have you?"

"Two—the best in the world. They've taken everything off my shoulders, so that now I can be a Harold Skimpole and enjoy a second childhood."[15]

---

[15] Childish, selfish character from *Bleak House* by Charles Dickens.

He laughed like a boy.

By this time they had arrived at the little thatched house.

"I live here," he said. "Won't you come in, friend, and be introduced to my wife?"

Celia felt a slight check. She could not account for it, but it was as if a shutter had come down suddenly between her and one she had known all her life.

"How can you introduce me? You don't know my name," she replied, smiling.

"Don't I? Are you not Celia Grey?"

Of course, she realised, if he knew all the villagers so well he would have learnt the name of a new-comer.

"My name is Pearl," he went on, "John Pearl, at your service. I will now show you my mate and mistress."

She came from the kitchen accompanied by an appetising smell of baking cake; a little roly-poly woman with a dimpling face, like a child's, clad in a shapeless lavender print overall.

"This is Ruth Pearl," said her husband. "I've brought friend Celia Grey to see you, wife. We have been peace-making together."

"That is good hearing." She put out a plump hand and smiled at Celia, a smile of great sweetness. "I was wondering if you would care for me to call. But I do not like making calls. It is good of thee to come first."

Celia liked the sound of that 'thee.' It made her feel as if she had fallen back on old England for a moment. So they were Quakers, these Pearls. She knew nothing about Quakers, but liked their name and connected it with things she loved, tranquility, simplicity, gentleness.

"And do you like your new home, friend Celia?" said John Pearl, when they were seated in a small room on the right of the hall, where a fire of logs burned, and daffodils were set upon the sill and tables, in narrow-necked vessels and a brown jug.

"Very much, friend John," she replied promptly, and they all laughed.

"Good. I feared it might be lonely there at night."

"It is lonely. Especially after hearing queer things about the house. Before I came to live there I was told it had 'a bad name.' "

"I suppose you mean the rumour that it is haunted?" he said, smiling.

"Oh, John!" his wife expostulated. "It is not well to repeat village gossip. People say that about all old houses, don't they?"

"And it is true enough," he observed. Celia gave him a startled look.

"Every old house is haunted by spirits of the past," he said. "Longfellow has expressed well the experience one has in them of 'impalpable impressions on the air.' You know his *Haunted Houses*, of course."[16]

Celia did not remember it. She would certainly look it up. John Pearl advised her not to do so. "Better not, if you're in the least nervous," he said, "and I am sure you do not need any such suggestion as the poet makes. You have imagination enough of your own."

"How do you know that?"

"I do know," was all he replied.

And then, involuntarily, Celia found herself telling this Quaker couple of her nocturnal experiences, how, that night, she had fancied she heard something moving in her room. When she concluded

---

16 The poem 'Haunted Houses' by Henry Wadsworth Longfellow, in which 'All houses wherein men have lived and died' are haunted in some way by their previous inhabitants—'Impalpable impressions on the air/A sense of something moving to and fro'. See also p. 245.

with the sentence haunting her mind that morning John Pearl looked thoughtful. Presently, in a pause, he said:

"That is very curious. For many years, in the memory of the oldest inhabitants of Misty Vale, there had been a legend of buried treasure about Clew Lodge. It has tempted several persons to live there from time to time, besides your uncle—the last tenant was your uncle, wasn't he?"

Celia nodded and John Pearl continued: "Then I suppose you know that he bought the house—or so it was generally supposed—because he had heard there was a treasure concealed somewhere about it, or its grounds. How he first heard of this, I cannot say. But he convinced himself that the said treasure was coal. There is coal under us somewhere, I believe, according to expert opinion. He made up his mind it was under the Clew Lodge demesne, and was so far certain that he actually had a shaft sunk at the far end of the garden—where, no doubt you have noticed the ground is broken up. Nothing was found: nothing but rock. He told me it was a great disappointment to him."

"You knew my uncle?" Celia looked surprised.

"Quite well. He was a queer stick—by your leave—and not kind to his wife; though he was really devoted to her, and heart-broken when she died. He couldn't stand the house without her—so he told me."

"He told me he couldn't stand the whispering," said Celia.

"I expect while she was alive it did not worry him. But I know he—well, he fancied he heard whispering about a buried treasure. I thought it was an echo from his *idée fixe*, for he was certainly possessed by the idea that the old house had a secret. He often spoke of it to me. He believed it was in the earth—or under it. When his attempt to find it failed he grew more morose than ever: and when Mrs. Grey died he got worse. It eded in his leaving quite suddenly."

Celia was silent a few moments before she said:

"My father always thought that he and Aunt Emily were ill-mated: that he had married the wrong woman."

John Pearl shrugged his shoulders.

"Who can ever tell that? There's no 'right woman' for the self-centred man. I only know he was lost without her. She was someone to cast all his burdens on. When her poor back broke he was appalled. Did he not separate her from her children? Poor wretch!"

"I've always been very sorry for Aunt Emily," Celia declared. Mrs. Pearl echoed her, and John Pearl said: "Perhaps he was more to be pitied than she was. He had nothing of his own. She had, at least, the love of her children."

His voice sank. Celia thought of the letter she had received from her cousin and agreed.

Mrs. Pearl rose then and said she must return to her cooking. Her sweet, rather vacuous, smile had shown that her thoughts were with her cakes, rather than with Celia's ghosts.

"But do not hurry away, friend," she added. "John will talk to thee. He loves talking."

John laughed. "Very true," he said. "The dear soul has a lot of my talk to put up with, I fear. You remember who said: 'We've all a parlous lot too much pulpit in us.'[17] And the worst of it is she never really knows what I'm talking about, bless her!"

"She is sweet," Celia exclaimed impulsively. "I think she has the kindest face I've ever seen."

"And you can imagine the girl she was—the prettiest, most

[17] From *One of Our Conquerors* by George Meredith.

charming . . . But you'll see our daughter soon, and then get some idea of what Ruth was at her age. Only Faith is—different. Not so placid. She has my tiresome, questing spirit."

He talked then of Faith. She was trained as a nurse, and had been fortunate enough to obtain the post of District Nurse to Misty Vale and other villages and hamlets nearby. Celia showed keen interest, and he went on to tell her his family history. How his father had inherited, and handed on to him a linen-draper's business at Millborough, and how he had managed it till his sons had grown up and then left it to their management. How trading had irked him at first, but he had gradually become interested in it, "because everything is interesting, more or less, if you apply yourself to it," he concluded with the frank boyish smile that pleased Celia so much. He had bought this cottage, with its adjoining piece of ground, a paddock and a garden, some few years back. He had dug up some of the ground himself and made a garden, to keep himself fit by physical exercise, he said, and had bought fowls and bees to amuse Ruth, who loved her little feathered family and storing her own honey. They were all interested in the Women's Institute, he said, and he had formed a dramatic group. Celia would have to join and act with them next winter.

Her eyes shone. She had loved acting, as a girl. They talked of plays for some time, and then he told her something of the history of Misty Vale and its environs. In the course of his remarks he said something about The Blue Idol, of which Celia had already heard.

"The oldest Meeting House in England, probably," he said. "Anyhow, it was called, 'The Old House' in William Penn's day. You know, of course, that he had a house not very far from Misty Vale?"

She hesitated. "You mean William Penn, the founder of Quakerism," she said, mentally rubbing up her history. He smiled.

"Not exactly the founder. He founded Pennsylvania, though."

"Oh, yes, of course I remember now. I should like to see his house."

"That you cannot do, I'm afraid. But you can see the site and the old barn. I'll run you over some day in Phyllida, my little old car. We call her Phyllida because she flouts me.[18] William Penn was not often there, but his wife and family lived there some time, and his mother-in-law died there. No doubt they visited the Selcrofts, who lived then at Clew Lodge. It is said that his decision to visit America, and his scheme for a new province, were formed while he was in this neighbourhood."

"I'm afraid I know very little about William Penn," said Celia.

"Then you know very little about one of England's greatest sons," he said gravely. "We owe much of our civil and religious liberty to him."

Mrs. Pearl returned to them at this moment. She had doffed her pinafore and appeared in a sober cloth gown with white linen collar and cuffs.

"I wonder what kind of people the Selcrofts were," Celia questioned thoughtfully. "Would they be court folk, likely to wear a very rich dress I found in a closet?" And she told them about it, saying: "I don't know what to do with it, Mrs. Pearl. What would you do?"

The little lady laughed. "Send it to a museum, I suppose. Or have a glass case made for it. You say it is fragile."

Celia turned to John Pearl with an unspoken query. He advised her to keep the dress carefully, as air-tight as possible.

---

[18] 'Phyllida Flouts Me' is the name of a 17th century ballad (see J. Woodfall Ebsworth, *The Roxburghe Ballads*, vol 6, 1889, p. 460). It is also the name of a novel by Mary L. Pendered (published 1913).

"Don't you think it possible," he said, "that while it is in the house you may learn something? You must listen for more whispers. How if it were 'the treasure'?"

Celia's eyes opened widely. Was he jesting? There was certainly a faint twinkle in his eyes. Mrs. Pearl observed, laughing, that John was full of fancies, and she advised Celia to take no heed of them.

A swift step was heard outside, and through the little hall a girl came in. It was as if something bright and very full of bounding light had entered. She was rather tall and of slender grace. Her brown uniform, with its close bonnet and floating veil, threw into exquisite relief a skin like apple-blossom, and little curls of hair at the ears; of that ash-blonde which is no more yellow than a primrose. Such Scandinavian fairness Celia thought she had never seen. It made her think of china shepherdesses, little delicate figures in Faience paste. But oh! so richly alive. She brought a fresh atmosphere with her.

They were introduced and clasped hands. The girl's blue eyes—the pale blue of riverside forget-me-nots—met Celia's with a frank and friendly welcome in them.

"I'm so glad you've come to Clew Lodge," she said, when they were seated. "The poor old house looked so forlorn with no one in it. I hate to see old things neglected."

It was so exactly what Celia had felt that her heart warmed towards Faith Pearl. But the girl had obviously come in for a meal, and Celia felt she might be tired and hungry after her morning's visiting. So, when they had talked together a few minutes, she rose to go. They begged her to stay and dine with them, but that she would not do. John and Faith went out with her and along the street till she turned into her road. They parted, promising to meet again soon, and Celia went on blithely to her home.

It seemed dark and somewhat dreary after the house she had just left. Her fire was nearly out and her clock showed a surprising lateness. She could hardly believe it had struck two. Lob was clamouring for his dinner. After she had fed him and started on her own meal, Celia had time to think over her morning's strange happening.

For was it not a strange happening? To meet a man in the street and go home with him? And it had all passed so swiftly, like the scrambling action of a cinema film, or a scene in a rollicking farce. Suddenly new friends, a new interest, had jumped upon the stage of her life, to colour it with fresh tints. She felt excited and uplifted.

Celia had never boasted to herself of being unconventional: indeed she had not thought of it. But now she definitely enjoyed the sensation of freedom from convention, being clearly aware that her action in going with a stranger into a strange house would shock many of her friends. They would say she ought to have waited for Mrs. Pearl to call on her and suggest, probably, that Mrs. Pearl was secretly disconcerted by the sudden appearance of an unknown lady in her parlour. But they did not know Mrs. Pearl, she reflected, and, surely, there was not another John Pearl in the world.

That was her first conclusion about him. And she could not regard him as a stranger. From the moment when he had turned his penetrating grey eyes upon her she knew that they had always been friends, although they had never met before. On some other plane, perhaps. She pondered over that. But certainly they belonged—they fitted together: they would never need to explain to one another. By some queer intuition she realised that. It could not be reasoned out, but there it was—a positive conviction. When he had replied to her first question she had felt ashamed of having asked it. She ought to have known what he meant, why he had not interfered between the boys. Not that she agreed with him, exactly: she would have to think it over; but she ought to have grasped his reason without explanation in words. She knew him instantly as the man her soul had longed for: and, while she felt a pang of regret for the lost years and opportunities, there was, nevertheless, a sense of exhilaration in the thought that she had found him at last, and her long waiting was justified. She was jubilantly glad that she had never accepted a makeshift.

Sometimes she had called herself a fool for letting the business go by in pursuit of her dream, giving up substance for shadow. But now she was satisfied and proud of her resistance to a common temptation. It was true that John Pearl had not waited for her, as she for him. He was happy with his wife and children. Celia thought of the lovely girl she had seen and reflected that she, too, might have had as beautiful a daughter had she married Leslie Hale—as strong and handsome a father as any woman could wish for her children. But not this, nor any other intervening consideration, could shake her sudden and overwhelming conviction that no other man than John Pearl ought ever to have been the father of her children.

A little trill of laughter escaped her lips as this thought took shape. What nonsense was she thinking! She had but known the man a couple of hours. He was attractive; he made appeal to some inner self she had never analysed; he seemed different from all other men. But she might yet find all that difference, that freshness and charm, wear off on closer acquaintance. It might be all on the surface, nothing behind but disillusion. Who could tell?

But however she argued with herself, Celia could not escape from John Pearl. She found herself continually dwelling on his words, his face, the deep and gentle inflections of his voice.

She thought also of the setting in which she had found him,

a setting after her own heart. The softly-tinted room, with its air of homely comfort; the grandfather clock in its corner, the harpsichord (she thought of it as a spinet) by the wall; the deep settee by the fireplace; the many book-shelves and straying books everywhere; the two low windows back and front, the back one looking out on flowers and grass. Lines she had always loved swam into her memory:

"Give me, ye merciful Powers,
A house full of books and a garden of flowers."[19]

Well, she could have all that here, in her own house now, thank goodness, and there was no need to envy anyone. Some day she would have the spinet, perhaps, or, if not, a little cottage piano. Her music had gone. She was not even sure she could play now, as her last rooms contained no piano, and before then the only instrument available had been a painful travesty. Somehow she began to think of music now and long for it.

Perhaps she would, some day, have a radio set, which would be even better than a piano. But when would she be able to afford such a luxury? She was already faced by the difficulty of keeping house on her slender income, depleted by the necessary raid on her little capital. There was but one prospect of adding to it, and that of the vaguest uncertainty. If she could earn anything by writing—if she were only sure of that—but her past failure haunted and daunted her.

In the afternoon, however, she was able to bid avaunt to that shadow of doubt. Wandering round about the stone paths of her garden into the wood beyond and back again, the vitalising sap

---

[19] Based on lines from 'Ballade of True Wisdom' by Andrew Lang: 'And I'd leave all the hurry, the noise, and the fray,/For a house full of books, and a garden of flowers.'

of spring seemed to ferment in her and fertilise her mind. Or was it the thought of John Pearl that inspired her, set ideas sprouting? The aspens had begun to whisper a love-story to her. She stood beneath them listening to their soft rustle, for as yet their leaves were very young, and the sound they made was faint as fairy wings. A dark cloud swept suddenly between sun and earth: a heavy shower followed, pattering a little chorus on the trees, and Celia had to take refuge in the woodhouse near the stables. From it she watched the cloud pass over and a lovely rainbow shine through the silver, slanting rain, and she heard herself murmur aloud: "Thank God for it—for all such perfect things." The glorious primary colours, shading off to the delicate tints of primrose and lavender and shell-pink, seemed to satisfy an appetite within her, as perfect beauty can do to some of us. It brought tears of thankfulness to her eyes. She watched it fade into the milky blue of the sky and went back to the garden, where the delicious smell of wet earth and grass greeted her, and raindrops glittered on every leaf and twig.

There were buds on the lilacs, the mock orange and guelder rose, quite tiny but full of promise; forget-me-nots, primroses and wind-flowers were blooming where they could find their way: a wallflower in a sheltered corner had put out a little orange flag among the green, and fox-glove steeples were rising from their flat beds on the earth. A mulberry tree still remained stark and black in an emerald world: in the wood oaks had started in their race against the ash-trees, and Celia thought of the old rhyme:

"If ash-leaves come before the oak,
We shall surely have a soak:
If the oak's before the ask,
We shall only have a splash."

She had, as yet, but scant knowledge of trees, and knew them only by their foliage; but she fancied the oak had won in the spring race, and devoutly hoped so.

As the sun set slowly behind the wood, gilding the tree-tops and showing a delicious glow through their branches as it sank, the world grew cold and Celia was glad to go indoors to her fire. Over tea she pored upon a florist's catalogue and heard another gentle shower tapping at the window-panes. The coloured pictures of delphiniums, roses, sweet-peas and all the rest of the flower world evoked visions of her future garden: she could almost smell the roses and sweet-peas; vegetable marrows, beetroots, cauliflowers, giant peas and gooseberries made their several appeals. She could savour them in fancy.

But as the twilight fell on her mood of sweet content and lassitude, and she could no longer see to read, Celia fell back on her thoughts again and the thronging ideas that had seized her in the garden. She looked round the room with happy eyes and felt that she loved it dearly. The glowing fire threw shadows into its corners, but they were not menacing shadows now: nothing lurked in them but little elves like Lob-lie-by-the-fire, whose living representative lay purring on her lap. Her thoughts grew hazy, and she dozed.

CHAPTER SEVEN

SO absorbed was Celia in pleasant thought, enjoying sensuously the warmth and silence, that she did not note the gathering shadows until they had thrown a black mantle over the room. Only one log glowed in the fire, like a wonderful red eye. And then the terror sprang at her throat again. She could not bear the dark in this strange old house of hers. It was as if something lurked in its corners ready to pounce on her. She shook herself and sprang to her feet.

"Brrr——" she shivered, and spoke aloud: "How cold it is with the fire nearly out! And how lazy we are, thou little Lob of spirits, to have let it out."

She threw on a fresh log and some coal, lighted her lamp and drew the curtains. When that was done, and little dancing flames spurted from the kindling wood, she lost the sensation of fear, till a gentle push at the door set her nerves tingling again for a moment. Only for a moment. She knew it was the wind rising. A strong breeze had sprung up and, from open windows, swept about the house. Celia took a candle and went to close the downstairs casements, which she kept wide open all day to sweeten the decay-laden air that had been, at first, so stifling.

The wind was eerie though. It began to moan down the chimneys and whine through the keyholes. As she sat down to her last meal, with a sense of increasing dread of the coming night, Celia evoked the sturdy, matter-of-fact figure of Miss Flack and the tones of her dry voice, to support her battle against 'nerves.' Miss Flack had no respect for nerves or vapours. They filled her with contempt, as did all superstitious tales of haunting. There might be more things in heaven and earth than dreamt of in her philosophy, but she knew nothing about them, and did not want to know aught about them. She did not believe in them, nor did she ever intend to believe in them.

It was an attitude, Celia felt, that had a certain wisdom behind it. But it was not, obviously, the attitude taken by John Pearl. She thought of his suggestion that she should preserve the old dress she had found and listen for more whispers. Was he joking? There was a twinkle in his eyes, as if he were not quite in earnest, and yet she thought he believed there might be *something*—something not quite normal and natural in her house. But she would not think of that, nor of him. She would think of Miss Flack and her strong common-sense, her entire freedom from fancies.

It was not easy to banish John Pearl from her mind. She recalled all he had said about her house and about William Penn. She must learn more about William Penn. In her bookcase there were several volumes of an old Encyclopedia, relics of her father's library which she had dragged from lodging to lodging in her dreary pilgrimage because she could not bear to part with them. She sought the volume devoted to O's, P's and Q's and found Penn. It was a brief account but stimulating; she wanted to learn more.

She had eaten her light supper and was reading the story of Quakerism, as expounded by the writer in the old Encyclopedia, when a sudden sound brought the blood pounding to her head and set her heart beating wildly. Yet it was only a gentle knock at her front door.

"That shows the state of my nerves," she muttered, and her hand shook as she applied a lighted match to her candle. Then she thought: "Who can it be at this time of night?"

Wondering and still rather alarmed, she pushed back the bolt of the heavy door and turned its big key in the lock. Outside, in a shadow, stood a tall graceful figure, carrying a small bag.

"I hope I haven't startled you, Miss Grey," said a young, sweet voice. "Father thought you might be lonely and nervous, and might like me to sleep here. I told him you would probably think it a great impertinence—my coming—but he's so sure about things and so determined. He was positive, from something you said, that you didn't like being alone. I should have come sooner, but was called out. Do tell me if I am a nuisance and send me home at once."

"You are not a nuisance—you are a godsend."

Celia felt a great longing to throw her arms round Faith's neck and kiss her, as she stood smiling on the doorstep. But she refrained. That might be an 'impertinence' truly. And she had a vague idea that Quakers did not care for demonstrations of emotion.

"Your father was quite right," she said, as they entered the sitting-room and she put out her candle, "though how he knew I cannot tell. I am sure I did not say I was nervous. I must have implied it. But I am, horribly and senselessly. So ridiculously scared that I actually went to Guildford, the day before yesterday, to try and get an old friend to come and live with me. I felt I could not sleep here another night alone. But I conquered the feeling last night and hoped to do so to-night."

"I expect Father knew all that," the girl said laughing. "He always knows things. You don't need to tell him. He seems to have an extra sense for perceiving what is in other people's minds. I tell him it is uncanny. Have you an extra bed for me, or shall I sleep on that nice comfy couch? I can sleep anywhere."

"Indeed you will not. Rather should you have my bed. But I've a second bedroom leading out of my own. These funny old houses always seem to have economised passages. It is only a question of bringing sheets and blankets down to air."

She lighted the candle again and they went upstairs together. Faith helped her carry down bed-clothing, leaving her cloak, bonnet and bag in the room she was to occupy. Celia saw her then in her ravishing fairness, and felt the spell that beauty always cast upon her. The pale amber hair, the apple-blossom tints of her skin, faintly pink lips, rather pointed chin and delicately arched eyebrows gave her a faery look. But there was an earnest depth in her blue eyes, a kindness in her smile that no soulless elfin thing could ever show. This girl could feel, and feel deeply.

Celia told her, with a laugh, that she had just been reading about Quakerism in her cyclopedia, and confessed her ignorance on the subject. Faith read the account in the fat, mottled old book and said: "You can't learn much from this, I'm afraid. But we can lend you stacks of literature on the matter, if you care to read it. Did Father say anything to you about the book he wants to write on this village?"

"He said he was collecting facts for a book, but no more."

"He has actually begun it—sketched it out. A sort of romance. Of course we, Mother and I, think it very good—his idea—but whether he will ever do it or not, who can say. It is about a family who has lived in this village for hundreds of years and has interesting traditions. Of course all the names have to be altered!" Celia's eyes shone. "Has he ever written a story?" she asked. Faith shook her head.

"No, though he used to tell us wonderful stories, when we were children, and he is full of romance. I believe he has read all the novels ever written!" she ended smiling.

"He must have done nothing else."

"Oh, well, of course"—Faith laughed—"one takes a certain license."

"Have you ever wanted to write?" Celia asked. And Faith replied promptly: "No indeed. I have no literary pretensions whatever: no more than Mother has. I don't believe she had used more than a hundred words in her life! Father revels in words. If he finds a new one, or one he has forgotten, he is quite excited."

"I should like to read something he has written. Is any of it printed?" said Celia.

"Very little, and only in our own papers. You shall read some."

There was a pause, during which Lob jumped on Celia's knee and begun to play with a bead chain she was wearing.

"I have written two books," she said abruptly, "two poor little dead babes—in another life. Or so it seems to me."

Faith's eyes shone. "You are an author—how lovely! I've never met an author before. Tell me the names of your books. I may have read them."

"Very unlikely. They both departed this world when you must have been an infant in arms. I have almost forgotten them myself."

"Never! Can a mother forget her child? Please tell me their titles."

"The first," said Celia, "was called *Enchanter's Nightshade*; the second *Or So it Seemed*."

"How old were you when you wrote them? As old as I am, or older, or younger?"

"I don't know how old you are."

Faith said she was twenty-six, and Celia told her that she was the same age when her first novel was written. She was nearly thirty when the second was published.

"Why wasn't there a third?" Faith asked; and Celia told her the outline of her sordid history. She had to earn a living and could not afford to wait for a speculative success. Failure had daunted her; she had no confidence in herself, as a writer, and no heart to go on. Sorrow, too, had flooded her mind and sapped her inspiration. She could no longer concentrate.

Faith mused, with a troubled face. She earned her own living, but from choice, not necessity, and she realised that this was a different matter. It had been her ardent desire to lead a useful life, and she had gone through a nurse's training for that purpose. But the profession had attracted her and she had been interested in it. What must it be like to have to work only to keep yourself alive, and at a job in which you were not interested? Her face was full of sympathy as she said gravely: "I think you should have stuck to your writing, having a talent for it. Couldn't you get any other work to do—journalism?"

"I did try," Celia smiled, "and proved myself quickly the world's worst journalist. I have no great talent: only a poor little creeping thing without wings. Nobody wanted it. I wrote a saccharine novelette, with love on every page, and got ten pounds for it. But it nauseated me, and I felt too ashamed to write another. That was the end of me, as a writer."

They talked on for a while, Faith asking innumerable questions. She was one of those rare girls who are not entirely interested in themselves, and one of those nurses who are not entirely interested in their patients. Suddenly her eyes grew brighter and she flung out a suggestion.

"Why shouldn't you and Father write a book together—a romance? He has the idea and you could weave the plot and write the dialogue. I wish you would."

They talked till midnight. Celia asked Faith about her own work, and a kind of spiritual exultation seemed to emanate from the girl as she spoke of it; of her ministrations to the sick and suffering. Of the humorous side that sometimes lightened the way; of the gratitude she met with and the kindness of poor folk to one another in affliction. Behind it all Celia felt that there lay an undercurrent of personal sadness. Faith did not speak of her own inner life at all, and Celia did not like to probe; but some intuition told her that Faith was not as happy as a girl in her situation ought to be; a girl with love in the home and satisfaction in her life of noble service to her kind. Knowledge of the reason why was to come later.

As a little clock on the mantelpiece struck twelve they both paused in their talk.

" 'The witching hour when churchyards yawn and graves give up their dead,' " Celia quoted.[20] "I should not have dared to sit up so late alone. We must really go to bed."

They went upstairs, each carrying an armful of bedclothes, with a hot-water-bottle for Faith's bed, against which she had protested, but Celia insisted, afraid of any damp there might be. The old house seemed much more normal to her as they went up; its stairs creaked less, the wind's voice sounded less dolorous and menacing. The window at the top of the staircase, which had made her heart jump the night before by the flash of her candle back from its dark panes, now seemed to be peeping kindly from behind its rosy curtain, stirred by the draught. There was nothing uncanny, nothing to make her breath come short or set her nerves trembling. She realised how traitorous those nerves must be, to be thus calmed and mastered by the presence of another human creature.

---

[20] Based on lines from 'The Spectre of Tappington' from *The Ingoldsby Legends* by Richard Harris Barham.

Faith approved the rose-coloured curtains. She confessed to a love for bright colour which, she declared, ought not to exist in her, but ought to have been quenched long ago by the generations of Quaker ancestry. The Pearls had been Friends for two centuries at least, she said, and during all that time, up to the present, had never worn anything but greys and drabs.

"I am sure my grandmothers would turn in their graves," she said laughing, "if they could see my party frocks. I have one almost as bright as your curtains. I love pink, especially the colour of the rose."

"I should like to see you in pink and yellow, like a dainty columbine, pink petals and amber spurs," said Celia.

They made up Faith's bed together and agreed to leave the door open between them. Then they kissed each other. To both it seemed as though they were quite old friends.

"I pray you may sleep well, dear ministering angel," said Celia.

"Oh, I shall. I always do," the girl declared. "And I am not psychic, you know. I never hear or see anything everyone else doesn't hear and see. Quite a commonplace type am I, with hard-strung nerves."

"So I thought mine were till I came here."

"I admit it is an uncanny house," Faith laughed, "but all very old houses are, I think. When we first took our cottage I felt it was rather spooky, and lay awake expecting to see things, but nothing ever appeared. The only scare I had was from birds in the thatch, which I took to be rats. Probably that is what you've heard."

Celia told her she had heard nothing that could not be accounted for. All the terrors were in her own mind. She paused, then went on: "Only in my dreams things seemed moving in the room, and I woke with a fragment of speech floating in my head. Why should that haunt me?"

"Why do we dream at all? And why do we dream such idiotic things?" asked Faith. "The other night I woke up crying because I dreamt Mother would not let me feed the hens. It seemed such a monstrous slight and injustice."

They parted, laughing, and both slept well. But when Celia was dressing she suddenly became aware that the door between their two rooms was closed, and she had a qualm of discomfort. Why had Faith shut it? She knocked, and the fresh young voice cried: "Come in."

"Did I disturb you in the night?" asked Celia anxiously.

"I was just wondering whether I had disturbed you and you has shut the door," was the answer. "I hope I wasn't snoring."

"Then you didn't shut the door?"

"No."

"I did not," said Celia.

They stood staring at each other a few moments.

"It must have been blown to by the wind," Celia suggested.

"Should we not have heard the bang? I am a light sleeper."

"So am I."

Again they paused, looking at each other with puzzled eyes.

"I expect one of us walked in her sleep and shut it," observed Faith, as she brushed the long pale waves of her hair. And they left it at that.

But neither of them felt convinced. Faith no more than Celia. They did not refer to the matter again, but Celia, who had more time on her hands than the District Nurse, found herself pondering more or less all day on who, or what, had shut that door noiselessly in the middle of the night.

CHAPTER EIGHT

FOR a week Faith Pearl went every night to sleep at Clew Lodge. But she and Celia did not again leave the door open between their rooms. It was enough for Celia to know that another human creature was near, a living barrier against the dead, as she felt it to be. But, nevertheless, she remained strangely conscious of 'impalpable impressions on the air,' and inwardly believed that one was active. Not merely a quiescent ghostly thing of the past, but something still sentient, and, in a sense, alive.

One night, when she was lying awake, she heard, in the dead silence of her room, a whispering sound like that of leaves rustling, or a soft wind blowing the waves of the sea upon a shingly shore. It gathered strength and presently became articulate in a murmur of speech. And then she heard distinctly the words that had floated through her mind one morning: "I had to leave it there—I had to leave my treasure." In a low plaintive voice, little more than a whisper, these words were repeated twice—thrice—and then died away into the silence, and she heard no more.

She was surprised to find that this did not rouse in her any sense of superstitious fear. At the first recognition of articulate words she shivered a little, as if with sudden cold, but after that her only sensation was of sadness. To have to leave one's treasure—what could be sadder? And yet it is what we all have to do, sooner or later, whether the treasure be a living thing or something laid up that moth or rust can destroy. She, too, would have to leave her treasure, her home and newfound freedom, before many years were over. Youth had long gone by, middle age was going, in twenty years she would be old, if she lived so long. Celia hardly knew whether she was pitying herself or the unknown entity that lamented in the stillness the loss of a treasure it had left centuries before. How many centuries? And why was it still lamenting? What kept it here? Was it really a spirit chained to earth, or merely an echoing voice from the past, strangely held afloat in the air by some mysterious agency.

Celia said nothing of it to Faith next morning. Why should she? The girl would only think she had been dreaming. And talking about it would, she felt, only lend it a spectral terror it had not yet caused her. Perfectly convinced, as she had now become, that Something invisible moved and spoke in her house, she felt a queer shrinking from putting this belief into words. The fact that the door between their rooms was set open in the night more than once, when both were sure they had closed it, was disconcerting and puzzled Faith; but they agreed to suppose that it had not really been closed, that the latch had not caught, or that one had opened it to speak again and forgotten to shut it. They tacitly agreed not to talk about it.

During the week Celia's friendship with Faith Pearl ripened into a strong mutual affection and sympathy. Faith was out on her rounds all day, dressing wounds, attending to new-born babies and their mothers, washing or dressing invalids of both sexes, but in the evenings she returned to Clew Lodge after supper at the Thatched Cottage, and John Pearl always brought her. He had left her at the garden gate the first night, waiting there in case Celia had not wished her to stay. Now he went in, and the three spent pleasant hours together. Never before had Celia met a man who shared every taste and pleasure of hers as this man did; who was interested in every subject she found of interest; who loved beauty and loved the past for its beauty of romance; yet while steeped in its glamour, kept a modern outlook with a vivid sense of future development, in art, in sociology, science and psychology. Faith sat and listened to their talk, rarely interpolating a remark, and sometimes, it must be confessed, scarcely following them. She had her own subjects to think of, personal and impersonal; but if appealed to, she answered with smiling interest, real or feigned. And she was both pleased and amused to see the spark she had kindled catch fire between them—the suggestions she had thrown out that Celia and her father should collaborate in a book. At first they had laughed as if it were a jest, but before the week had fled a plan had been sketched out which they were eagerly filling in—the plan of a romance in which they could enjoy themselves, and which they hoped to make enjoyable to others. Faith, who had inherited so much of her mother's temperament that she could not invent or throw herself back into the past, found this unconcealed excitement of her elders over imaginary people and situations delightfully amusing. It is always difficult for the young to realise that the old can have thrilling excitements of their own, less ardent or poignant, than those of youth, but none the less engrossing. Faith, who adored her father and thought him truly wonderful, could yet laugh at his almost childish joy in the thought of writing a romance. But it was tender, sympathetic laughter. She could not enter into that joy of imagination, it seemed rather absurd to her; but she loved him the more for his boyishness, just as she loved her mother for her childishness. Ruth Pearl had never really grown up. She lived in a little world of her own: occupied by the simplest interests; devoted to her husband and children, without in the least understanding them, or sharing any of their ideas. She thought her husband 'queer,' and was satisfied to leave the matter thus, since she could never, by any possibility, enter into his world or know what was in it.

Her children knew all this. They had no illusions about their parents, and were perfectly aware that their father had no companion in his wife. Sometimes they wondered if he realised the fact and ever, secretly, longed for the companionship of a woman after his own kind. If he did, they never discovered it. Either he was self-sufficient or he was too loyal to betray a regret.

Ruth had decided by now that Celia Grey was as 'queer' as her husband, and having come to that decision she was perfectly satisfied in their friendship. It was only natural that two 'queer' persons should fraternise.

When Celia went to the Thatched Cottage and held long conversations with John Pearl, Ruth smiled on them, serenely knitting or sewing while they talked, and taking in no more of what they said than if she had been stone deaf. She had her own thoughts to occupy her mind, thoughts of her children, her work, her cocks and hens. The past history of the district, its traditions, customs and superstitions, did not offer the least interest to her. That people should get excited and talk ardently about witchcraft, faery lore, dialect and all the lumber of ancient days afforded her a mild wonder; for she took everything mildly. She could understand John's interest in the book he was writing; as part of him she tried to feel interested, too, and was glad that Celia was going to co-operate with him. But that they should both wax enthusiastic over musty old books and documents, collected by John, over Hermetic science, alchemy, magic, astrology, psychology and suchlike, was quite incomprehensible to her. She classed those subjects with fairy tales, and wondered what grown people could find in them. Perhaps she felt a little private apprehension that such subjects were impious; but her faith in John's religious convictions overcame this fear.

John Pearl and Celia were, by the end of this week, so lost in their study of a day long past, and their project of fitting the ideals and problems of that day into the mould of romance, that they became practically unaware of Ruth's presence, or, indeed, her existence. She was there in the room with them, but with no more substance than a shadow. If she moved out into the kitchen or elsewhere, they were unconscious of the fact. Ruth was such a quiet, unobtrusive little person, and she would not have disturbed their conversation for worlds.

Celia was so engrossed with her new companionship and the work she was doing, that she had ceased to speculate about Faith and wonder, as she had done at first, why there was sometimes a look in the girl's eyes, a droop at the corner of her mouth, that spoke of sad thoughts. But she was pulled up in her egoism on Saturday evening, when Mr. and Mrs. Pearl had gone to see their sons at Millborough and Celia took a walk through the village alone.

Wrapped in her own thoughts, as she strolled back in the fading twilight, scarcely noting the approach of night, she came suddenly upon two young people leaning over a gate. Their backs were turned to her as she passed by on the road, and they did not turn at the sound of her footsteps: being, apparently, as absorbed in their own interests as she had been in hers. It was not an uncommon sight, on these fair spring evenings, to pass lovers on the road, and Celia would not have taken special notice had not the sound of their voices—or, at least of one familiar voice—arrested her. The words spoken were barely audible, but she heard them, and she heard also the note of despair in them. The voice was Faith's; the words were:

"It can never be."

"It can never be?" Words fraught with pain, Celia felt, as the phrase that haunted her: "I had to leave my treasure." Did they mean that Faith would, also, have to leave her treasure? And why?

Someone has said that the most poignant word in our language is 'never.' It seemed so to Celia now. There is in it the passing knell of hope, a tragic acceptance of the inevitable. She felt a little shock as she walked on. Faith, so lovely, so useful and sweet-natured, was she unhappy in her love, and why? Celia did not doubt that the man with her was Faith's lover. The tone of her voice was enough to betray that fact. But why was she meeting him thus, clandestinely? It seemed impossible she could wish to conceal anything from the father and mother who adored her: she so frank by nature, and unafraid. Yet it seemed to Celia like a stolen meeting of lovers.

She was determined to discover the truth and, in their nightly talk, told Faith that she had seen her that evening in the twilight.

"Whom were you talking to?" she said. "I could not see, in the dusk. Indeed, I had nearly passed when I heard your voice."

A lovely wave of colour began to rise under Faith's skin to the roots of her primrose hair.

"I was with Michael Staniforth," she said. "I had been to tea with his mother, and he walked home with me. It was such a lovely evening that we had a stroll first."

"Oh." Celia could not think of anything to say for a few moments. She was thinking: "I was wrong, then, it was not clandestine." Aloud she said: "I did not know you were friendly with the Staniforths." And Faith replied: "Oh yes, we've known them ever since we came here, in a way. The Vicar didn't call, knowing we were not Church people, but he and Father are on the Parish Council and quite good friends. Mr. Staniforth has been good to lots of my patients and we have met at their houses. I often go to tea at the Vicarage, especially when Mike is at home. He is my . . . friend."

"Only friend—nothing more?" suggested Celia, smiling.

"Nothing. There never can be."

She spoke with decision. In that firm answer, however, Celia detected a note of sorrow.

"I heard you say that, as I passed," she said. "And I wondered what it meant. Is there, then, some obstacle between you?"

"The greatest possible obstacle. He is in the army."

Faith's lips closed tightly on the last word. The flush in her face deepened, and there was a shadow in her eyes. Celia did not speak at once. She rose to put a log on the fire. Then she asked:

"Surely that is not an insuperable obstacle."

"To a Friend! What do you think? Could I marry a soldier?"

There was a hint of scorn in her upturned lip as she spoke. Celia made no response. After a pause Faith went on, in a torrent of words poured out from a full heart.

It was foul luck, she said, that the only man she had ever cared for should be a soldier. She loathed soldiers and war. The loathing was in her blood: it had come to her through generations of pacific ancestors. She would rather die unmarried than be the wife of a murdering soldier. She regarded them all as murderers. And Michael loved his profession. He had even dared to regret to her that he had been too young to serve in the Great War.

"I told him that I looked upon him as a horrible bloodthirsty brute," she added, breaking into a little rueful laugh that had tears in it: "It wasn't true, of course, because he has the kindest heart in the world and wouldn't hurt a fly. I've seen him climb to the top of a high chimney on a rickety ladder to rescue a frightened kitten. But he has no imagination—not a fraction. He can't realise the horrors he was not in, or visualise the hideous cruelties and sufferings he did not see. War to him is something fine and glorious and heroic, with chances of doing great deeds—and all that. What can you expect when boys at school are taught to admire great conquerors, generals and admirals? Who are the heroes of history books? Alexander and Napoleon and Wellington and Nelson—all barbarous survivals of savagery, and only one remove from lions and tigers! I tell him that if 'dogs delight to bark and bite, and bears and lions growl and fright' it is time men knew better—after twenty centuries of Christianity.[21] But so long as they think that fighting is glorious and patriotic and noble, men will continue to behave like bears and lions—of course they will. The spirit of adventure urges them on. War is a great adventure—perhaps the greatest of all. Risk tempts men. They love it. It's a form of excitement. I know all this, but I want to forget it. And how could I ever forget it with a husband in the army, drawing pay for his willingness to go out and slay his fellow-men? How could I?"

Celia gazed at her. She had not a word to say. Like most of us, she had accepted the facts of war, and the maintenance of armies and navies, as part of an ordered scheme in every State; maleficent but necessary. It had never occurred to her to doubt this, and she could not, even now, believe that our present condition of civilisation could dispense with them. Moreover, she had certainly not outgrown her youthful admiration for a soldier; especially for those who had led armies to victory. To hear Wellington and Nelson branded as savages gave her a real shock. She had always regarded them as the saviours of England, men of whom England was justly proud. One does not shed the beliefs and adorations of a lifetime so easily that Celia could agree with her youthful

[21] Based on lines from the poem 'Let Dogs Delight to Bark and Bite' by Isaac Watts.

friend. She disagreed profoundly, though her scaffolding of faith rocked a little.

A long silence followed. Celia knew that if she stated her well-stereotyped opinions a long argument might ensue, and it was late to begin arguing. All she said was, when she thought the silence had lasted long enough: "But don't you think, Faith dear, that the difference between you might be got over in time. If you love him . . . "

"I don't," interrupted Faith quickly. "I refuse to love a soldier."

Celia smiled. "As if one can help loving!" she exclaimed.

"Surely you are not so sentimental as to believe that!" Faith said with an uplift of her delicate golden eyebrows: "Surely you do not dignify by the name of love a feeling that is not based on perfect understanding and reciprocity! That may be passion: it isn't love."

"Do you feel any of that passion?" asked Celia frankly.

The girl's eyes fell. "Perhaps I do," she said, "but I don't give way to it—not an inch. Michael has a sort of attraction for me, I own—a sort of primitive attraction. He's good-looking, you know, and . . . compelling. But I am not so weak and foolish as to let this passion dominate me; to give up a happy useful life for it. I don't call it love."

Celia quoted softly:

> " 'That is an essence far more gentle, fine,
> Pure, perfect, nay divine;
> It is a golden chain let down from heaven.'[22]

But, darling, how many women would ever marry if they waited for that? And look at the thousands of happy marriages there are

---

22 From the poem 'Epode', from Ben Johnson's *The Forest.*

between men and women who are not . . . who have not that perfect understanding you speak of."

"I know. Like Father and Mother," said Faith, calmly. "They have never understood one another in the least. Father married Mother chiefly because he knew she wanted him, and he never could be unkind to anyone. She was pretty, and attracted his fancy at first, I suppose. Fancy has a great deal to answer for. I believe it influences many men more than passion. I've often wondered what would have happened if they had not had children. After we were born, of course, they had one great subject of interest in common. But they have never been companions in any sense of the word. And that would not do for me. I could not differ from a man continually and go on loving him."

Celia mused. "I should have said your father and mother were a very happy couple—a real Darby and Joan," she said.[23]

"Oh no. You and Father are the real Darby and Joan," declared Faith, surprisingly. "I knew it directly I saw you together. Of course, Mother has not the least suspicion of it. She's such a sweet, innocent child. But she would not mind, anyhow."

Celia felt the blood rising to her cheeks.

"My dear, you must not say things like that," she protested. "It is great nonsense, and, of course, you don't mean it. I am sure you would not have things other than they are."

"Oh, I do not say I would. I should not be what I am if I had a different mother—you, for example—and I like to be what I am, naturally. Besides, if you had been my mother, Father would have been all yours and not mine, as he is now. I was only thinking of it from an abstract point of view—the fact of your obvious one-ness.

[23] Darby and Joan: a devoted married couple living in domestic harmony.

If he had not been led astray by Mother"—she laughed—"but had kept single, as you have, what a 'marriage of two minds' it might have been."

"I don't know," said Celia, meditatively. (It did not seem queer to her then to be discussing John Pearl with his daughter, as it seemed when she thought of it afterwards.) "You see, Faith, your father and I do not hold the same views on everything. On religion, for example, and on military defence. We might find ourselves as opposed as you and young Staniforth."

This gave pause to Faith. She considered it gravely for a few moments.

"No—it's not the same thing," she finally said. "With us it is a fundamental separation, rooted within. I could never change him, nor could he change me. Father would soon make you think with him. You are rational and imaginative. Mike isn't. He cannot argue and he cannot visualise. He can only see and believe what he has been taught to believe. And it's the same with me. We can never be Darby and Joan for that reason."

She went on, after a pause: "You are rather shocked, friend Celia, at the way I've spoken about my parents. But you will not misunderstand, will you? Saying exactly what I think is my most fatal habit. I am not disloyal to Mother. I think her the kindest, best and most unselfish of women. Father is kind. He would never do anything to hurt anyone; but Mother has no self at all. She just lives for us. And that is why she is so happy. Isn't it the essence of living—to lose your tiresome, ever-exacting self, altogether? You said just now that Father and Mother seemed a happy couple. Of course they are. Each tries to make the other so, and that's the whole secret. But it doesn't make them *one*. They are *two*, and always will be. So would we be—Michael and I. But I am not like Mother.

I have a self—a very aggressive and determined self, as you must have discovered by now."

Celia laughed at that, and they went to bed without further discussion. But she did not sleep for hours. Faith's words, "you and Father are the real Darby and Joan" haunted her mind. She felt them to be true and yet felt no great pang of regret. Suppose, she thought, they had met twenty years ago, when they were both young and passionate, what misery they might have endured, mental struggle and spiritual torment! Celia, as she dozed off to sleep, realised how the years provide a soothing balm for all such fevers of the spirit. Poor Faith's agonising conflict, torn in two between her heart's desire and her soul's resolve, made Celia's own lot seem strangely happy by comparison. She had found her Darby at last. Faith had still hers to seek, or must succumb to a conventional conquest.

Would the old Quakers hold their own, or would Michael Staniforth, in his panoply of youth and passion, break down the walls they had raised and take the citadel? Celia wondered, and was glad that problem was not hers to solve. There are times when we may be thankful to have passed youth's passionate turmoil.

CHAPTER NINE

THE courtyard at the back of Clew Lodge had once held a substantial wooden dovecote, whose strong stem, made from the trunk of a fair-sized tree, still remained untouched by the years, though its little round house had fallen into dilapidation. A small space at its base had been left unflagged, and this Celia had resolved to make into a flower-bed, with a pillar rose to preside over it. She desired a shining vision of colour from her sitting-room window, which now looked out on grey stone, with only a few trees to break the monotony. For this she had chosen wallflowers, forget-me-nots, nasturtiums and a Scarlet Climber; the wallflowers and forget-me-nots as heralds to the later flowers, the delightful old 'lark's heel', with fruit easy to grow and useful to pickle. Reds and yellows, she thought, would show up well against the grey walls beyond, in which wild things had already seeded themselves and were beginning to show signs of bloom. But the nasturtiums were making a tardy appearance, and Celia thought to remind them of her expectations by a gentle shower from her watering-can. The earth there was friable and dry; there had been only light showers for a week, and she was impatient to see the little green discs appear.

She was absorbed in looking for them when the sound of footsteps coming up the path from the north side of the house arrested her, and she turned to see Miss Flack walking towards her, with a suitcase in one hand, an umbrella and hand-bag in the other, looking very hot and moist.

"Well, this is a pleasant surprise!" exclaimed Celia, as she took the suitcase and set it down with her watering-can, before offering her hand. Miss Flack grinned.

"I wondered if you had been scared away," she said, seeking a handkerchief to mop her face: "I don't know how long I've been pulling your bell and banging on your door. I had almost given up hope when I saw a black kitten frisking round the side of the house, and thought there might be a path to the back. Have I surprised you?"

She spoke in her usual dry, toneless voice, but her small eyes shone with friendliness, and she was evidently relieved to find Celia.

"You have indeed. Why did you not write? I am so sorry you could not make me hear. That is the worst of being cook and parlourmaid and all the staff of a large house—and head-gardener to boot," said Celia, laughing. "But do come in, and rest. I expect you have walked from the 'bus. It's a long way when one has anything to carry. You must be tired."

When she had divested Miss Flack of her wraps and made her a cup of tea, Celia enquired:

"Has anything happened? Mrs. Crump——"

"Is dead."

"Oh dear! Was it sudden? When?"

"Last Sunday morning. I was with her, and——"

The little woman grimaced and turned her face aside.

Celia, seeing her moved to tears, occupied herself in the kitchen for a few minutes.

"I ought to have let you know," Miss Flack said when she came back, "but there has not been much time, what with making arrangements for the funeral, getting rooms ready for the relations—and black clothes. Second cousins, they are, another generation. Quite nice young people, and very civil to me. They always have been. Of course the nurses didn't know where anything was, or when the servants had been paid, so they sent for me. We had to go through her things together. They were hoarded in all sorts of places, all over the house. Such a business—and so painful to me," her voice cracked again—"it seemed to bring her back—and the old days, when she wasn't so . . . I felt I must get away from the house as soon as possible, and, as you said you would like me to come here, I've come. I always take people at their word. If you don't want me, you must say so."

"Of course I want you. You must tell me all about it when you've rested. Let me take your hat and coat. How heavy it is! You must be tired."

They sat talking over the early tea, for it was only three o'clock. Celia told Miss Flack about Faith Pearl's nightly companionship, and Miss Flack instantly proposed going to the inn to sleep; but this Celia would not allow. It was extremely doubtful, she said, whether there would be accommodation at the Pack Horse, and Faith would be only too pleased to sleep in her own bed. Her visits had been of pure charity. After tea she, Celia, would go and tell the Pearls she had now a companion.

But this was rendered unnecessary by the appearance of Faith herself. One of her patients had seen a lady with a suitcase going towards Clew Lodge, and she concluded it would be Miss Flack, of whom Celia had spoken to her. She had come to find out.

The first sight of Miss Flack gave her a slight shock. The small person in a black frock and hat grotesquely unbecoming affected her unpleasantly. She thought she had never seen a woman so ugly and repellent. For Miss Flack, sallow, red-eyed and grim-looking, gave no indication of the heroic goodness with which Celia had credited her. On first view, it appeared impossible that she could be kindly. Her set mouth and rasping voice suggested a hard nature. And Faith loved beauty. She said to herself, "I could never live with anyone like that," and she doubted whether Celia could. But before she left, this opinion was modified. She had seen Miss Flack's eyes suddenly fill with tears, and her harsh voice had faltered when she made some reference to her late employer. A wave of compassion flooded the girl's kind heart, and when Miss Flack smiled at her, in saying good-bye, Faith saw her with different eyes. That rare smile transformed her plain little face.

When she had gone Miss Flack commented on her prettiness. "Yes, and she deserves it," declared Celia. "Her soul is as lovely as her face. She deserves the pleasure she must find in her looking-glass!"

Even as she spoke Celia accused herself of tactlessness. Such words seemed to emphasise the lack of good looks in her friend. There could be no pleasure for *her* in her looking-glass. But Celia need not have been troubled. Miss Flack showed no sign of perceiving the implication. She said callously: "I suppose people get too used to their own looks to notice them much, whether they're pretty or ugly." And Celia thought, for the first time, that the pity she had always felt for the plain woman had been misplaced. It had seemed such a terrible thing to be ugly that the sight of an ugly man or woman, especially a woman, had always given her a pang of compassion. Now she began to wonder if they ever realised their lack of comeliness; if Miss Flack, for instance, had ever really minded seeing her sallow little puggy face in her glass. Probably not. Her words suggested this. She was so used to it!

They sat discussing matters more important, however. Miss Flack told Celia about Mrs. Crump's will, in her own dry and impersonal fashion.

"She has left me a hundred pounds. The old servants got only ten pounds each. One has been with her as long as I have. She can't have saved much, as Mrs. Crump never raised her wages from the time she first went. The rest of the money goes to the nearest of kin and a few charities. But though she wasn't generous, poor soul, the cousins are. They say they are making my legacy up to five hundred pounds and giving Sarah ten shillings a week till she gets the Old Age Pension. It's very decent of them."

She screwed up her face, and her eyes grew red again. Celia agreed: it *was* decent.

"Of course I have't got it yet," Miss Flack went on; "and I may never get it. They may change their minds. 'There's many a slip,' you know, and I've seen too much of life ever to count on anything that isn't sure.[24] But if I do get it, and it brings me in ten shillings a week invested, I have a proposal to make to you. I've thought it all out, and I'll pay you seven shillings and sixpence a week for two rooms, if you'll let me have them, and help with the work of the house. I can't pay more, because I haven't saved very much, and I must keep it against a rainy day. But I can work. I know how to do most things in a house, and can cook a bit. I don't want to be idle. If this scheme doesn't appeal to you, I shall look out for another engagement. But as you said you wanted companionship, and your house is big, I thought perhaps——"

"I'm not going to take your money," Celia burst in. "I was wondering how much I could afford to pay you for living here and helping me. I am not very expert in a house, though I am learning the work gradually. If you'll stay, as my companion, and give your

24 'There's many a slip 'twixt cup and lip', an English proverb, meaning that even when a good outcome seems certain there is a lot that can go wrong before it is reached.

services, I shall be more than satisfied. It will save the expense of outside labour."

But Miss Flack turned down this proposal with decision. She was a very decided person, and had made up her mind what she wanted before coming to Clew Lodge.

"I should like to live with you and make a home here," she said. "I believe we could get on all right together, if we had our own rooms. But I've always determined that if ever I had the chance of being my own mistress I would be. I can feel that, if I pay for two rooms, and do as I like in them; but not unless. I want to be quite free; to shut myself up if I choose, or go out when I like, without a by-your-leave. Not to have to talk when I don't want to talk, or to be agreeable when I feel disagreeable. I expect that sounds very selfish to you. But if you had led the life I have for twenty-five years, you would understand."

Celia did understand and said so emphatically. Moreover, she recognised at once the commonsense of Miss Flack's proposal. Here she, Celia, had been ready to take into constant companionship a woman she really knew very slightly, confident of her own power to please and readiness to be pleased. But, on sober reflection, she realised that close intimacy with this prim person might bring them into conflict. They were of different temperaments, different views, different tastes, and friction might easily arise between them. It is, perhaps, she thought, more difficult for two women to accommodate themselves to such a union than for a man and woman, or happy marriages would be less common than they are. Before she and Miss Flack went upstairs that night they had practically settled the question of living apart under one roof.

"There is one thing I want to ask," Celia said, when they had re-made the bed for Miss Flack, "and that is your Christian name.

I can't go on calling you 'Miss Flack.' "

"Mrs. Crump called me 'Flacky.' "

"But do you like that?"

"I detest it! I was not consulted. Even the maids called me 'Flacky' behind my back. I overheard them. But my Christian name is so silly and inappropriate that perhaps you'd better call me 'Flacky.' I am used to it."

Celia declined to call her Flacky, and was told the 'silly' name —Anabel.

"Even Mabel would not have been so bad—so romantic and unsuitable," Miss Flack said, with a grimace. "And to make it worse, I was always called Belle at home. You may call me Ann if you like."

"I don't like," Celia said, laughing. "I prefer Anabel. I love romantic names. But I shall call you Belle to remind you of old times. And you must call me Celia, for the same reason. I've been Miss Grey for so long now, and I want to feel young again. Miss Flack and Miss Grey are so obviously dull old maids, whereas Belle and Celia are quite happily gay and youthful!"

After this they parted, and closed the door between their rooms. But in the middle of the night Celia was awakened by a sound that she recognised as the click of a latch. All the doors had latches upstairs, and only a few downstairs had more modern fasteners. She turned to see the door between their rooms open slowly. No one entered, and Celia was shaken by a slight tremor for a moment. It passed and she told herself it was not fear. The night-light twinkled, on her washstand; there was no sound except a faint jingle from the rings of the window curtains moved by the April wind; nothing to disturb the sweet serenity of the night, or cause the least alarm. Yet she was glad to hear, in the stillness, a creak from Miss Flack's bedstead next door, giving an assurance of friendly company.

She had, by now, become accustomed to strange nocturnal happenings in her room; but in spite of that fact, and the near presence of another human being, Celia could not force herself to get out of bed and shut the door. A sudden dread of feeling, something touch her—something cold she could not see—held her fast. It would be dreadful, she thought, to feel anything you could not see. It was bad enough to *hear*, but to *feel* . . . no. She could not summon enough courage to rise from her warm bed and cross the cold boards that lay between her and the door.

She closed her eyes and presently dozed. But just as she was falling asleep a soft, sighing voice penetrated her consciousness, and she heard the words now becoming so familiar:

"I had to leave it there—my treasure."

. . . . .

"Our door must have blown open in the night, unless you opened it," were the next words Celia heard, as she was putting on her shoes. Miss Flack stood at the doorway in her night-gown, with her hair screwed tightly up for washing.

"I did not open it," said Celia. Then, defiantly, she added, "and it was not blown open, either. That is what happens continually. Something—something unseen—opens or shuts the door between these rooms."

"What nonsense! You don't expect me to believe that," said Miss Flack sharply, as she shut the door.

CHAPTER TEN

AFTER living with Anabel Flack for a week, at close quarters, Celia decided that she was not an ideal companion, and was glad they were to live apart. She possessed none of the graces that smooth the everyday passage through life. It never occurred to her to gloss over any difference of opinion of feign agreement. Dissembling, even in its kindest form, was as foreign to her nature as it was essential in Celia's. Long training as a saleswoman had cultivated her natural urbanity, and she smiled to think what her employer would have said if she, Celia, had spoken to a customer as, doubtless, Miss Flack would have spoken.

To Celia it needed no effort to be pleasant and disguise any dissension or distaste she might feel. To Miss Flack such disguise appeared dishonest. Horror of pretence had bred in her a habit of being unpleasant which years of subordination had not succeeded in quelling. She had learnt the wisdom of holding her tongue, and doing as she was bid without comment; but, as she told Celia, it was always an effort to make herself agreeable when she felt disagreeable, and one reason for wanting her own apartments was that she need not then make that effort.

Celia soon realised this and was sorry for it, on Miss Flack's account. She knew the little woman yearned for affection, and she also knew how far the gentle graces of life go towards winning it. Experience in the world had worn off the rough edge of uncompromising sincerity, and she believed that to be always absolutely frank one must be perfect in a perfect world. Although you may be feared and respected for your goodness, you are loved for qualities that may exist without it. Affection rarely comes to the man or woman who wears a rigid front, and conceals a soft heart under a hard manner. It was, she reflected, one of life's minor tragedies that women like Anabel Flack, kindly sympathetic beneath the surface—women who long for affection—go through the world misunderstood and uncared for because they lack the gracious arts by which so many selfish and superficial women command love.

But Miss Flack, if uncompromising, was not obtuse. She was quick to see when her blunt speech offended or irritated Celia; to take herself off when it occurred. In the house she was a valuable ally. Celia had scrambled along in a disorganised way till she came; but now method began to be exercised, and the work shared between them.

But she knew, all the same, that Miss Flack had not forgotten what she had told her of strange whispering, and her uncle's remark about it. If Anabel disguised nothing in herself, she was an adept in penetrating the disguises of others.

At the least suggestion of uncanny manifestations in the house she scoffed unstintedly.

"Nothing will ever make me believe in such things," she declared. "All the stuff one hears about hauntings, and séances and mediums and the dead coming back, I look upon as just a pack of foolish lies and deceptions, only fit for the feeble-minded. And what's more, it's all against the Scriptures and the teaching of the Church. God never meant us to come back, once we've passed away, and He never meant people to dabble in all that spiritualistic rubbish—concertinas and table-rapping and such nonsense, and I tell you plain. So don't expect any sympathy from me over your whispers and things. It's all fancy."

"And yet if we *are* spirits, and do live again, why should we not revisit the place in which all our interests were once centred?" Celia contested; "it seems only reasonable."

"And it seems to me most unreasonable. As if we shall take any further interest in this miserable world after we've left it!" Miss Flack retorted, with that crisp articulation of her words that always reminded Celia of dry chips.

"You think, then, that love doesn't last beyond the grave," she ventured.

"I don't know anything about love or——" the little woman paused abruptly. She went on: "Of course earthly love, and all that, will be over. We shall have something better."

"I wonder!"

Is there anything better than love? Celia was thinking. But she perceived the folly of arguing with her friend on a subject of which she, confessedly, knew nothing. Had Anabel ever loved anybody—even that old woman she had served? Celia queried pitifully, again realising the strange inequalities and injustices of this life which, it would seem, could only be adjusted in another. For she thought it must be worse never to love than never to be loved.

"Better to have loved and lost, than never
to have loved at all."[25]

was not a sentiment she had previously echoed, but now, in the face of Anabel Flack's unguarded admission that she knew nothing about love, Tennyson's platitude seemed justified.

With regard to the supernatural manifestations in her house, Celia felt comforted by Miss Flack's scorn, which gave her a sense of security and support, though she could not share it. When she

---

[25] From *In Memoriam A. H. H.* by Alfred, Lord Tennyson.

asked: "Who, or what, opens the door between our rooms?" Belle promptly declared it was either the wind, or that one of them had walked in her sleep. And nothing would shake this conviction.

But they did not waste much time on discussing the matter. Miss Flack was busy for a week after she came, scrubbing her rooms, and making them ready for the furniture she had to buy. One whole day she spent in London hunting in Marylebone Road for cheap things she wanted. And when all this was done, and she had vacated the chamber next to Celia's to take possession of her own furnished ones, Celia saw very little of her for some days. Obviously she was revelling in a sense of independent possession and enjoying her own society. Celia could appreciate that condition of mind and sympathise with her. They had agreed to share their midday meal together, and in the evenings, when it was cold, they shared the comfort of Celia's fire. Miss Flack had invested in a little oil-stove, upon which she could boil or fry, but the heat it threw out was not great. On sunny days her rooms were warm enough.

One cool evening when Anabel came down she found John Pearl and Celia, poring over documents by the fire, and talking excitedly about 'our book.' Their greeting of her was perfunctory, and she soon became aware that her presence made little mark upon their consciousness. It struck her as surprising, and rather absurd, that two grown-up, rather elderly people should be so absorbed and eagerly interested in matters that appeared to her childish—old lore and legend, quaint superstitions, primitive beliefs in spells and charms, taboos and customs.

"You know that queer corner-house by the four cross-roads," John Pearl said. "There are old women in the village who still believe that the witch, Sukey Martin, called up the suicide who was buried there with a stake through his breast, and was seen talking to him at midnight, with a blue musty vapour surrounding them. They brewed much mischief between them, and he gave her one of his chest-bones to work spells with. I was told that, quite seriously, by old Mrs. Browne, who has lived in the corner-house most of her life and has seen queer things, she says. Her grandmother remembered seeing Sukey Martin when she was a child. I can't find out the exact date of her birth and death, but she must have lived about the middle of the eighteenth century, because she is spoken of as a contemporary of Malkin Evans, who was hanged in 1753. So we can bring her into our book quite reasonably. Indeed one can hardly write a book about that period without a witch in it. And certainly in Sussex, where such legends persist."

"I rather wonder that you listen to such silly tales, Mr. Pearl," observed Miss Flack, without looking up from the towel she was hemming.

"Listen! My dear friend, I listen with all my ears for such tales. They are the very music and colour of the past," he said, smiling, "and have you never thought there must be something, some strange truth, behind them? Witchcraft was certainly recognised by the Church up to quite recent times as an evil thing; a Satanic influence and a menace on society. I believe the Roman Catholic Church still uses a form of exorcism against it. And I sometimes wonder whether our modern spiritualism does not bear a close resemblance to it. The 'control' of the medium, is it not practically identical with the 'familiar' of the witch? Was a witch a medium, according to our nomenclature? Had she a curious, odic, hypnotic power, the gift of thought-reading, and of suggestive direction? We hear a great deal about suggestion and auto-suggestion to-day; about thought transference and the sub-conscious, suppressed complexes and so forth. It is more than probable that witchcraft had its bases in all this, only the science of psychology had not developed, and we use different terms for the same ideas."

He was not addressing Anabel Flack particularly, but she replied, with a little sniff, that in her opinion it was all nonsense together—witchcraft, spiritualism and the rest of the mumbo-jumbo. Then she returned to her sewing, with the satisfaction of knowing that she had settled the matter for good, and only very foolish and childish persons could go on considering it seriously.

With a twinkle in his grey eyes John Pearl asked her whether she did not love all the old myths with delicious names? He picked up a book and read some out to her. "Bull-beggars, elves, hags, fauns, sylvans, brownies, hellwains, puckles, firedrakes, spoorns and other delectable goblins; such as Robin Goodfellow, Tom Tumbler, Kit-with-the-Candlestick, Lob-lie-by-the-Fire, Will-o'-the-Wisp and the like." Wouldn't she like to see a sylvan, a spoorn or a hellwain, just for once? He would.

He could not resist teasing Miss Flack, and she was never quite sure whether he was in earnest or not. If he were, she certainly ranked him with the foolish and childish.

Celia delighted in such childishness. Years had passed over her since she had read Scott's *Demonology and Witchcraft* (from which he had quoted above), but she had been interested in the subject at the time, and John Pearl had revived that interest; co-ordinating these things, which Miss Flack dubbed 'silly superstitions' with the religions of the old world; religions still existing among backward races. He lent her an abridged copy of Frazer's *Golden Bough*, and she had shuddered over its mass of collected data about the slavery of the savage mind to ghastly fears, taboos, inhibitions and cruelties. A whole world of fascinating and fertilising ideas had been opened up for her, and she was thrilled with fresh interest in matters grown stale from unquestioned acceptance. John Pearl was fertilising fallow places in her mind. She began to conceive the kind of romance that might develop from them.

"We will have a Quaker family," she said to him, "set down in this district when it was a little rookery of ignorance and superstition. I had not thought of it in connection with magic and witchcraft. The influence of William Penn and the Inner Light of the Friends, which seems to have given them a little world apart, can be woven into the story. I see it all. And if we can give a clear picture of the strangely confused thought that credited your great man with Jesuitism because of his desire for religious freedom and tolerance, we ought to make the book of some interest historically. But I shall have to depend upon you for all that, about which I only know so much as you have told me. I will paint the *outside* of our characters and write their dialogue. Oh! but how hard that will be to do: to steer between 'tushery' and our modern speech; to know when they used 'thou' and when 'you'; to give colour to their period without making ourselves ridiculous.[26] I wish we had some old MSS. to show us how. But they could not give us much idea of actual talk, could they?"

"I think so," John Pearl replied thoughtfully. "We should have something to go upon, anyhow. But let us frame out the story first; and let us avoid unnecessary dialogue. It can be very tiresome in a story."

Celia agreed. "If I open a book and see many pages of talk, I don't want to read it," she said. "It looks so frothy that one suspects very little good liquor underneath."

Briefly the story was to be concerned about a young man of

---

[26] Tushery: the use of affectedly archaic language when writing.

good family destined by his parents for the priesthood, from a vow they had made to God after his recovery, as a child, from a dangerous illness. A great Catholic family in the neighbourhood, an ancient Castle and an Abbey, had suggested a background full of enchantment. Add magic and witchcraft, civil war, the battle of religious freedom versus ecclesiastical authority, and the foundations would be laid for a thrilling psychological romance. For it was not, they had decided, to be the old kind of historical novel, full of sword clashings, impossible adventure and sentimental love. The day for them had passed, or was passing: the *Prisoner of Zenda* type giving way before the type first conceived in *Esmond*, the more subtle and subjective type of *Queen Dick* and *Witchwood*. The title they thought of was *Mansoul*, since the story was to be of a soul in conflict between two opposing forces; those forces that were responsible for the religious upheaval in Europe.

When they discussed these questions before Miss Flack she could not refrain from occasionally expressing her very decided views. She would have no truck with the Roman Catholics, and she deprecated the mild and tolerant way in which her companions spoke of the old religious houses, the monks and nuns, with whom they seemed to feel much sympathy. Once she was mystified by a burst of Homeric laughter from John Pearl at a speech of hers: "I would even rather be a Quaker than a Catholic." It implied a black pit on either side of a narrow way: one a trifle less black than the other!

She was, moreover, puzzled by the friendly relation that existed between Celia and John Pearl. Nothing like this friendship had ever been presented to her mind; that maidenly mind of the past which regards a man always as a male rather than a fellow-soul. And yet it would have shocked her to be told she ever thought about sex.

"Why doesn't Mrs. Pearl go out with her husband?" she asked Celia one night, when John had gone, and Celia had bolted the door after seeing him off.

"I don't know. You had better ask her."

Celia smiled, guessing what was to come.

"I always think it is very foolish of wives to let their husbands go out without them," pursued Miss Flack.

"Then you don't believe in freedom for married folk? Suppose Mr. Pearl likes going out and Mrs. Pearl prefers her own fireside—what then? Must they both sit at home, or both go out?"

"A sensible wife would certainly go with her husband. What I meant was that it is not good for married men to seek distraction outside their own homes and away from their wives."

"What you really meant, my dear Belle," said Celia, with laughing bluntness, "was that you do not approve of married men calling and staying late, with seductive young things like you and me. You think it is improper. Now own up."

Miss Flack relaxed into a grim smile.

"Well, so it is, even if we're not seductive or young. You can't be too careful in a village, where people have so little to talk about."

"If I can provide the poor dears with something to talk about, so much the better," Celia declared: "but I don't flatter myself. I am too old to be interesting. There are plenty of young people to provide the necessary gossip. Besides, we're not in the village."

In Mrs. Pearl, Anabel Flack found a satisfying companion, and she went often to the Thatched Cottage, where she always found a friendly welcome. She was interested in Ruth's fowls and her fine handicraft; in the village affairs, to which Ruth gave up much of her time. Before midsummer the little spinster had her finger in many pies and visited many cottages. She learnt what babies were expected, what babies clothes wanted; what men were out of work or on half time; which girls were 'keeping company' and which ought to be married at once; whose cottages were clean and whose were dirty; whose children were neglected, and whose husbands took a drop too much. Faith provided a good deal of information, albeit discreet, as became her calling. She was of course, admitted to a certain degree of intimacy, and could have unfolded many domestic tragi-comedies had she been so minded. But she was wise beyond her years, ruthful, sweet-natured and sympathetic. Malicious gossip never fell from her lips, or from her mother's. It was from the village women themselves that Anabel obtained many spicy items of gossip.

She went to church, and was soon on friendly terms with the Vicar and his wife. It surprised her to hear the way they spoke of the Pearls, especially of Faith Pearl. Michael Staniforth she had not seen, as his leave was up before she came to Misty Vale, and so she knew nothing of his relations with Faith.

When Miss Flack talked about the village folk and their affairs, Celia felt a little wistful and dissatisfied. Happy as she was in her home, which had not ceased to entrance her, but grew dearer as the weeks passed, she felt a certain self-reproach when she heard of the work done by Ruth and Faith Pearl—by John Pearl too—in the village. Their usefulness, while it impressed her, seemed to reflect on her own selfishness. Here was a young girl, nearly half her own age, she thought, spending her time, her youth and all her energies in serving, taking a very necessary and important part in the world's work; while she, Celia, was playing, like a child in a meadow, living only for herself. And yet, strange to say, she was conscious of being much happier than Faith. Doing good continually should, she felt, be rewarded by happiness; should be, indeed, its own reward; but she knew, by that sympathy which is a psychic gift, that Faith was not recompensed for her devotion to duty by radiant joy or exaltation. Some recompense she must have, of course: a sense of self-satisfaction, an interest in her work; but there lay a shadow in her lovely eyes that spoke of sadness, and Celia knew her thoughts were often with the young soldier she had forbidden herself to love.

To Celia, a 'romantic' to her backbone, the situation was inconceivable. That is to say, she could not conceive of a love unready to cast away every other consideration for its fulfilment. The idea that a conscientious objection could intervene between two lovers was contrary to her creed. "Many waters cannot quench love" was her definite belief, and it seemed incredible to her that it should be quenched by a pious opinion.[27] She did not, perhaps, take Faith's ancestry and upbringing sufficiently into account. But then, whoever does? Celia could only wonder and sympathise. She was even annoyed at the unfairness of it. Why should that exquisite girl—exquisite not only of face and form but of mind and soul—be unhappy while others less deserving, herself for example, felt as blithe as birds in a garden.

How they sang, those days, the birds in her garden, through "April, May and sunny June," as the old song ran:

"I sowed the seeds of Love,
It was all in the Spring,
In April, May and sunny June,
When small byrdes they do sing."[28]

---

[27] Song of Solomon 8:7 (King James Version).

[28] From 'The Seeds of Love', a traditional British folk ballad.

She learnt to know them by degrees, thrushes and blackbirds, willow-wrens, tits and robins, chaffinches and fly-catchers, garden warblers and, last but not least—the nightingale. When he first began, in the tree by her garden gate opposite her sitting-room window, Celia felt a thrill of joy: but after he or another had kept her awake for nights, pouring forth his delirious rapture hard by her bedroom window, she grew so used to his song that it ceased to disturb her, and certainly gave her no more thrills. At the end of April and beginning of May Philomel sang nearly the whole day through: only for a few hours after noon was he silent.[29] He drowned the whispering voices of the aspens by day as well as night; and for that Celia loved him the more. She could not get over her strange dread of the murmurous leaves, associated in her mind with her uncle's words, and with the voice so often heard in her room.

But the nights grew shorter and shorter as May month ran through its rainbow hours. Celia was able to work late in her garden, and Miss Flack often helped her. Her interest was centred in the vegetable garden, with its beds of onions and potatoes, lettuces and broccoli, peas and beans and turnips. She was always willing to weed these beds, while Celia grudged the time from her precious flowers. Coles came once a week to do a strenuous day's work, and Mrs. Coles scrubbed for many hours at the same time.

There were delicious moments for Celia when she first shelled her own peas and gathered her own strawberries. Nor dd she disdain the beauty of beetroot and carrot leaves, nor the purple and green flower of the potato. But she loved best her lilacs and guelder roses, her delphiniums—poor dwarfed things though they were, outworn by the years—anchusas and fox-gloves, roses and lilies,

[29] Philomel: poetic name for a nightingale.

as, one by one, they unfolded their charms to her adoring eyes. Life seemed a very perfect dream to her just now.

She was sitting one evening with Anabel after supper, when she heard John Pearl's now well-recognised knock, and opened the door to admit a strange-looking man with a queer nose and a hand held to a white face—John Pearl, indeed, but with a difference. She started back in alarm at the sight of him.

"Have you any butter to spare?" he asked, with a little boyish laugh.

"What *have* you done to yourself?" she asked, in great concern.

"I haven't done anything to myself; but, very foolishly, I've been interfering between man and wife." He added after a pause: "And I'm afraid I should again, under the same provocation. Do I look anything like a prize-fighter? I feel like one. And have you any butter—cooking butter—to rub in my bruise. I will not waste your best on such a bad cause."

"You are the last man in the world I should have suspected of fighting, Mr. Pearl," observed Miss Flack, as Celia went to her larder.

"Ah, but you don't know me, friend Anabel," he said gaily. "You don't know how weak I can be under temptation. Original sin breaks out in all of us at times, doesn't it?"

"You haven't been fighting, of course," said Celia, gently applying butter to a bruise that had inflamed his cheek and was swelling his nose, "but what has happened?"

"Precisely what I've already told you. As I was walking here Mrs. Clayton came running out of her cottage—you know the one at this end of the village—followed by her husband the worse for drink. He struck her once and then I put in my oar, and caught one of the blows intended for her."

"I hope you gave him as good as you got—the brute!" cried Anabel.

"Quite. Much better, in fact. He received from me a drubbing he is not likely to forget."

"I am glad to hear it. I thought Quakers never did such things, but I am glad you can use your fists in a good cause."

He laughed gleefully. "Oh, I didn't use fists. That wouldn't have done a ha'porth of good. He would merely have knocked me down and taken it out of his wife afterwards. I chastised him with the Sword of the Spirit, and made him feel about as small as a son of the Living God can feel—poor beggar! He didn't know what he was doing, of course, and it gave him an awful shock to find he had hit me. You should have heard his abject apology."

"Surely you don't make excuses for him because he was drunk," said Miss Flack, disgusted.

" 'We are all frail, but thou ought'st to esteem none more frail than thyself,' " he quoted.[30] "There is no man more to be pitied than the unhappy wretch who cannot overcome his own weakness. I am sure you agree with me, friend."

"My pity is for the poor wife," she answered briskly. "I can't imagine anything worse than to be married to a man who drinks."

He made no reply to this and the subject was dropped. But next day, in the Stores, Mrs. Moore asked Celia if she had heard about Job Clayton giving Mr. Pearl a black eye, instead of his wife. Mr. Pearl, she said, had stood between them, and Job did not recognise him.

"He was proper upset this morning, Mrs. Clayton told me," she added. "Swears he'll never touch a drop again. Just fancy hitting Mr. Pearl, as sat up nights with him when he was ill last winter,

30 *The Christian's Pattern; Or, a Divine Treatise of the Imitation of Christ*, book I, chapter II, by Thomas à Kempis.

and half kept him when he was out of work. He's ready to go out and hang himself, like Judas!"

"I suppose Mr. Pearl did not hit back," said Celia, concealing her own knowledge of the affair.

"Oh Lord, no! As if he would—and him a Quaker. It would be against their religion you know, Miss. Quakers don't hit back. But he spoke so serious and kind to Job that he made him cry, Susan Clayton said. Not preaching like, but friendly and sort of sorrowful. Job was like a bit of wet rag after it. All the fight was gone out of him!"

" 'The Sword of the Spirit,' " Celia pondered. "Is it always so powerful? Or does it depend on the man who wields it?"

A wave of exultant pride passed through her. "And that man is my friend," she said to herself, "my dear true friend. How lucky I am!"

CHAPTER ELEVEN

CELIA laid by in lavender the memory of her first summer in Misty Vale. The loveliness and rapture of it were to live in her mind to her last day on earth. Like a young girl united to her lover she felt united to her precious house, the longed-for home of her dreams for twenty years or more; and even its faults were dear, as the faults of a loved person. How far her joy in it was increased by the new friendship that had broadened her outlook and refreshed her spirit who can say? Or how much was due to an ideal spring and summer. The time and the place and the loved one together had come to her, she thought, and she counted herself fortunate in the conjunction.

No fears oppressed her now. Since those first few nights of haunted terror, when she had trembled at a sound and dared not open her eyes in the night, the phantoms of the old house had ceased to trouble her; although she still heard occasionally the faint, windy whisper, like a voice through a keyhole: "I had to leave it." No longer did that whisper cause a moisture to break through her skin, or make her heart beat to suffocation. The nights were short now, as the 'midsummer pomps' came on, and when the nightingale ceased his singing there was still the strange cry of the nightjar, the quivering whine of the little brown owl, or the queer flat bark of a fox to break the dead silence, to give it life.[31] Celia liked to hear these sounds of living creatures in the night watches;

---

31 Pomps: splendid displays. From 'Thyrsis' by Matthew Arnold: 'Soon will the high Midsummer pomps come on,/Soon will the musk carnations break and swell...'

even the crowing of cocks in the distance at 3 a.m. was a comfort sometimes, though it could be an irritant too, when the wind brought it too near. Lob-lie-by-the-fire, now grown lanky with indulgence in flies, which he caught with amazing dexterity, still slept in her room; but he had now learnt to rise early and depart through her window as soon as it was light, using the creeper outside as his staircase.

It was a poet's summer, without doubt, such as are rare in our climate; with many golden hours of sunshine and brief thunderstorms, never very high. Celia loved to watch the violet lightning in the distance of an evening, flashing in and out of a dark sky without any sound to follow; to see the quivering heat rise from her garden mould, and the purple mist deepen at the horizon after sunset.

She and Miss Flack went several times to the sea by the omnibus that passed along a road not far from Clew Lodge. They took tea in a thermos flask, hard-boiled eggs, bread and butter for a meal, breakfast or lunch according to the tide, and had delicious bathes. They would have gone often, but Celia could not spare the time from her book and her garden. One or the other swallowed up her hours voraciously: the book more voraciously than the garden—or so it seemed; for time never passes so swiftly as it does in creative work. She could echo the plaint of lovers as to the rapid flight of time in their meetings. An hour flies like a minute in trying to mould even one perfect sentence. And Celia was, for the first time, trying to write prose. Her other books, she found, had been written in—what? She hunted a word for it. But John Pearl was a critic; he had an eager craving for *le mot juste*, a contempt for the facile. The obvious word was apt to make him shudder. Celia recognised in him a certain chastity of taste that she felt might be partly due to his upbringing. The Friends, she had begun to realise, dislike tawdriness, over-emphasis, or any form of extravagance.

Garden toil seemed mere child's play after her mental travail in the house. And it brought reward more quickly. Heaven only knew how long it might be before she would see the result of her literary labour; whereas the result of her manual labour was soon to view. And not only to view, but to taste. The peas she had seen Coles sow, and had herself 'sticked,' had sweetly flowered and grown plump. She had eaten her first dish and found them very good, with mint from her own garden and a few very tiny potatoes, just from one root. Who can ask more for pleasant work? One's own peas, one's own potatoes, one's own mint. And even a little gooseberry pie; tender and rather tasteless, too young to be sour, but still a pie! It was warmly encouraging. She could go on weeding and sowing and sticking for ever with such a goal in view. And flowers. She watched her fox-gloves shoot up and up their angelic steeples, hang them with pinky purple bells—gloves for fairies, thimbles for little fingers, larders for bees to rob—and then dry off to seed vessels, with as many atoms of life in them as would serve to grow an army of fox-gloves next year, if left to fall of themselves into the garden mould. She tried to count them once. There were over ninety in one pod and thirty pods on a stalk. And she fell to musing over Wild Nature's exuberant fecundity, her resolute determination to propagate. Gather her flowers, destroy her seed-vessels, and she would keep on blossoming to re-supply what was lost. Celia picked off her dying Canterbury Bells and lo! fresh ones began to form a few days later. Leave her sweetpeas to form pods and the vines instantly ceased to flower. "What's the good?" they seemed to say, "when we have done our business, accomplished our Mother's design?" The garden was thickly carpeted with tiny seedlings long before midsummer was over: forget-me-nots, primroses, wallflowers, as well as weeds. The 'gold-dusted snapdragon,' that had set itself among the wild things of the garden here and there, was now in bloom, throwing out its delicate lemon scent on the evening air; a flower and a fragrance Celia loved: it was so unobtrusive, so insinuating. Not like the rich honey of the woodbine or evening stock, or tobacco plant; scents that breathe boldly and almost attack you. The antirrhinum suggests only that it is sweet and lovable, as the roses do, being, as Bacon said, "fast flowers of their smells, so that you may walke by a whole row of them and find nothing of their sweetness: yea, though it be in a morning dew."[32] But the snapdragons' breath is not so 'fast' as that. Celia was caught by them as she passed in the morning's dew, and by some of the roses too, the dark red ones and the thornless Zephyrine Drouhin and, of course, sweet-briar. But Bacon set the eglantine apart from roses, though it might be called the mother of them all.[33]

The more Celia worked in her garden, the more she marvelled at its miracles of fertility, its beauty and inspiration. It brought ideas thronging to her mind, and fresh, beautiful words flowered with her roses and delphiniums there.

There was but one shadow to cast itself over this blissful time, the shadow of debt, the difficulty of paying her way. She was forced to contemplate the necessity of giving up even the one day of hard work that Coles served her garden. She had refined down her needs to the lowest possible ebb, and yet it seemed as if she must draw on her slender capital before the autumn set in. The result of this anxiety had a nearly fatal result for her.

---

32 From Francis Bacon's essay 'Of Gardens' (XLVI).

33 Eglantine: *Rosa rubiginosa*, sweet briar.

The small plots of grass had to be mown or left unkempt to fling their seeds all over the garden. Coles had mown them once a week till now; but one day, early in July, she decided to do it herself, in the evening after the sun had gone down. It was a warm evening with little breeze, even in its oncoming twilight, and when Celia had pushed her mowing machine (one of old and heavy build she had found in an outhouse) she suddenly collapsed in a dead faint upon the grass.

When the sound of the mower ceased suddenly and did not start again, Anabel, who was ironing in the kitchen, went out to discover the cause, and found her friend, to all appearance, dead beside her machine.

When she had brought her round, Anabel censured her severely.

"You ought to know better at your time of life," she said, in her most clipped and acid speech, "than to think you can mow a lawn unaided. Why, a young girl could hardly do it—and on an evening like this, without a breath of air. It's nothing but conceit and vanity. You think you are so young because you look young. Drink up this wine. I'll never be without brandy in the house again."

There was in Celia's store cupboard a bottle of strong dandelion wine made by Mrs. Coles, and given to her months before. It was, like many home-made wines, well reinforced with alcohol and therefore stimulating. The first gulp revived Celia, who had lost consciousness entirely only for a very few minutes. She swallowed the rest now and coughed.

"You are probably right," she said then, sitting up against her friend's shoulder. "I am an old fool, no doubt, but not vain, Belle. Why should we be vain of being young? I can't help being so young, can I? It is no fault of my own. And even young people have weak hearts." She laughed.

What could one do with such a woman? Anabel frowned and then laughed too.

"I didn't say you were young: I said you *looked* young," she corrected. "Of course you're old, as I am; only I don't pretend not to be and do silly things—like mowing lawns. I hope this will be a lesson to you, Celia, not to play such tricks with yourself. I shall order Coles to come and mow the grass once a week, and pay him, if you can't."

"I can," Celia lied promptly. Anabel grunted.

"By far the best plan," she declared, "might be to let the grass grow and have it scythed every few months. Some man with a horse or a cow would be glad to do it for the hay. You might even make something by it."

But the idea of letting her fine old grassy turf turn into hay did not commend itself to Celia, and he said so plainly.

"You are a great dear," she concluded, kissing her friend's sallow cheek, "and I don't know what I should do without you; but I must keep my little lawns for the fairies to dance on nightly, or they would pinch me black and blue. Next time I do any mowing it shall be when you are out—see?"

"And when I come back I shall find a corpse!"

"No fear! You will find me sitting triumphantly by a lawn all shaven and shorn, with a brandy bottle on one side and a syphon on the other, smoking a Craven A, and feeling that 'something attempted, something done has earned a bibulous repose.' "[34]

But she did not mow the lawn again; only a bit at a time, and she took care to do it when Anabel was within hearing. Her collapse

---

[34] Based on Henry Wadsworth Longfellow's poem 'The Village Blacksmith': 'Something attempted, something done,/ Has earned a night's repose.'

had really frightened her. She was not so strong as she thought, and her youth was youth of the spirt, not of the flesh.

About this time they had a call from Mrs. Staniforth—not the first, but a less formal, more friendly one. She saw them at church on Sunday mornings, Anabel regularly, Celia according to mood, or the time to be spared from her work. Celia liked her. She was a motherly woman, wrapped up in her husband and son, with a side interest in her husband's parish. After talking of that parish with Miss Flack, who had become a district visitor and went to mothers' meetings, Mrs. Staniforth glided into talking about her son, and that interested Celia more.

"We should have preferred him to go into the Church," his mother said. "He is all we have, you see, and although all my people are Army or Navy—the Vicar's too—we did not want him to be sent abroad. A soldier may be ordered off at any time, you know, Miss Grey. But, of course, he had to make his own choice, and he chose the Air Service—the worst of them all, from a mother's point of view," she smiled and made a little grimace, "more dangerous even than the sea, don't you think? But danger seems a lure to young men."

Celia agreed. It had been better to stop there, but something urged her to say more.

"Yes, the danger seems to obscure the other side. In the glory of adventure and risk our young men do not see the horror of killing others—the awfulness of taking life."

Mrs. Staniforth's face underwent a sudden and startling change. Its smiling urbanity gave place to a severity alien to its plump and gracious curves.

"I cannot quite see it in that light, Miss Grey," she said coldly. "Those who enter the services do so in defence of their country's rightful liberties. There are some causes in which the taking of life is a necessary, even a religious, duty."

Celia was silent a moment, seeing her mistake, and feeling deeply conscious of its source, the influence that had recently overcome her mind. She had once thought like this herself. Now all that had been curiously, imperceptibly changed. She knew herself now in flat opposition to the old tenets, the tenets Mrs. Staniforth was upholding. A sense of the utter futility of argument in such a case restrained her from contention. She could but say mildly: "I know many people think so."

"I do, for one," put in Miss Flack, feeling that it was her turn. "I've no patience with people who won't stand up for their own country, and would take insult and dishonour lying down—as it seems with some folk."

The speech was unfortunate, since it took shape, in Celia's mind, as an attack on John Pearl.

"I seem to have read somewhere," she said, smiling rather unagreeably, "of an injunction to turn the left cheek after a blow on the right, and something about loving one's enemies."

Silence for half a minute.

"It does not do to take everything in the Bible too literally," then said Mrs. Staniforth stiffly, and set down her cup.

"But Quakers do," remarked Anabel sharply, "at least in some things—when it serves their purpose."

Celia saw red.

"I suppose they are not the only people who do that," she said. "It sometimes seems to me that they are the most consistent Christians, since they try to practise what Christ insistently preached—love your neighbours and forgive your enemies. Perhaps you can explain away that sentence in the Lord's Prayer, Anabel: 'forgive us our trespasses as we forgive them that trespass against us.' Are we not to take that literally, Mrs. Staniforth?"

"Of course we are, but——" the guest paused as she rose and shook crumbs off her skirt, "but I do not think it applies in this case, Miss Grey. You should have a talk with the Vicar about it. He does not know you are a Quaker."

"I am not. I was christened and confirmed in the Church of England," Celia replied, taking the big soft hand extended to her. "It was there I learned all the Christian tenets I've been quoting, and to worship the Prince of Peace. But do you think He would approve of murder—even the killing of our enemies, Mrs. Staniforth?"

Her smile was disarming. Mrs. Staniforth gave a little, embarrassed laugh as she replied:

"Oh, well, it is too big a question for me to answer, Miss Grey. I only wish there were some other way of settling international disputes. Perhaps the League of Nations will find one. You believe in that, of course. But you must really have a talk with the Vicar."

"I shall be delighted."

At the door, the Vicar's wife opened up the subject again:

"You must not think, Miss Grey," she said, "that I have a word to say against Quakers. They are quiet, law-abiding citizens and not aggressive like some dissenters. We should miss them in this village—especially the Pearls. They are loved and respected by everyone. The Vicar thinks very highly of John Pearl. They are on the Parish Council together, you know, and quite good friends. I buy all my household things at their shop in Millborough. They are not very cheap, but wear for ever. And Faith Pearl is really a godsend to the village—a veritable Fairy Godmother. Not only is she a very nice, well-mannered and well-educated girl, but she is good and unselfish, so kind to the poor sick people. I am really fond of her."

She looked at Celia as if inclined to say more, but thought better of it. Evidently she was prepared to accept and cherish Faith as a daughter, despite the difference in their creeds and outlooks. Important difference as it obviously was, Celia felt that it might—that it ought to be—overcome. For where could the girl find a kinder or more affectionate mother-in-law? She sighed to think of the barriers that thought puts up against feeling, and realised how much happier are simple minds than complex ones; how much easier it is for the simple to find a mate.

But that was not the real dividing line between Faith and Michael Staniforth. Had she been as doltish as any maid in the village who browsed on sickly novelettes, and had no aspirations higher than a visit to 'the pictures,' this same barrier might have been raised between her and her lover. It was not so much a question of intellectual reasoning as of heritage. And the silliest girl in the place might have come of pacific Quaker ancestry; might have been taught from babyhood that fighting was an evil, introduced by the Devil himself. Faith had reinforced this early teaching with intellectual stuff from her own brain, arguing that violence breeds violence, hate, hate, and vengeance, revenge. Rationally she saw the utter futility of war as the last remnant of the animal in man, a survival of the day when it was literally necessary to take life in order to live. But hebetude would not have saved her. The barrier would have been there even without the brain, a very solidly constructed barrier between a Quakeress and a professional 'man of blood.' Had not her ancestors suffered persecution for their faith, their rebellion against authority and refusal to bear arms? In her, pacifism had become an instinct, part of her very being. Nothing, no human love, could tear it from her soul.

As a 'romantic' Celia mourned. She longed to see the beautiful youth and girl united. Their open engagement would have added the last idyllic touch to an idyllic summer. She would have enjoyed their happiness vicariously, revelled in the beauty of it. Love ought to be everything to youth. Nothing should stand in its way. As it reigned in romance, so it ought to reign in real life, all conquering. But real life is so full of contradictions, of cross threads and entanglements. That is what makes it so absorbingly interesting.

CHAPTER TWELVE

THE garden had been washed in a thunder shower, and breathed delicious odours of wet earth and grass, with pine and juniper, mignonette and clove, thyme and lavender. On every leaf a jewel sparkled. The stone-laid paths shone in the sunlight. A faint arch of many colours was beginning to show in the sky. Catmint and pinks, flattened out in their borders by the sudden deluge, were trying to lift themselves up again, and Celia gently helped them to shake off the weight of moisture. She felt very happy and relieved. The garden had needed rain badly, and she had feared it would be necessary to water some of the wilting flowers where the earth was driest—as in her nasturtium bed round the dovecote. The hedges, too, had cried out for a bath to freshen their dusty leaves. How gratefully the holly and hawthorn sparkled now! She snuffed their virile scent and the sweetness of a bay-tree that reminded her of custard eaten in her past, when they used the aromatic leaves for flavouring. She must make a custard pudding with bay-leaves to flavour it one day—perhaps to-morrow. The perfume of the dark bush brought her old home vividly to mind. She saw herself again, slender, pretty, in a preposterous white nainsook gown flounced almost to the waist with lace-edged frills and a folded scarf of the muslin round her hips, knotted in a great bow behind; with elbow sleeves frilled and a frilled fichu about her shoulders. She realised now the amount of labour required to 'get up' such a costume every time it was washed, but it never troubled her then.[35] What

[35] Nainsook: lightweight muslin. Fichu: a scarf worn about the shoulders.

were servants for, and laundresses? She could see herself, as in a glass—her face rosy with tennis under a large hat: not jammed on her head after the present fashion, but coquettishly tilted on one side like the hat of Gainsborough's famous portrait of a duchess, showing the thick coils of her auburn hair. And always with a swain by her side, looking ardently at her. Not always the same swain, but in the distance of past years they all become mysteriously merged into one, and that one was Leslie Hale.

Perhaps because of his personal splendour, his tall athletic figure and dark handsome face. He was hardly more than a boy then—ten years younger than herself. She recalled his carrying her upstairs in his arms one day amid shrieks of laughter from the other girls, of whom she was the tallest and heaviest—she must have been well over ten stone then—and how he had flung her on a bed, kissed her ear and stalked off downstairs again, with no more than a slightly quickened breath.

"The impudent scamp!" she said to herself, a smile curling her lips, as she thought how little she had cared and how little anyone had thought of the matter at the time.

"One loses something when one is past kissing time," she reflected, with a memory of the old rhyme they used to say when they blew thistledown:

> "It's half past kissing time,
> And time to kiss again."[36]

A fugitive recollection of Leslie's kisses was wafted to her on the scent of the bay-tree. It might have been an evocation. For, at the sound of a footstep behind her, she turned to see Leslie himself

---

[36] From 'Kissing Time' by Eugene Field.

standing on the wet grass, with the rainbow behind him.

Celia gave a little gasp. It was so unreal, so uncanny. This materialisation of memory!

"Leslie! Where did you spring from?"

He took her in his arms and kissed her.

"Lovely! Lovely as ever!" he ejaculated.

"Don't be so silly. I'll tell your wife, you absurd villain!" she said, trying to frown but blushing like a girl. Her instinctive commonsense told her to treat the caress lightly.

"She wouldn't care. She's got me safe, and she knows I've always loved you, Celia. I've made no secret of it."

"Of course she does not believe you. Who would? But even if she did, I have no doubt she would raise no objection to you kissing old ladies you knew in your youth."

"Old ladies! You're a girl—a child."

"Quite. I'm only half a century old and years your senior. Old enough to be your mother, in fact, as you've never grown up. How is Dora—and the children? Why didn't you bring them to see me? And why are you here anyhow?"

"What a question! To see you, of course. I was driving through on business—at least my business brought me within ten miles or so. I thought I'd take my chance of finding you, and my luck hasn't failed this time."

"How did you get in? There's no one at home, and the front door is locked."

"I didn't get in. I banged at the door till I was tired, and then marched round the estate till I found a gate open. I caught a glimpse of something green that moved, and it was you. You are as fond of green as ever, Celia, but I like you best in white."

"White is too expensive for me now," she said, smiling.

"Curiously enough, I was remembering myself in white when you pounced on me. Do you recollect carrying me upstairs once at your house, when I was staying with your sisters?"

"Don't I? Shall I ever forget? You were pretty hefty, too, in those days, let me tell you, my lady. You are lighter now, I'll warrant. Let me try."

He made as if to put his arms round her again. Celia repulsed him and turned serious.

"No more of that nonsense, Leslie. It is undignified at our time of life, to say the least of it."

He looked at her sentimentally and sighed.

"I haven't altered, Celia," he said.

"Nonsense! Of course you have; we both have. You can't put the clock back, Leslie. Now come in with me and help me get tea. Miss Flack will be in directly, and she will be glad of a cup with us. She has gone to the village, and it is a long, dusty walk."

"Miss Flack! Oh, crimes! You don't mean to say you have that old frump living with you?"

Celia was suddenly annoyed. Why should this man speak insultingly of a woman who was her friend, simply because she was plain and elderly? Leslie became a stranger, a rude boor who failed in respect for womanhood.

"Miss Flack is only a year older than I am," she said icily, "and she is my friend. I object to hearing her called names."

"Sorry," Leslie said lightly. "But what on earth made you saddle yourself with such a——?"

"That's enough, Leslie." Celia's snubbing tone checked his levity. He followed her silently into the house.

They were at tea when Anabel Flack entered, hot and tired. She put her head in at the door and said: "I thought you might like to know I've not been struck by lightning. But I got held up by the rain."

"Come in and have tea," cried Celia. "I have a visitor here you know."

Leslie jumped up. "Good afternoon, Miss Flack. You don't remember me," he said.

Miss Flack replied that she remembered him very well, and extended a limp hand. Her speech, dry and staccato as usual, made him feel guilty, as if she might have heard his previous remarks about her. Anabel, after a moment's hesitation, and a protest that she could get her own tea in five minutes upstairs, sat down at the table, drawn irresistibly by the teapot's aroma, and perhaps, a little by her sense of propriety. She could not escape from the feeling that it was indecorous for Celia to sit at tea with a former lover—and he a married man!

"You know what oil-stoves are," said Celia, " 'linked sweetness, long drawn out.' Take the goods the gods provide when you find them, Anabel, and don't be perverse."[37]

"Miss Flack," she went on, turning to Leslie, "is one of those preposterously independent persons who hates to take so much as a pinch of salt without paying for it. She will probably insist on giving me tuppence for her cup of tea! Did you know, by the way, that Clew Lodge has now become a kind of tenement house? I let apartments, and Miss Flack is my first lodger. So you will know where to come when you want rooms for yourself and family."

"I'll take one myself and stay a month," he exclaimed promptly.

"You won't mind sleeping on bare boards then?" she replied, laughing. "I don't let my rooms furnished."

---

[37] From the pastoral poem 'L'Allegro' by John Milton.

"Nor to gentlemen," put in Miss Flack, with a prim smile.

"Of course not. We are models of propriety," said Celia.

"I've found that out already."

Leslie's look at Celia was caught by Miss Flack, who stored it in her mind.

They talked then—or, at least, Miss Flack and Leslie talked—about the weather and Guildford people; the sort of talk that held little interest for Celia. She slipped into her own thoughts, smiled at the memory of a remark once made by her mother. "It amuses me," she had said, "to hear how you prattle with Leslie Hale. Nobody would ever think you are a clever girl." And Celia had quoted, in reply, the words of an American humorist then in vogue: "If a woman wants to get the whole of a man's heart, she must either be a bigger fool 'n he is, or make him think so." Everyone has forgotten Josh Billings and his aphorisms now, but this came back to Celia as she was pouring our Leslie's third cup of tea.[38] She had no faith in them; they belonged to another age and generation. Men to-day show little preference for fools, she thought, and certainly Leslie never had. Her cleverness had attracted him. But one could only prattle with him; he could only prattle himself. She looked at him with some admiration. How handsome, how healthy, how athletic and manly he was! A whimsical idea seized her. Were not her old heroes of romance, Ivanhoe, Coeur-de-Lion, Amyas Leigh, just like him? Would they not have prattled in the same way? Men of action, not of thought—and, perhaps—as dull as Leslie, who had won cups for rowing and shooting, and played cricket for his country?

[38] Josh Billings was the pen name of Henry Wheeler Shaw, a comic writer whose philosophical comments, misspelled and written in plain language, became very popular after the American Civil War.

A puckish spirit suddenly possessed her, and she asked Leslie what he thought of the Government's new housing scheme. A flat look came upon his face as he replied that he hadn't thought much about it. He added that he didn't think much of the present Government anyhow, and he brightened as he said this, as if he had disposed of a difficult question. But he was not to be let off so easily as that. Celia plunged into the subject of slums and houses and Parliamentary procedure until she saw that he was thoroughly bored. He betrayed no sign of interest in any of her speculations or suggestions, but, stooping down, took Lob upon his knee and amused himself by alternately stroking him and pulling his tail. Celia quickly took the little cat away from him.

"Why did you do that? I wasn't hurting her," he said.

"No, but you were teasing him. I don't allow my cat to be teased. It spoils his temper."

Leslie laughed contemptuously. "Nonsense! They like it. Cats are such silly things: they haven't the sense of dogs," he declared, and began telling her stories of his own dogs and their wonderful intelligence, till Celia was wafted back to her girlhood's days when Leslie had told the same tales and talked the same talk.

"Dear old Leslie! He hasn't grown an inch," she thought, "his brain is still microscopic." She made one more attempt to interest him in a subject outside the little things of everyday life, and then gave it up in despair. Her description of the ancient monastery near, of various interesting discoveries and the survival of ancient customs, merely brought to his face the 'gingerbread rabbit expression' she had formerly known so well.

It was a relief when she heard John Pearl's three quiet taps on the front door. With him the atmosphere changed magically. It had become somnolent, but now it was charged as with an electric current. John Pearl's vitality communicated itself instantly to the three persons in it. Miss Flack brightened up, and even Leslie Hale managed to appear less dull.

"When I saw a car at your gate," Mr. Pearl said, after the introduction to Leslie had been made, "I debated whether I should come in or slink off. But I decided to make this an excuse for coming in. Look here!"

He took out of his pocket and laid on the table a curious-looking object made of rusty metal.

"A caltrap, beyond a doubt," he said. "It was found by old Ben Mills in a ditch, and he brought it to me, knowing I like 'all them sorter things.' Interesting, isn't it, a clear evidence of a battle fought hereabouts? These hedgers and ditchers have wonderful opportunities of finding such things."

"I am afraid I don't know what a caltrap is," said Celia, examining it.

"It is a nasty, mean instrument designed to injure the feet of horses in warfare."

"How do you know it is one? Have you ever seen one before? I haven't."

"I've seen them in museums, and have a drawing of one. Look at the little fiendish thing."

Leslie was interested. He knew a good deal about horses. He took the caltrap up and looked at it.

"Seems a bit old," he said, with an air of discovery; "it's quite rusty."

John Pearl gave him a queer look out of his grey eyes.

"Iron is rather apt to get rusty if it lies in the earth a few hundred years," he observed. And then the same instinct that had prompted Celia to tease Leslie, prompted the remark: "Rather worse than moly, isn't it, Mr. Hale? And that must have been trying for farmers."

"Moly! What's moly? Never heard of it," said Leslie.

"Otherwise moonwort. It can open locks and un-shoe horses when they happen to tread on it. A dangerous herb."

John Pearl's eyes twinkled.

"But you don't mean to tell me you believe a tale like that!" cried Leslie, taking him seriously. "What rot!" And he laughed contemptuously. John looked at him with amused eyes.

"I assure you it is well authenticated," he said. "Nicholas Culpeper tells us that on White Down, near Tiverton, there was found thirty-two horseshoes pulled off from the feet of the Earl of Essex his horses. And who can doubt Culpeper?"

His laugh enlightened Leslie. "You're pulling my leg, sir," he said. "I've never heard of anyone called Curlpaper, but he can't have much commonsense if——"

The rest of his speech was drowned in a squall of laughter from Celia and John Pearl. Whereupon Miss Flack explained that Culpeper was a silly old herbalist who wrote books a few hundred years ago, which our great-grandmothers believed in.

"He made out that all the herbs were governed by the stars," she concluded. "Such nonsense!"

"You don't seem at all excited about my find," said John Pearl. "Not half so excited as old Ben was over the five shillings I gave him for it."

"Five bob for that bit of rusty iron?" exclaimed Leslie, incredulously.

"He would have been satisfied with one," Miss Flack suggested.

"It is not a question of what would satisfy him, but of what it is worth, friend. I don't know its museum value, but it is worth five shillings to me and has given me five pounds' worth of pleasure."

"Why?" demanded Miss Flack.

"I don't know," said John Pearl. "Does anyone know why he enjoys anything?"

There was no answer to this. They all gazed at the caltrap, as if expecting to find some reason there.

"Horribly barbarous—the thing, anyhow," Celia murmured at last.

"No worse than poison gas," said John, wrapping up his treasure. "And I think if I were a horse and given the choice, I would rather have been in a twelfth-century battle than a twentieth-century one."

This remark led to a discussion on modern chemical discoveries, and in the course of it he spoke of Ben Johnson's *Alchemist*, which, he said, threw curious side lights on modern chemistry. Just as witchcraft bore a certain relation to spiritualism, so alchemy bore some relation to metallurgy—even to such discoveries as that of radium, or so it seemed to him. Who could say where the next missing link would turn up, or what still lies in the womb of earth? Celia discussed this with him animatedly while the other two sat silently wondering what all the talk was about, and feeling extremely bored. Leslie Hale had no idea what alchemy was, and he was, as people usually are, exasperated at hearing many words he did not know. He might have been listening to a strange language. After yawning once or twice he said he must go.

Celia went with him to the garden gate, feeling a sense of compunction. What bad manners to speak in a foreign tongue before a guest who did not understand it!

As he took her hand, Leslie asked abruptly:

"Are you going to marry that old Johnny?"

"My dear Leslie, how absurd you are! Mr. Pearl is a married man and a grandfather."

"His wife alive?"

"Very much so. The dearest little Quaker lady you ever saw."

He let go her hand and stood looking down at her with troubled eyes. It was getting dark, and a gibbous moon was peering over the trees. The aspens trembled and whispered mysteriously behind them, though there was little breeze to stir their leaves, and Celia experienced the usual eerie sensation their murmuring always roused in her. What were they saying? Was it: "I had to leave my treasure?" And was that treasure life, slipping so fast away? Youth gone, middle age going, old age and death stealthily creeping on. Leslie had a curiously paradoxical effect upon her. He made her feel strangely young, and yet more conscious of those creeping footsteps than she ever normally felt.

His voice broke into her thoughts.

"But you are in love with him," he said, "and he with you."

Celia turned upon him an angry face. But it was no good being angry with Leslie or trying to explain anything to him. He was but a child who would never grow up.

" 'What is love? 'Tis not hereafter,' " she quoted.[39] "No, I'm not in love, Leslie. I leave that to the young. It is their prerogative. All I want now is friendship—and sympathy. I find these in John Pearl—that's all."

"And where do I come in?"

"You are a friend, too, a dear old friend."

There was no sound for some moments save the gentle rustle of the aspen leaves and the belated flute of a blackbird. Leslie's

[39] From the clown's song, Act 2, Scene 3, *Twelfth Night* by William Shakespeare.

handsome dark head bent a little lower to look into Celia's eyes, so candidly raised to his.

"More than that," he said; "you know I love you, Celia."

"Yes, I know. You always have, Leslie; it has become a habit. But you love your wife more."

He repudiated this as if it were an insult.

"You don't believe that!" he cried.

"I do. I am sure of it. She is your right woman. I am not. Your love for me is based on fancy. I am romance to you, as you are to me."

He was out of his depth at once and floundered, seizing the only spar of plain sense he could capture.

"Nonsense. Fancy has nothing to do with it. I fell in love with you when I was eighteen. I don't change, Celia."

His tone was so consciously virtuous that it made Celia smile.

"I suppose it is estimable never to change," she said reflectively, "but I am afraid it is a virtue I don't possess. I've changed a hundred times since I was eighteen—I'm always changing, one way or the other. But, granting that you're the same Leslie you were at eighteen (or at eight, she said to herself), nevertheless I am only your romance, your dream, your fancy. And I want to be only that. I hope I may always be. But your wife—no. I should bore you excessively."

Her rider to that remained unspoken.

"You would never bore me," he declared.

"I should, inevitably. I've been doing it all the evening. Why attempt to veil the truth, my dear Leslie? Have you ever thought why Dora is not jealous of me? Of course she knows what she is to you, and what I am. She knows her place, and I know mine. You married her before all the world, and she is the cherished mother of your children. I am an impalpable shade beside her.

Let me remain that mere vision and be still romance to you."

He said nothing. She wondered how much of her speech had reached him. Suddenly he turned on her fiercely.

"I am going to kiss you, anyhow," he said.

"Why not?" She lifted her face. "It will do nobody any harm. I am not going to be coy and struggle, Leslie."

He kissed her and held her tightly in his arms. But in spite of the convulsive strength of that embrace she recognised quite well it only simulated passion.

"I wish you were not so damn clever," he muttered. "It is that keeps us apart—always has done."

She laughed. "That's one way of looking at it."

"How can you laugh at me when I'm so miserable," he groaned.

"You're not in the least miserable. You are only sentimental, and like to think of yourself as a forlorn lover. Be honest, Leslie. Before you've driven ten miles you will be thinking of your business, your home and children. Confess."

After an attempt to remain scowling, Leslie's strong white teeth began to show in a smile—a very attractive smile.

"I believe you can make me do anything you like—witch!"

He turned from her and sprang into his car.

"But you don't know everything, Celia, clever as you are, and you needn't think it. And you haven't seen the last of me. Good night."

He whirred off. Celia walked up her garden in the moonshine, smiling and feeling very light, as if her feet wanted to dance.

"Romance and moonlight—how lovely they are together!" she thought, "even when it is not the real thing, but just a misty rainbow with its feet in the clouds. What an ideal hero of fiction he is! Yet an hour in his company reduces me almost to pulp. In a film he would make a perfect lover. In real life a perfect bore."

She added: "What a foolish old woman I am, to be sure," but she did not feel like one. She felt like a girl, and, indeed, looked like one as she entered the lamp-lit room; her cheeks glowing and her greenish grey eyes holding points of light. John Pearl looked at her with smiling interest, as he might have looked at a happy child.

"So you've said good-bye to Lubin," he said.[40] "What a handsome fellow! He looks like a hero of romance."

With a sharp glance at Celia's flushed face Miss Flack asked why she had been gone so long? "Wouldn't the car start?"

"It wasn't asked to," said Celia gaily. "There it stood, patiently waiting, poor thing, while Leslie talked. I wonder if cars do get tired of waiting sometimes—such energetic creatures as they are."

"What on earth had he got to talk about?" Anabel demanded, ignoring the foolishness about cars.

"Was it surprising," said Celia, "considering how he had been bottled up for hours while we talked?"

"Yes, it was too bad," said John Pearl. "I fear I must have bored him abominably. You shouldn't let me talk so much, Celia. It is my besetting sin—so my family say. They frequently put the stopper on me. But you and Miss Flack encourage my garrulity—out of politeness no doubt. Now shall I go, or shall we set to work?"

"Let's work," was Celia's prompt reply. And Miss Flack, with some misgiving, left them to it.

---

[40] Lubin: an inept, talkative country bumkin in the play *George Dardin* by Molière, and a conventional name from pastoral literature.

CHAPTER THIRTEEN

AS usual they bemoaned the difficulty of making seventeenth-century people talk naturally, to avoid making them appear like characters in a book rather than living men and women.

"I am dissatisfied," Celia said, "with that last dialogue. We seem to have mixed up different centuries. Isn't it terribly hard to make people talk even as they *may* have talked three hundred years ago? To say nothing of as they *did* talk. That, of course, we cannot know."

"*Cannot* and *never* are two words I don't admit to my vocabulary. Who knows what the future holds? There is a new theory being mooted now that we may be able to catch up the echoes of the past in the ether by means of some delicate wireless apparatus that will give us fragments of the speech of long ago. Any why not? We can hardly hope for it to be perfect yet, or, at least, in time for our romance. But one never knows. Inventions and discoveries crowd upon us faster and faster every year."

They discussed this idea with eagerness and polished their dialogue in the last chapter till Celia suddenly felt hungry, and laid her usual meal on the table. They shared it, scarcely knowing what they ate, being so absorbed in their discussion. It was past eleven o'clock before John Pearl rose and said, with a sigh, that he supposed it was time to go. They walked to the garden gate together.

It was dark now. The moon had sunk behind the trees and only stars were shining.

" 'Look how the sky is thick inlaid with patines of bright

gold,' " said John.[41]

" 'On such a night did young Lorenzo swear he loved Jessica,' " added Celia, thinking of Leslie.

"He, or another like him, has been doing so ever since. We must have a scene between our lovers in starshine, Celia, not moonshine. There is something about the tremulous light of stars more delicate and subtle than the blue glare of Luna."

"It seems impossible, doesn't it, that sin and disease, sorrow and shame can ever exist in such a lovely world as this?" said Celia, dreamily.

"Shadows thrown by the light," he responded. "Our consciousness of sin and ugliness is due to the Light behind. Life is full of mysteries, Celia. One can but wonder and worship."

"And question."

"Yes, and question everything. Everything but the supreme fact of the Light shining through."

"You know it to be a fact?"

"Why yes, of course." His tone had surprise in it. "Don't you know it too?"

She hesitated. "When I am with you I do. Sometimes . . . I've questioned."

"Doubts come to us all. But never doubt that. If it were not true, why should sin and sorrow trouble your mind? In a world ungoverned by a force divine what would they matter to you?"

They fell into a long silence. A car passed along the road full of chattering, noisy people. It seemed to make a smear on the tranquil night.

---

41 Based on lines from Shakespeare's *The Merchant of Venice*, Act 5, Scene 1: 'Look how the floor of heaven/Is thick inlaid with patens of bright gold.'

"They remind me," said Celia, "of what I have left behind. I can hardly believe—here in this delicious silence, with the stars above and flowers below, keeping watch by day and night, as O. W. Holmes fancied—I can hardly realise that three months ago I was spending most of my days among such people as those who just passed, strutting about a show-room, exhibiting clothes for their inspection and choice. Over-rich, over-fed, idle women with nothing in their heads, and no interests in life, but to be always changing their costumes, showing themselves off, playing silly games, and trying to make other women envious."

John Pearl laughed. "Oh, come now, friend Celia, that speech is not like you," he said: "it is far too caustic and uncharitable. How do you know what their interests are—what emotions fill their hearts, what aspirations are in their minds? Give them, at least, credit for a sense of beauty, in colour and design. You would not have women dress, as men do, in drabs and browns, all of the same form and cut, would you? It would make a sombre world."

"This from a Quaker!" cried Celia.

"Why not? The earliest Quakers, you know, dressed like other folk. It was probably the extravagant foppery of the eighteenth century that set the pendulum swinging towards sober raiment."

"And it may be why I would rather wear sober raiment all the rest of my days than have to show off fine clothes in a shop," she said: "I sometimes feel that I never wish to enter a draper's shop again."

He gave her a whimsical look.

"And yet I could affirm that you love to go prettily clad as well as any other woman living."

She had to laugh, but made no reply.

"When I was called upon to go into my father's business," he went on, "I felt a great distaste for it, and inwardly rebelled. Nothing but the fact of my mother's widowhood, and the necessity of keeping a roof over our heads, would have made me do it. Like all young men, I had spectacular visions of more soul-satisfying careers. But, as I told you before, I soon became interested in it. The variety, the ingenuity, the very change of fashions in the drapery trade, give it a certain charm. And people must have clothes, you know."

"I had forgotten you had ever been a draper. You are not like one."

"How do you know that? I am probably like a great many. 'Because a man has shop to mind . . . " how does it go on? . . . 'need spirit lack all life behind, all stray thoughts, fancies fugitive?'[42] I forget the rest, but you will remember. Now I must depart. Ruth will be very severe with me for keeping you up."

"And for keeping her up?"

"Not I. She goes to bed, and I sneak upstairs without shoes, like a burglar. Good night, friend Celia. God be with thee."

The soft air fanned her face, no longer hot. She looked after him as he walked down the road, with that quick, boyish step she had learnt to know so well. As his footfalls died away, she felt suddenly tired, a little old and lonely; not as she had felt in Leslie's presence, a young heroine of romance. And she felt, moreover, nervous. The night was full of mysterious voices, whispering, with the aspens, to her soul. She wished she might find Miss Flack sitting up, but knew that was unlikely. Her house, although dear to her, was not companionable at night. It seemed then to forsake her for its past, to be full of strange haunting shadows. Through it, as she

42 From 'Shop' by Robert Browning.

entered, a chill current of air seemed to meet her, and glide like a snake about the dark passages. It suggested to her mind the cold dews of death, and she shivered with apprehension; the uncanny sensation of terror she had felt at first but had not known for some months. As she went into her sitting-room and Lob came forward to meet her with piteous eyes for his supper, she thought how she had then regarded her house, with compassion, as forlorn and deserted. Now she felt forlorn and deserted herself. Her two friends had gone home to their wives and she was left with only her cat and her house for company. And the cat thought of nothing but food: the house had its ghosts and dreams. She felt forsaken and useless.

But then her tired eyes fell on the papers and books that, a short time before, had been engrossing her, and the flame of her spirit leaped up again. If only she might create a beautiful thing, something of permanent value, she would not feel that she had lived in vain and missed her natural woman's destiny. She would not feel barren.

Comforted and restored as she was by the sight of her work with John Pearl, and the thought of his unfailing sympathy, she could not shake off the creeping sensation of terror that had assailed her on coming back into her house. She assured herself that it was due entirely to her nerves and physical exhaustion; but there was no quelling the premonition that some fresh manifestation of immaterial phenomena lay in wait for her. As she climbed the staircase, with Lob dancing before her as usual, peeping through the banisters at the turning corner to catch at her skirts when she went by, the atmosphere of mysterious dread deepened, and her own shadow, cast by the flickering lamp in her hand, took on the fearful aspect of a weird succubus. She drew back from it with a sudden start of fear, and then laughed at herself. By now she ought to know her old house well, with all its strange possibilities. But even accustomed as she was to the acceptation of its haunting shades, as part of its mystery and beauty, she could not repress a shuddering dread of what she might see or hear.

In bed, feeling Lob's warm little body at her feet and his movements as he assiduously washed himself, Celia was no longer shaken by strange terrors and prepared to sleep. But before she could do so there was a rustling by her bed, as of a silken gown; a chair was pushed across the floor; a door opened and shut: the room seemed full of light. But she dared not open her eyes, and drew the sheet over her head.

More clearly and plaintively, than she had ever heard it before, the whispering voice sounded in her ears.

"I had to leave it—my treasure."

Celia knew that Something stood beside her bed, and she held her breath.

Presently the tension was relaxed. All sound ceased. She felt a sudden release from fears and fell asleep.

CHAPTER FOURTEEN

"I DON'T wish to worry you," said Miss Flack next morning, "but are you aware that there are rats in your house?"

Celia was not. She did not believe there were, and said so emphatically.

"You may not believe it, but there are," Anabel declared, even more emphatically. "I heard them overhead last night."

Celia felt a little tremor creep up her spine.

"Nonsense! You were dreaming," she said.

"I was till they woke me. I wonder you didn't hear them. They made a horrid noise."

"What kind of noise?"

"Oh, thumpings and things being pushed about. I thought, at first, someone had got into the house and was burgling it. But I knew there was nothing to burgle, and they were not likely to start in empty attics."

"I expect you heard me coming to bed late, and Lob scampering about. He makes a noise like a regiment of horse."

"What time did you come to bed?"

"About twelve."

"It was one when they woke me. What were you doing up to midnight? Surely Mr. Pearl didn't stay so late. What must his wife think?"

Celia ignored this question.

"If there were rats in this house Lob would have caught one by now," she said, "you know what a mighty hunter he is. And if there is any sharp noise in the night, he is on the alert in a moment.

Once I thought I heard a mouse, but when he did not stir I knew I must be mistaken."

"Then he couldn't have heard what I did last night, or you either. They may not be over your room."

"If there were rats in the house, I should certainly have heard them before now."

Miss Flack bristled.

"If you think I am a liar, Celia—" she began, her dry voice trembling slightly.

Celia hastened to apologise. "I didn't mean that, Belle. You must have heard something, of course."

"What else could it be?"

Celia was silent.

"What is there in the attic over my room?" asked Anabel, "is it empty or not?"

"I believe there are a few odd things I haven't cleared out—boxes, a broken chair, and so on. You see, I haven't done much in the top storey. There was so much to do downstairs and in the garden."

"Well, it is time something was done, that's all. I'll help you clean them up. We shall then see if there are any rat-holes."

Celia thanked her for this offer of assistance, and the subject was dropped for the moment. She concluded it were best to say nothing of the thought that had instantly crossed her mind when Anabel told of her disturbance in the night. Among the books John Pearl had shown her was one by Camille Flammarion on haunted houses. He had refused to lend it to her, saying that it was not the kind of book to read at Clew Lodge; but she had dipped into its pages and read various accounts of supernatural manifestations, examined and attested by this famous French scientist. Among these were instances of curious physical phenomena such as Miss

Flack had heard—material things being moved about, showers of stones, knockings and other noises, impossible to explain by natural causes. But to tell this to Anabel would be to court scorn and ridicule.

The puzzle in Celia's mind was to know why Anabel had heard the noises and not she herself, since she had been awake and sensitively aware of other ghostly phenomena at the same time. Moreover, the experiences quoted had seemed to show that a medium is usually involved in such cases, and Anabel as a medium was inconceivable. Celia knew it would be impossible even to make her believe that the sounds she heard were attributable to anything less material than rats. All she could do was to try to avoid an immediate hunt for these rodents, was to urge that midsummer was hardly the time for working under the roof; and as this suggestion was received with a mere grunt, she hoped the matter would end there, at least for a time. But she reckoned without Anabel's ingrained obstinacy. At the end of the week, which had turned rainy and much cooler, Miss Flack opened fire again.

"It is just the day to clean out those garrets," she said, plunging in upon Celia after breakfast, when she had settled down to work. "I vote we have an early tea and start this evening, Celia. You can't do anything in the garden: it is too wet."

"Oh, let it be," exclaimed Celia, irritably. She did not wish to be interrupted, nor to clean out her attics.

"Surely you don't want the place to be overrun with rats," said Anabel, sharply. "The sooner they are routed, the better. You know how they propagate."

Celia, in spite of her irritation, wanted to laugh. The absurdity of the situation tickled her sense of humour. Miss Flack's belief in rats against her own belief in ghosts—which was to conquer—the natural or the supernatural? There was, after all, only one way of putting the matter to a test.

"Oh, hang the rats!" she said, laughing. "You will be seeing them crawling about the walls next, Belle, since you have them on the brain. It may clear up this evening, and there is a lot to do in the garden."

"In that case," said her friend stiffly, "I will mind my own business and not trouble you any more with offers of help."

She went out, shutting the door rather noisily. Celia jumped up, full of compunction, and was going after her friend when the door was opened again and Anabel put in her head.

"But I am not suffering from D.T.'s—if that's what you meant," she flung out, and would have departed in a great dudgeon had not Celia seized her.[43]

"Silly old dear!" she said, "you ought to know me by now and take my little jokes as they are meant. Let us turn out the attics, by all means. It will be a good thing over, and it is very kind of you to help. I really could not afford Mrs. Coles just now."

For two hours that lovely summer evening, for the rain had ceased and the chastened sun shone out, Anabel and Celia toiled in the hot and dusty attic over Anabel's room, sweeping, scrubbing, dragging old boxes and useless things downstairs to be burnt for firewood or given away. There was a common chair with a broken back and another without its cane seat, which Anabel said could be mended and used in the garden. There was a painted wooden washstand, having holes for crockery and but little paint left upon it. There was a camp-stool with canvas rolling from it, and a small iron bedstead, in sections, covered with rust. All these things had

[43] DTs: delirium tremens, alcohol withdrawal.

to be moved down a very narrow staircase, with twists and corners and low beams to catch the head. The window had stuck fast, and they had to spend nearly half an hour on prizing it open with a hammer and screwdriver, so that the heat at first was insufferable. And even when they had opened it very little air came in under the low eaves. Long before they had finished Celia was in a state of sticky moisture, longing for a proper bath-room. Their apology for one involved long and hard pumping up of cold water from the well. All she could do, therefore, was to change all her clothes and wash in her room.

Even when they had worked for over three hours the attic chamber was not completely finished, and they agreed to leave it; for the dusk fell quickly there, and the oak floor had to dry. They were, moreover, very tired. They agreed to sup together, and by tacit consent did not speak of the matter in both their minds—the fact that no sign of a rat had been discovered by them; no hole in the floor or skirting boards. There were plenty of spiders, moths and maggots, but nothing more.

The next evening they went upstairs to finish the work begun; clean the window and wash the paint. When they were there Anabel declared suddenly her conviction that the rats must be domiciled in the low cupboards that, on either side of the garret, were set in the wall. These were partly concealed by the old-fashioned pattern of the wall-paper, and Celia had hardly noticed them before. They had knobs, but no keyholes, and were easy enough to open. Miss Flack had, indeed, pulled one open and glanced in the day before, but, seeing nothing, had closed it again. Now she announced her intention of groping under the eaves with a candle. Celia protested, alarmed, seeing in anticipation her precious house set afire; but the little electric torch she possessed had run out a few days before, and so the only light available was that of lamp or candle. She begged Anabel to wait till next week, when she could obtain a refill for her torch; but Anabel's will was too strong for her. The candle was fetched and the search begun.

Groping through the aperture in the wall on her hands and knees went the intrepid Miss Flack, pushing the flat candlestick before her. Celia stood behind, anxiously. When her friend disappeared entirely there was no sound for several minutes. Then something between a shout and a grunt reached her. Celia knelt down and peered.

"I can see something—a box," she heard Anabel say, her harsh voice slightly muffled. "Oh!"

"What is it?"

"I'm smothered in dust! But the box is quite light. I'm bringing it out."

First her feet appeared, then her body and the candle; after which an oblong box, about two feet in length, came in view, thickly covered in dust and smelling of soot.

The next action of Miss Flack, after she had put out the candle and shaken herself, was to give the box a kick and stand back; in obvious expectation of seeing a tribe of rats run out of it, Celia fled to the door, but nothing came from the box save a cloud of dust.

"I expect this was the thing they moved about," observed Anabel. "No doubt they have their hiding places by day. What a pity we did not look for this yesterday and save our nice clean floor. It will have to be swept again."

Celia made no reply. Once assured that there were no rats in the box she felt no more fear, nothing but excitement and elation.

The Treasure! What else could it be, hidden away there beneath the roof? She fell on her knees beside it and began to examine it closely.

It was a wooden casket with a domed roof, roughly but strongly made, and had evidently once been covered with some substance, paper or cloth, that had rotted away, or been eaten, as Miss Flack suggested, by rats or mice. A rusty padlock held it locked.

Its light weight disconcerted her. She remembered certain words John Pearl had spoken. "A treasure need not be gold or jewels. Other things are treasured—old love letters, a baby's tiny robes, things precious to the heart"; but she had secretly hoped for gold and jewels, especially jewels—glowing rubies, cold flashing diamonds, vivid emeralds, things of beauty and material value. But, she reflected, anything three hundred years old must be full of interest, and even of some worth. Of course the coffer might be empty—just an old box stowed under the roof to be out of the way; but the fact of its being securely fastened contradicted this belief. Surely no one would lock up an empty box.

She lifted it and tipped it sideways. Something moved slightly inside. Her spirits rose again.

"Turn it right over," Miss Flack suggested, "to see if there are any holes in the bottom."

There were no holes in the bottom. It was clamped with two strong pieces of wood laid across. All hope of discovering a rat nest in it left Miss Flack's breast. She sighed, perplexed.

It was growing dusk in the attic. The lozenge panes they had just cleaned admitted but little more light than before. Celia lifted the casket in her arms, not without some inward shrinking, and carried it carefully down the break-neck staircase. She took it first into the courtyard, where they thoroughly dusted it, and then into the parlour. There they tried every key they could find between them, but found no one to fit the ancient, dusty padlock. By this time, past eight o'clock, they were both tired, hot and thirsty.

Anabel declared she could do nothing more until she had had a cup of tea, and Celia was not loath to pause. Both of them rather dreaded opening the box, in spite of their eagerness to see inside it, though for different reasons. Celia felt a strange fear of something undefined; Anabel was afraid there might be something in the casket that would encourage Celia in her foolish superstitions. If there should be actually a treasure in it, Miss Flack sapiently concluded, Celia would evermore believe that she really had heard strange whispers, and her uncle too. In which case Celia would triumph over her, Anabel's, scepticism, and commonsense would be flouted.

And so it happened that the two women lingered over their tea, and it was not until the lamp was lighted that they brought a screw-driver into play, and unscrewed the hasp of the metal flap that fitted over the strong loop, held by the padlock. It was attached to the lid by four screws, and it seemed, at first, impossible to turn them, as they had rusted in their sockets and were deeply imbedded in the wood. But at last they yielded to the screw-driver, and, with a quickly beating heart, Celia threw open the lid.

A layer of quilted silk met their eyes. It had probably once been white, but was now discoloured with age and brownish at the edges. Celia lifted it gingerly, and dropped it again with a little cry. For that which lay beneath it gave them both a shock. One glance was enough. Celia shut down the lid quickly and turned horrified eyes on Anabel.

"It couldn't be . . . " she quavered.

"A baby!"

"A mummy!"

Beneath its coverlet they had seen lying a little weird creature with a yellow waxen face and strange eyes staring up at them. One thought rushed through both their minds. It must be—it looked like the embalmed body of a newborn babe!

So this was the Treasure, Celia concluded, of the pathetic spirit that haunted the house: some unhappy girl who had thus concealed her shame from prying eyes. And then, maybe, had died herself, in lonely agony.

They fancied they could smell the odour of corruption, long pent up, with the scent of ambergris and musk.

Anabel recovered herself first.

"Horrible!" she exclaimed. "I wish we had left it alone. The best thing we can do now will be to put it in the shed and bury it to-morrow. I don't want to see it again."

Celia did not either. She could not bring herself to open the lid again, but she wanted to know more about the contents of the coffer before thrusting it outside the house. There might be something else underneath.

"No," she said firmly, "I shall not do that. I am going to fetch John Pearl. He will know what it is, and what to do with it."

"Absurd! It is dark, past nine o'clock, and will be nearer ten by the time you reach the Thatched Cottage. They will be going to bed. You don't want to fetch him out."

"Indeed I do. He never goes to bed early, and he will be tremendously interested. You need not come with me. It is not very dark,"

"If you think I am going to be left alone with *that thing*," said Miss Flack emphatically, "you are much mistaken. If you go, I go too."

It was quite light outside, though with no moon or stars. The last pearly glimmer of twilight had not yet faded into the midsummer night. The village seemed asleep as they passed the first cottages, whose front rooms were rarely used, and, in many cases, stood with their gable-ends to the road. But they found the Pearls' little house lighted up as usual, and the sound of quaint music issued from the open parlour window. It continued after their first knock, for John Pearl was playing a Handel Suite on his harpsichord, and the lively Gigue drowned all other sound.

Their second knock brought Mrs. Pearl to the door. She welcomed them with her usual sweetness. Celia could hardly respond in her excitement. Almost before they were inside she cried:

"We've found it—in the roof! Oh, can you come at once and see it?"

She spoke to John, who sat on the music-stool, his thick silvery hair shining under a light over the harpsichord. In his eyes the spell of music lingered. But he sprang up quickly at her words.

"Not the Treasure!" he exclaimed.

"Much the reverse," declared Anabel, "the horrid thing!"

He looked at her a moment and turned again to Celia. "Tell me exactly what you *have* found."

"It may be the Treasure," said Celia, with a nervous laugh, "but it gave us a turn. We found an oblong box in the garret—in a cupboard under the roof—and it happens to be a—coffin!"

"A coffin!" ejaculated husband and wife as one.

"So it seems. It was padlocked and we unscrewed the hasp. When we opened the lid and took off a sort of coverlet we saw what looked like a small mummy—of a baby."

He looked grave. Ruth Pearl gave a little gasp and sank into a chair, very pale.

"Such a weird, waxen, pathetic little face," Celia went on, in a low voice, "with round, shiny eyes staring up at us."

"Did you notice anything else about it?" asked John.

"Only that it had a cap on and long whitish clothes, like a baby." She shuddered.

At this moment Faith entered. She had been out at a maternity case. When the story had been related to her she was full of burning interest and wild to set off at once to Clew Lodge. Ruth preferred to stay at home, but Faith and her father went back with the two women in his little car that he called Phyllida.

"The thing that puzzles me," he said, "is why a mummy should have 'shiny eyes.' I've never seen them in a mummy, have you?"

"What else could it be?" Celia asked. But he had no suggestion to make.

The box stood on the table as they had left it, with its padlock and the screw-driver beside it, and Celia felt a curious sensation, something like surprise, at the sight of it. The whole incident—the finding of the casket, the shock of its opening—was of dream-like consistency in her mind. When John Pearl went up to it and raised the lid, both she and Miss Flack turned their eyes away to avoid seeing what lay there.

A hearty peal of laughter from Faith and her father brought their eyes quickly back upon the opened box.

"Why, you dear simple women, it's a *doll*!"

They all looked closely as he lifted out the little figure for inspection, and Celia laughed as heartily as the Pearls at her own silly conclusion. Although rather ghastly of aspect, with its yellow waxen face and beady glass eyes, the thing did not bear any real resemblance to the mummy of a baby. It was a crude little object, very stiff, and clothed in yellow satin. The cap tied under its chin was of fine lace; its hard waxen hands had no thumbs and only four pointed fingers; it was almost flat, and the red of its mouth had nearly faded away.

They gazed at it with an interest in which a sharp sense of something eerie was blended. The dead past seemed to have thrown up a fragment from the sea of time at their feet. No mummy could, indeed, have spoken more eloquently of that past. Their laughter froze to gravity as they regarded it.

"A 'puppet,' " he said softly, "that was what she would be called in her day, this little lady. They seemed to have had no word like doll. I wonder how long she has lain buried under the roof. By the style of her dress I should think——ah! what have we here?"

While speaking he had taken some layers of silk and paper from the box, and there, under his hands, lay a thick, leather-bound book, with tarnished clasps.

"Behold the Treasure!"

He lifted it out and placed it in Celia's hands. Miss Flack and Faith drew nearer. The excitement was immense as Celia undid the clasp and cried: "A diary—a real old diary! What a find! How perfectly delicious! John, it is just what we want. Now we shall know how they talked and wrote."

He smiled. The diary, he thought, would be like any other diary of the past and tell them no more than they knew already. Moreover, judging from the doll's attire, its period would be much later than that they had chosen for their romance. But he would not damp Celia's enthusiasm by such cold doubts, saying only that it was indeed a valuable and most entrancing discovery. He added, with a mischievous glance at Miss Flack, that she would now probably hear no more whispers.

"Now, pray don't encourage that nonsense, Mr. Pearl," Anabel exclaimed, falling at once to his lure in her most rasping voice. "To hear you talk one might really think there was something in it."

"Well, isn't there? We have found the Treasure—that you cannot deny, and the whisper was always of a Treasure."

"And we have not found any rats," added Celia. She and John Pearl had laughed together over Anabel's obsession, and she felt so childishly delighted with her trove that an impish desire to tease her friend overcame her. "Surely you must now be convinced of my ghost, Belle."

To which Miss Flack promptly replied: "When I begin to believe in ghosts, Celia, I shall certainly be in my dotage."

"There speaks your true-born Briton, who never acknowledges defeat," said John. "Good night, friend Anabel. I hope all this excitement will not keep you both awake. If I were you, Celia, I would put the doll back in the box and cover it up carefully, excluding the air as much as possible. Screw on the padlock again. Keep the diary out, as we shall want to study it. Come, Faith, you look half asleep."

She did indeed look tired. Anabel and Celia were tired too, but so excited they felt disinclined for bed. It was past midnight when they went upstairs.

Celia lay for a long time wide awake. She felt a great longing to go downstairs again and bring up the diary, which she had locked away, to read in bed. But she dared not venture. At any moment, she knew, the strange, undefined Terror she had experienced before might seize her by the throat and paralyse her reasoning faculties. It might be that, now the Treasure was found, the uncanny agencies would cease to operate; her whispering 'ghost' be laid for ever. But she could not be sure of that, or of her own nervous fancies. She had become conscious of certain innate sensibility to impression that made her a medium for ghostly manifestation; a psychic quality of which she had been entirely unconscious before coming to Clew

Lodge. And the finding of the casket so strangely had not lessened her perception of the supernatural. 'Ghost,' she told herself, was a vague and elusive term. It might mean anything one liked to make it mean. To Anabel it meant something in a white sheet with a turnip-head. To Celia it meant 'a palpable impression on the air,' some emanation of etheric matter surviving from the past. As a phenomenon, she thought, although unexplained, it might not be inexplicable. But, in spite of her philosophical reasoning, Celia dared not go downstairs again to fetch the diary; not even when the darkness began to melt into dawn's grey light. The chirp of a sparrow on her window-sill made her draw a deep breath of relief, and she fell asleep.

CHAPTER FIFTEEN

THE diary, to which Celia now applied herself, was not easy to read. The ink had faded to a pale brown, almost yellow, and although the script was tidy it was very small and full of unaccustomed abbreviations. Letters were formed differently from the way in which we write them now, and it took some time to get used to the flourishes, the long tails of ss, the queer loops of ll's and the still queerer spelling, which seemed to be under no rules. 'Heart,' for example, was spelt herte, harte, hearte or heart quite indiscriminately; 'courage' was sometimes corage, corrage or currage; and capital letters were profusely sprinkled over the pages. By degrees, and by the time John Pearl came that evening, she had mastered most of these stumbling blocks, and was able to read aloud to him some pages of the diary.

It began thus:

> "This is the book of Lavanda Selcroft wherein I do set down all that is in my Heart but can never leave my Tongue, for those in authority over me forbid me to speak of that I Love best and Honour most. And having no Ear open to me ever these pages shall be an Ear and no Body shall ever know, for I have found a Hiding place in Secret where they will not deign to look. So may I ease this troubled Heart of its Woe and when that Fond Heart ceaseth to beat, I pray that Whoever findeth this Book will deal with it Kindly and make no Sport or Jest of its Foolishness, for I am indeed a very foolish Maid and that I know full well. I do confess my Folly and ask for

pity in my Trials and Sorrows, and hereupon do I begin to write this First Day of February in the year of our Lord 1744."

"Eighteenth century—I thought so," muttered John Pearl.

Celia read on, turning over the pages reverently till she came to a passage that made her eyes smart and her voice falter. It was written about a week later, and it transcribed a letter received from one very dear to the writer.

> "There were Words in Thy valued Letter which, while not fostering any certainty, yet give a Hope and Cordial to my Courage. If in the Depth of my Heart existed a Doubt as to the Truth and Reality of my Affection or its perseverance, that Doubt hath been for ever laid to Rest by the knowledge that we twain are one in Heart and Soul. Thou hast said my Name is forbid to be spoke in thy Home. So be it. Thou shalt Honour thy Father and Mother and I would be the Last to wish it otherwise. But nor Father nor Mother nor Law of Man can set aside those whom God hath joined together, as thee to me, till Death and after, in the Life of the Spirit and thus are we united. May God be ever with Thee my only Dear.
>
> Thy true and faithful Servant,
>
> Richard Butler.

Celia's speech failed, and she let the book fall in her lap.

"It seems almost a sacrilege," she said, with a little break in her voice, "to read what was intended for no eyes to see but those of——" she broke off and bit her lips. John Pearl did not speak for some moments. From out the dim, forgotten past the aroma of a tender romance seemed to fill the room, and its pathos touched both their hearts.

"I think," said John, "that Lavanda will not mind our reading her diary, or fear that we shall make a jest of it. It seems to me that she has set all this down in confidence, hoping that one day it may be read and understood with sympathy. Her restless spirit would scarcely have haunted this place for centuries had it been satisfied to know her secret was hidden from all eyes."

"You really believe, then, it is the ghost of Lavanda Selcroft that haunt this house?" said Celia.

It was the first time he had committed himself so definitely.

He smiled. "Yes, I believe it. Perhaps partly because I like to believe it. But, also, because my mind can postulate no other reason for the curious phenomena that have given the house its reputation. It may be, of course, but the echo of a voice that whispers through the rooms. But I think, at least, we may be sure that the author of this diary would raise, if she could speak to us, no objection to our reading it. Why should she?"

They pored for hours over the crabbed writing and came across many passages that excited them. Here is one:

> "I have still kept my little Poppet which delighted my Childhood's years, and which I named Gulielma after Madame Penn who lived at Worminghurst, and is remembered still by old Dame Wiggins who saw her when a child. R.B. says she was most Beautiful and most Beloved, tho' of course he saw her not, being born in the same House long after her Death. His Grandfather did hear Mr. Penn discourse at the Blue Idol Meeting House, whither he went on the Lord's Day in an Ox Wagon when residing in his House. He had surely the Gift of Tongues for R.B. saith he did convert his Grandfather to the Faith of the Quakers, albeit he was before of the old Faith

and regular at the Church Communion. Alack! Would he had never heard Mr. Penn, for then my Dear Love would not have been bred amongst those strange People who are, my Father sayeth, false to their King and Country, refusing to take the Oath of Allegiance or bear Arms against our Country's Foes."

"Lavanda's story in a nutshell, and full of suggestion for us," said John, as Celia paused. "Is it not strange to think that whereas we shall cover hundreds of pages with words in the telling of our romance, this eighteenth-century girl can do the same in a few pregnant sentences? She sets the whole picture before us. Her father and mother, respectable Church of England and Monarchy folk; her lover, the son and grandson of a Quaker. Her own bitter regret that she must love one whose religious principles she cannot approve. Her love triumphing, nevertheless. The name she has given her 'poppet' of a woman, the fame of whose beauty and sweetness reached her childish ears. Gulielma and her family, including her mother, lived in the house at Worminghurst—or, as it is now called, Warminghurst—for about ten years, during William Penn's visits to Holland and Germany, and his first journey to America. Celia, we have indeed lighted on a treasure!"

He was like a schoolboy in his glee, rumpling up his thick grey hair, with eyes shining through his glasses. Pleased and excited as Celia was, her pleasure and excitement were not as keen as his. She was thinking of poor Lavanda's unhappy love story, and comparing it with Faith's. But she had promised not to speak of that to Faith's father, though she felt it was at the back of his mind as it was of her own.

"Our fortunes are made!" he went on, gaily. "When our immortal work is published all the critics will recognise some unknown source of inspiration, and wonder whence it is derived. The name of our book will be on all lips; its theme will be discussed in every home—worth calling a home. What shall we do with our wealth when we get it?"

"I know what I shall do," said Celia, falling into his mood and speaking as gaily. "I will make Clew Lodge a Mecca for Quakers—a hostel for pilgrims such as they have at Jordans; and the 'little poppet,' Gulielma, shall be shown, with the diary, in a kind of shrine. What do you think of that?"

"Perfect. If only we could verify and establish the tradition that William Penn once came to Misty Vale and visited Clew Lodge! It is said that he did, and that a Friend once lived here, one of those who accompanied him in the Welcome, on his voyage to America. Perhaps we shall learn something of that from Lavanda. At present it is but a very vague legend."

"There's always something in legends."

"Invariably. No smoke without fire. Isn't it thrilling, Celia, to think that he might have trodden your up-and-down floors, looked out of your leaded windows, bumped his head against the beams of your ceilings—he was very tall, you know—and, perhaps, ridden his horse up the cobble stones to your old stable at the back."

"Or even stabled his oxen and waggon here for the night," she suggested. "Aren't you glad, John, you do not have to go to Meeting in a bullock-waggon? I can imagine nothing slower or more bone-dislocating on earth. And that reminds me. When are you going to take me to the Blue Idol? I long more than ever to see it."

"When you please. To-morrow?"

"But I want to go to a service."

He frowned. "A service, madam! What do you mean? We do

not have 'services' or priests to serve: only meetings for worship. But I forgive you. And I will drive you over next First Day, if you like, and if you can get up early enough. It is a long drive as Phyllida takes it."

"Not so long as it would be in a bullock-waggon."

"Perhaps not quite."

They laughed and turned back to the diary.

Faith came in presently, to learn more about Celia's discovery of the Treasure.

"It is going to be a source of inspiration to us," said her father: "and when Celia has made a colossal fortune out of our book, she is resolved to turn this house into a hostel for Friends. We are about to discover that William Penn came here for a night—or two nights, or even three, and once we make that discovery known to the world, there will be no holding back the pilgrims who will want to come and stay here, from all over the world."

They talked a little longer, and then the Pearls left. Celia sat for long afterwards absorbed in the diary. At half past eleven Miss Flack put her head in at the door and asked if she were not going to bed.

"We were late enough last night," she said, "and I can't think why you want to sit up now the Pearls have gone. Have you found anything fresh in the book?"

Celia, still bemused, replied vaguely: "Oh, yes—what did you say?"

"Aren't you ever coming to bed?" was the impatient reply. Celia opened her eyes a little wider and looked at her. With awakened perceptions she realised a slight change in Anabel, who was not undressed, and evidently did not wish to go to bed until her friend came up. Why? Was she afraid? Celia thought she was and asked, slyly:

"Are the rats troubling you, Belle?"

A dull red began to patch Anabel's face.

"I haven't heard them again," she said, "if that is what you mean. But I feel as nervous as a cat to-night. I don't know why. This house is so . . . so quiet and lonely, and . . . I can't get used to the deathly silence, and it makes every small sound seem twice as loud."

This was very like a recantation, but Celia was too wise to say so. All she said was:

"You can sympathise now with my nervousness when I was alone here, coming straight form the noise of London. But you have been here three months now; you ought to be used to the deathly silence."

"Oh, well," Anabel snapped. "I'm not going to defend myself—my own foolishness, Celia. I expect it is your nervousness and superstitious ideas that have infected me. And Mr. Pearl seems to encourage them."

Celia rose and put away the diary in the little corner cupboard to which she had a key. Then she turned to Anabel, who had picked up Lob and was stroking him in her ungentle way.

"Belle," she asked abruptly, "are you still absolutely convinced that there is nothing supernatural about this house? Do you still believe that all phenomena ceased when Christ appeared to the women at the sepulchre? Tell me that."

"I am not going to drag religion into my discussions."

"But do you—yes or no?"

"I don't believe in ghosts, if that is what you mean."

Celia laughed. "Then you think the noises you heard were due to rats, and the whispers I heard had nothing to do with the diary?"

Miss Flack did not reply. She put Lob down and turned to

go. Celia extinguished the parlour lamp and lighted her own. At the top of the stairs she found Anabel waiting for her.

"If I were you," she said, "I should burn that box and all its contents. Then perhaps your ghosts would leave us . . . . leave you—in peace."

"Ah!" Celia cried, "then you do believe in my ghosts, Belle. Own up."

"I do not. It's all fancy and nonsense."

"Then why are you so scared? Because you are scared, you know. But why should we be scared? Isn't it simply because we do not understand certain laws that govern the spiritual world? They may not always be obscure to us. It is only their mystery that baffles and affrights us now. For why should we fear that gentle Lavanda Selcroft? Why should Uncle Jerrold have been scared out of his house by that soft whisper? Isn't it silly to be afraid of something we can neither see nor touch?"

She was trying to convince herself to argue away her fears of the night before. But Anabel did not know that. She agreed that it was extremely silly to be scared by imaginary ghosts, and declared that she did not intend to be upset by such nonsense.

"You may call it nonsense," said Celia, "but why should not a Personality remain about a house when its earthly shell has gone the way of all flesh? I feel sure that my spirit will haunt it when I am dead. I love it too well to quit it for ever. And I hope Lavanda will still whisper to me sometimes; though I hardly think she will, now that her Treasure has been rescued from oblivion."

"It is to be hoped not," said Miss Flack, crisply; "for I tell you plainly, Celia, that if I hear, or see, anything of the lady I shall clear out at once, and I should advise you to also, if you want to keep sane."

Celia shook her head. "I shall never leave my dear old house; be sure of that," she said. "I love every worm-eaten beam and creaking board of it. If I don't take care of it, who will? It would certainly crumble to pieces. You won't believe me, perhaps; you may know nothing of the love one can feel for a house—a home; but it has become inexpressibly dear to me. Its legacy from the past, its phantom voices, its strange lights and spectral rats—forgive my gibe, Belle—all add to its ineffable charm for me. And I know you will not leave me, dear. I was so lonely before you came. For a house, however dear, cannot give what human companionship can give, and I want you badly."

Miss Flack pressed her thin lips together and squeezed up her eyes tightly for a moment. Then she kissed Celia roughly. Her kisses were always like pecks, for she had no caressing ways.

"Of course I shan't leave you if you really want me," she said drily; "you know that."

"Yes, I do. You are a good friend, and will no more forsake me than I will forsake my house," declared Celia, and returned her kiss with a warm embrace.

CHAPTER SIXTEEN

IT was a perfect Sunday morning, and that is, perhaps, the most transcendental description one can give of an English day. For Sunday, in the heart of our country, is full of enchantment. When it falls in sunshine, with last night's dew sparkling on every leaf and blade of grass, and only the lightest of zephyrs to waft a foam of cloud beneath the sky; when the richly foliaged trees throw their shadows westward; when bees keep up a happy murmur in the scented limes, and little green apples thud the grass, then is this earth a forecast of heaven, and it must be a very heavy or morose spirit that does not respond to it.

Celia had heard much, during the past months, of the famous little Meeting House, with its unaccountable name, 'The Blue Idol,' so strangely at variance with the faith of its small congregation, and had been promised a visit to it. Good walker as she was, the distance from Clew Lodge was a little too far to take on foot, and whenever she had planned to go in John Pearl's car something had occurred to prevent her. Now, after reading Lavanda Selcroft's diary, she was more eager than ever to see the old place; so eager that she feared to be disappointed in it. But she was not.

When she alighted at the gate of a little field and saw, in the dip of it, the grey slabs of the old roof chequered with moving shadows from the trees near, she drew a quick breath of delight. She had expected something bigger, something more like a place of worship, than this quaint little homestead, as it looked, and as, indeed, it had been in the past. John Pearl had told her that, even in William Penn's day, it had been known as "The Old House," so that its actual date was unknown. But it touched her heart, as no building had ever touched it before: not even her own house had given her the throb of tender feeling that its littleness, and oldness, its air of modest retirement and sweet seclusion, gave her. Miss Flack observed that it was "very quaint," and remarked on its timbered and plastered walls.

But Celia could not speak a word, nor did the Pearls, as they entered through the low doorway to a small room containing about half a dozen oak benches with straight backs, and at one end a gate-legged table, with its flaps down; a rail behind, and slightly above it. On the table stood a bowl of carnations and mignonette, whose fragrance reached them as they took their seats, and beside it lay a few books. The stone floor was full of cracks; the long narrow windows looked out on trees and the rising green field. The walls were plastered and timbered inside and out.

Its dim coolness, and the absence of any decoration, gave it a chastity indescribable. Celia, used to the constant bobbing up and down of the Church service, feared that the inaction and silence of the meeting might get on her nerves, and, at first, she felt an inclination to fidget. But presently there stole over her a strange tranquility, resting body and spirit. She did not wish to move or speak, or even hear anything more than the buzz of a fly on the window panes, the caw of a rook flying over the house, and the distant bleat of sheep. When, after some time, there was a slight stir, and John Pearl rose to speak, she listened to his familiar voice dreamily. He said nothing very new or startling: she did not find in his simply chosen words any of those original or whimsical ideas that were to her so stimulating. But he seemed to fit the time and place and emotional atmosphere. It was all very lovely and godly, she thought. Yes, godly. She had been wont to laugh at the old word.

Now it struck her as beautiful, and John as a godly man took on a fresh aspect in her eyes. She had known before that he was good and kind and clever. Now she knew him for godly, as William Penn and George Fox had been, and this meant a man of the highest possible ideals.

When the meeting was over he took her into the other rooms of the little holy place, up the queer, crooked staircase and down into the small hostel built on to the side of the Blue Idol for the use of pilgrims to its shrine. That it spoilt the look of the ancient house from the outside she could not deny, but it was quaint enough within: very tiny and low-roofed and simply furnished. A ceiling had been removed over the room used for meeting, so that there was nothing above it, and a narrow gallery on one side had been left on that floor, wherein one could look down upon those gathered together beneath. But all other ceilings remained as they were originally, so low that one could touch them with a hand raised little above the head.

They walked round the house, and Celia was shown the small close at the side, where sunken headstones of forgotten graves crouched in the grass, and where William Penn used to pace up and down before meetings, pondering the subject of his coming discourse. Celia could clearly visualise the handsome, athletic man of thirty odd years old—in a long snuff-coloured coat, and knee-breeches, absorbed in thought and only half conscious of the assembling Friends about the door of the Blue Idol. The three hundred years seemed to roll away. He was still as much alive to his followers, and to her at that moment, as when he had stood thus among the graves and the daisy-sown grass. Were his cream-coloured oxen tethered close by, cropping that grass as he walked up and down? Celia stood smiling at the vision, till she was recalled to the present moment by some introductions John Pearl wished to make to her.

The spell of the place rendered her almost speechless. She could only smile, and say that she had fallen back into a dream of the past. Miss Flack, too, was subdued and lost in her own thoughts. She could not regard these Quakers as anything but heretical; but she had, nevertheless, been impressed by the religious spirit of the meeting and felt its peace in her soul. The little company melted away by degrees, and John Pearl drove Celia and her friend, with Ruth, along the deep and flinty roads to Misty Vale, only the main high-ways being smooth and tarred.

That night they went to supper with the Pearls. Afterwards John played some Bach on his harpsichord and they sang one or two hymns. Faith had a small, sweet voice and a good ear. She sang Tchaikowsky's *Legend* as a choir-boy might have sung it—very simply, without any pause or undue emphasis. It brought tears to Celia's eyes by its simple pathos. Then they talked of the Blue Idol and of Lavanda's diary, speculating as to its material value. Faith suggested that it might be not only a treasure to Lavanda, but a valuable relic of the past possessing a fictitious value in these days of antiques and curios. The mania for collecting, among rich people, she said, was altogether incalculable, and a fancy price might well be bidden for so unique a treasure of the past. Miss Flack's contribution to the discussion was the remark that "people were fools enough for anything," while Celia declared that nothing—no price offered—would ever induce her to part with the diary.

"Would you refuse a thousand pounds?" said Faith, laughing. "That would be a mere bagatelle to a millionaire who wished to gratify a whim."

"I'm afraid Mistress Lavanda Selcroft is not quite famous enough for that," said Celia, "but I would refuse it, anyhow." She paused, and went on: "At least I think I would. But the temptation is not likely to arise."

"I should hope you would not be so silly, if it did," observed Anabel sharply. "Think what you could do with a thousand pounds."

"Suppose you had such a chance, Miss Flack, what would you do with t?" asked John Pearl, who loved to draw Anabel out.

"Buy a nice cottage in the country and keep fowls," was the prompt reply.

"I would advise a pig too," he said gravely; "the pig is a very useful animal, friend Anabel."

"No. I should want a man to clean him out. And men are dear," said Anabel.

There was a ripple of laughter.

"Dear at any price, you think, perhaps," he said.

" 'What care I how dear they be, so they be not dear to me?' " Celia parodied.[44] "At present ours has to be a manless world, because of that dearness, hasn't it, Belle? But if you could afford a cottage, the pig would pay for the man, I imagine."

"If I had a thousand pounds dropped into my lap," said Faith, "I would take six months' holiday and travel. I would see Greece and Italy, Corsica and Japan . . . and Pennsylvania. What would you do with it, Celia, if you had it?"

"First I would have a bathroom," she answered, laughing, "and a man—at any price—to look after my garden and greenhouses—yes—I would have a permanent gardener and greenhouses. Then I would publish our book in a lovely edition, with perfect type and wide margins, on hand-made paper. After which I would make the

---

[44] Based on lines from 'Shall I, Wasting in Despair' by George Wither.

public wild to read it by subtly exciting advertisements."

"Your fortune would soon go in that," said John Pearl.

"Ah, but the dear, deluded public would give it all back," she declared gaily.

"And what about the hostel for Quaker pilgrims you promised?" asked Faith. "Have you forgotten that?"

"Certainly not. But I must have the bathroom and gardener first. You can't have a hostel without a bathroom in these luxurious days."

"There isn't one at the Blue Idol."

"That is unique. Clew Lodge could never bear comparison with the Blue Idol. Those who stay there step back into a past century."

"What would you do with a thousand pounds, Father?" Faith asked.

"Build decent cottages for decent folk to live in."

"And let them out at high rents?" said his daughter. They looked at each other and smiled.

"We haven't heard yet what Mrs. Pearl would do with a thousand pounds," said Anabel, turning to her as she sat in her corner with hands folded, and a smile on her lips.

"Yes, Mother, what would you do with it?" Faith enquired.

"Give it to John for his cottages, of course," she said: "What could I do better?"

Husband and wife exchanged a tender glance.

"I hope you'll put plenty of cupboards in your cottages, Father," said Faith, "and boilers, or coppers. Most of my patients have nowhere to put things, and have to boil every drop of water they need in kettles."

"My cottages shall have boilers and cupboards and baths," he declared gravely.

"One of them would do for me, perhaps, if the rent wasn't

too high," said Anabel, who had taken that assertion seriously.

"Oh no, Miss Flack; you would be much too rich for me. You must buy your cottage with your thousand pounds—or build it yourself. Mine would be let to labouring folk."

Celia rose. "I don't know how you feel, Faith," she said, "but I feel an inferior complex developing rapidly. Your father and mother put the rest of us to shame, for they are thinking of others, and our thoughts are all for ourselves. Why is that?"

"Because we already have all that we want for ourselves," said John, "that is easily answered. When you've got your bathroom and gardeners; when Faith has travelled and friend Belle has her cottage and pig—I mean fowls—you will have reached the summit of human bliss, and will cast about in your minds for a higher satisfaction. Must you go? I'll get out the car."

But that Celia would not permit. Anabel declared that the walk would do them both good, and they set off together finally, in the soft dark night; for the old moon had not yet risen, and the air was gentle.

"I never thought," observed Anabel, "that I could like dissenters so much. But, of course, the Pearls are exceptions."

Celia did not reply, and they walked a little way in silence. Something moved before them. A rabbit had run out of the hedge and was lolloping across the road; small white moths fluttered about them, like faery spirits. It was night to hush the voice and stir the heart.

Presently Anabel spoke again. She was not very susceptible to impressions of beauty or atmosphere.

"I wonder what makes Faith look so sad," she said. "Have you noticed, Celia, that when she is not talking and laughing, she kind of—droops and looks miserable?"

Celia was surprised to find her friend so observant. She said, after a short pause: "I'm afraid Faith isn't very happy."

"Why? Is she in love?"

"Well . . . I've no right to betray her confidence."

"I expect she is eating her heart out for that young Staniforth," said Anabel. "I met them together once or twice last time he was home. I hope he isn't playing with her."

"On the contrary——" Celia paused. Then she went on. After all, why shouldn't Anabel know the truth? "He is in love with her and wants her to be engaged to him, but she has refused him."

"Refused him! Why?"

"He is a soldier and she is a Quaker."

Miss Flack made a little, inarticulate sound in which several elements were blended—incredulity and disdain especially.

"It is better than if he were a Roman Catholic," she said at last. "She wouldn't have to bring up her children to be soldiers, anyhow."

"She will never marry a man who is not a pacifist," remarked Celia, not without a slightly mischievous intention. She knew the word 'pacifist' would give Anabel a shock, and it did, as her snort of disgust signified. But all she said was: "Well, I must say girls have altered since my young days. They would go anywhere for a red-coat."

"Perhaps khaki isn't so attractive!" Celia laughed. But her laugh was suddenly checked by Miss Flack's grasp upon her arm.

"Look, Celia!" she cried. "There's someone in your house!"

They had reached the brow of a rise in the road from which they obtained a view of Clew Lodge. And from its upper windows a faint light was distinctly visible. Celia felt an icy shiver run down her spine to the skin of her head, such as she had not felt since her first days in the house. Her hat felt suddenly very tight. She stopped abruptly and stared at the windows.

"Somebody has got in," Anabel exclaimed. "What impudence! Actually to light a candle. Of course they know the village policeman isn't likely to come this way, and they've found out we're not at home."

"It isn't candlelight," Celia breathed, "it is a kind of phosphorescent glow. There's no core to it. Surely this must convince you, Belle."

"Convince me of what?"

"That my house is haunted," said Celia boldly. She expected Anabel to contradict her flatly, but Anabel did not.

"Before I believe anything so . . . unlikely," she said, and Celia appreciated the mildness of this word, "I shall have to see over the house. Come on. We'll soon find out if anyone has got in."

They walked on, losing sight of the house as the road dipped again. When they reached it there was no light visible. Anabel marched up the garden path, after demanding the key from Celia, and flung open the front door. Inside the house they encountered nothing but darkness, and dead silence. A candle, with matches, stood ready for them on the table near the door. Anabel lighted it and stumped upstairs, followed by Celia, who, in spite of her quivering nerves, could not help laughing a little at the truculent air of the small woman, and her courage. If she really believed there was a burglar in the house, Celia thought, she was showing considerable valour.

At the top of the stairs a slight draught from an open window rattled the rings of a casement curtain, and the sound, in the unearthly stillness, gave them a start. The flame of their candle flickered; they feared it was going out. Sheltering it with her hand, Anabel moved out of the draught, and they both stood motionless, listening, with hearts that beat fast, and short breath. There seemed to be a faint movement in Celia's room. Anabel flung open the door and cried, in a loud voice: "Who's there?" And at that moment they were left in total darkness, their candle being blown out, as it seemed, by Someone or Something, in the room.

Dead silence followed, as they listened again. They stepped into the room and shut the door, when Celia struck a match and relighted the candle with a shaking hand. The casement curtain had fluttered down again, with the shutting of the door, but the wind had risen a little and rattled the rings. There was no other sound, and nothing to be seen in the room.

After searching the deep cupboard and the room beyond, they each took a candle and went to all the other rooms: but found no sign of a living soul. It was the same downstairs. Nothing in the house had been disturbed; nothing was missing. The burglar theory had to be dismissed by Miss Flack.

But she said, when they were in Anabel's room, after their tour of inspection:

"If I were you, Celia, I would have the telephone installed here. We might both be murdered in our beds and nobody be any the wiser."

"Can't afford it," said Celia.

"You could if you sold the old diary."

"I will not sell my Treasure."

Was it fancy, or did she hear the word 'treasure' like an echo, whispered behind her?

Anabel then suddenly announced that she was going to make tea. Her nerves, she declared, were all to pieces. She had lighted the lamp in her sitting-room while they were talking, and now proceeded to light her oil-stove. Celia, with Lob on her lap, whom she had fed downstairs, was glad enough to sink into a low wicker chair, and drink the panacea of all feminine ills. She felt tired and shaken. It had disconcerted her very much to find that the discovery of the casket and diary had not put an end to all ghostly phenomena in her house. She had felt so sure that the whispers would now cease, and there would be no more manifestations of the supernatural. But that light in the window had shaken her out of this comfortable belief. She was, therefore, perturbed and puzzled. Why should these things go on? Would they always persist? And, after all, why should they not? The fact that she had found that Treasure could not console poor Lavanda for having to leave it. And if, as John Pearl suggested, the eerie whisper had been but an echo of the past, preserved in the house by some strange agency, there could be no reason why it should not persist as long as the house lasted.

Anabel broke into these reflections abruptly.

"After all, I don't see that it is very likely anyone would trouble to break into this house. Everyone knows you're not rich, and it's not worth robbing. Besides, most people are afraid of it in the village, and wouldn't come into it after dark."

"How do you account for that fear, Belle?" asked Celia.

Anabel did not reply at once.

"Who can tell how tales get about? I suppose, in the first instance, somebody with too much imagination makes them up. Imagination can play strange tricks with us. No doubt the light we thought we saw was only a reflection of the moon rising behind the trees. It is due to rise about eleven."

"If you are satisfied to leave it at that, I am," said Celia, smiling.

After a short pause, Anabel said, with less precision than usual in her voice: "I won't exactly say I am satisfied, Celia. This is a queer house, I must admit. There are things I——" She broke off abruptly and changed the subject.

CHAPTER SEVENTEEN

CELIA was mournfully regarding her household account-books one day when Faith Pearl appeared at her parlour window. She often walked round to the courtyard to save Celia the trouble of opening the front door. It was the middle of the morning, and Faith had finished her round earlier than usual, having but few patients this summer.

"Am I interrupting important work?" she asked.

Celia welcomed her, both as a friend and as a respite from account-books. It was always a pleasure to see Faith; her lovely colouring gave Celia the same sensation she experienced from a blackbird's song. But one glance at her face to-day was enough to show Celia something was wrong.

"Is anything the matter?" she enquired anxiously, "your father—mother——"

"Both quite well. But"—she paused and pinched her lips together before going on—"Oh, Celia, Michael is ordered to India."

Her voice broke. Celia put loving arms round her neck, in mute sympathy. After a brief spasm, which she soon controlled, Faith said: "What a fool I am!" and sat down.

"It may not be for long. The trouble in India may soon be over, and he will come to no harm," Celia murmured.

"It isn't that," the girl said, vehemently, dashing the tears from her eyes with her hand, and feeling for her handkerchief. "I could bear that. I often don't see him for months together, and he will be as safe as any other airman, I've no doubt. But what I can't bear—what simply tears me to pieces, Celia—is to think of the horrible thing he may have to do there—dropping bombs on defenceless people. And he doesn't *care*—he doesn't *mind*! He tries to pretend he does, to comfort me, but he doesn't really. He will have no compunction, no sympathy for his victims—of course he won't see their agonies. And his conscience will be quite clear. He will merely think he is doing his duty."

"And isn't that true?" urged Celia, gently. "He has pledged himself to the service of his king and country: isn't it his duty to obey orders? Can you really censure him for that?"

"It is a monstrous pledge, and ought never to be given. Oh, why are we still savages when we call ourselves civilised? 'It makes a goblin of the sun.' "[45] Faith groaned. "And to think that the man I want to reverence and love and marry—because I *do*, Celia, I want him more than anything in the whole world—to think he could go and make that hideous pledge to slay his fellow-men; to think he is content to be a murderer, to break the law from Sinai, 'thou shalt do no murder,' with as little compunction as he would feel in putting his foot down on an insect. That is what crushes me. I can't bear it."

She was convulsed in another struggle against the sobs that choked her. Celia was speechless. What could she say to comfort such sorrow as this—a sorrow that was new to her, after all her long years of life. She had never known, never thought, that such a situation could arise. Its strangeness and its poignancy almost stunned her.

"If he were going to stand up against other soldiers, man to man, as they did in the past," Faith went on, when she could command her voice again, "it would not be quite so vile. But to sail

---

[45] A line from Dante Gabriel Rossetti's 'Jenny'.

high above the poor, helpless unhappy things, dropping death and destruction upon them as a cruel devil might do—oh, it is foul—it is not work for a human being, made in the image of God. To me it suggests a tail and hoofs! And yet—oh Celia—Michael is so naturally kind. He would never hurt anything, or see anything hurt, if he could help it. But he can't see what he is doing—he can't realise the suffering—the cruelty"—she choked and went on, in a strangled voice—"He is sent up in the sky to do abominable work, like Jove hurling thunderbolts. I suppose Jove had no compunction in slaying men. I sometimes wonder if God cares. If He does, why does He permit such horrors in His world?"

Celia could find no answer to this question. She could only suggest to the tortured girl that Michael might never be called upon to drop bombs on the defenceless people. It was necessary to have aircraft there, in order to keep order by a display of power, but probably, by the time Michael reached India, the trouble would be all over.

Faith refused to be comforted.

"It is the knowledge that he can do such a thing that kills me," she said. "When I think of it, I almost hate him. I can't believe he is worth loving, or ought to be loved, when he shows no love or pity for his fellow-creatures. One might as well be a bird of prey, a hawk waiting to swoop on a poor little sparrow, and caring no more than the hawk does what his victim suffers."

She paused a moment and then went on:

"I ought to hate and detest him for his inhuman ruthlessness. I ought . . . but I can't—I *can't*."

She buried her face in her hands as if stricken with shame.

"Of course you can't. How could any reasonable woman hate a man for doing his duty—or, to say the least of it, what he conceives to be his duty. And I think you are unjust to call him inhuman and ruthless. You cannot suppose, Faith, that any decent man today *likes* killing other men, and does not shrink from doing so. Of course Michael detests it—as most of our men did in the Great War. But he regards it as an awful necessity imposed upon him by the State. He goes into the Services, more often than not, with his eyes closed to what may happen. He does not expect to be called upon to fight—and kill; he hopes the need for active service may never arise, and he merely regards himself as part of his country's safeguard against danger. Surely you are not one of those foolish persons who talk of the soldiers' 'blood lust.' Believe me, it does not exist in normal men. It may in diseased or abnormal ones."

"I am not one of those 'foolish persons,' " Faith raised her head to say, smiling through her tears. "Of course I don't think Michael *likes* killing people—he wouldn't kill a kitten willingly. But he doesn't *mind*. Don't you see what I mean, Celia? You must. He does not lie awake at night shuddering to think he may be called upon to smash up some miserable native—perhaps a little innocent child. And when he has done it, the fact will not haunt his conscience. He won't feel the enormity—the sin of it."

Celia was silent. She had used all her arguments, and saw that they were as wax against Faith's solid convictions.

"I don't suppose it is possible," the girl went on, "to make you understand how *we* feel about this. Your point of view is so utterly different. From our point the man who takes an oath to kill other men when he is required is not a Christian, that's all. He may call himself one and make long prayers, like the pharisee: but he is a heathen nevertheless, and for him Jesus Christ might just as well never have come to this earth. For a Christian must be a follower of Him, and keep his commandments—to love all men and forgive all enemies."

There was a long pause. Celia wished she could tell Faith what she had said to Mrs. Staniforth, and how that lady had reproached her with being a Quaker. But she thought it wiser to oppose Faith. Some intuition told her that it would be a slight balm to her sore heart to hear Michael, and the soldier at large, defended. Faith would not agree, her conviction could not be shaken, but the opposite view might serve to lessen slightly the awful enormity of what she considered a sin.

"You have never told me," said Celia presently, "what your father and mother think about it. Have they any objection to Michael as a husband for you?"

"Of course they have. Is it likely they would wish me to marry a soldier?" replied Faith, "any more than the Staniforths wish their son to marry a Quaker—and a draper's daughter."

She added, with a modern girl's calm disregard of parental authority: "But they would not interfere if we decided to be engaged. In the first place they know it would be no good, and in the second place, they naturally wish their children to be happy."

"And you will be one day: it will all come right, you'll see," said Celia softly, taking in her own the little rough hand of her friend, hardened by constant work and continual washing. "I know I am dreadfully old-fashioned and behind the times, Faith darling, but I hold a firm belief in the power of true love to overcome obstacles. Try to share that belief: don't make yourself unhappy by struggling against it."

Faith clutched her by the shoulders convulsively for a moment and then let her go again.

"You are a great dear, even if you don't agree with me," she said, "but don't worry about my quite unimportant love affair. I suppose every girl has troubles of this kind, more or less, before she cuts her last wisdom tooth, and I shall get over mine easily enough if I don't brood on it. And I haven't time to brood. It would be ridiculous to let a purely personal thing like that obsess one in a world where there is so much to do. But it does one good to be silly sometimes, I think, and let one's self go. It clears the mind to talk of one's troubles. What is it Hamlet says? 'Cleanse my bosom of its perilous stuff.'[46] I have discharged some of my perilous stuff on you, my dear, but don't let it distress you; throw it off, as I am going to do."

Before the girl left her she exacted once more a promise from Celia not to tell her father of this interview, or to speak of her trouble to him. He, and her mother, she said, were deeply concerned at her unhappiness, but spoke of it as little as possible. No amount of discussion, they all felt, could alter the situation, and talking about it only made them more unhappy.

"It was because of that, and because I felt so bursting with misery that I came to you," Faith concluded on parting. "You feel with me, and yet my trouble does not make you so wretched as it does Father and Mother. It almost kills them to see me cry, I know. I never hardly do—and never before them, if I can possibly help it."

"Promise me always to come here when you want a good cry," urged Celia, "it will do you no end of good to 'cleanse your bosom of its perilous stuff'; and your dear people need never know. I shall not say a word. I have never discussed you with your father,

---

[46] This is actually based on a line from Shakespeare's *Macbeth*, Act 5, Scene 3: 'Cleanse the stuffed bosom of that perilous stuff'.

in all our long talks. We go into another world, where we can make the lovers do just as we like. It is so much more satisfactory than real life, in which obstinate people—like you—will go their own way," she concluded, smiling.

This last speech was not strictly true. The lovers in their book were, at this time, giving trouble to Celia and John Pearl by their refractory behaviour. They refused to conform to the original plan of their authors, and were altering the scheme as first conceived. The foundation motive of *Mansoul* had been, as the title suggested, soul conflict—the struggle in their hero's mind against parental and religious authority in favour of religious liberty. The love story had been a side issue, and they had thought less about it than they had about the atmosphere in which it was set, the seventeenth century men, women and ideas, and the like. Now the book was becoming a passionate love drama, to which its whole setting became subdued and subservient. It was even calling for a melodramatic treatment, since modern writers cannot deal with the romance of past days without introducing a somewhat hectic atmosphere. Matters that, probably, appeared commonplace to the individuals of their day, take on haloes of vivid colour in modern eyes, and historical romance is written either with a dry regard to chronicled facts or coloured by an imagination that, while it may slightly distort, gives a prismatic effect.

This effect—this warm colouring of love-emotion was certainly, both John and Celia felt, due to Lavanda's diary. Their gentle puritan, Mercy, was drawn after their imagined conception of Lavanda, and began to dominate the romance, as well as the heart of Aloysius, her lover. And thus *Mansoul* did not seem the right title. It was too heavy, too stern and moralistic. In casting about for another they found a suggestion in the diary.

> "Through all this gloomy Darkness," wrote Lavanda, "the Crystal Lamp of our Love shines bright as ever and nothing can quench its Beams. Though R. and I be parted in Spirit we are never asunder."

Celia declared at once that *The Crystal Lamp* must be their title, and they thereupon adopted it.

Every day they came upon something in the diary to arouse fresh interest and discussion. One passage especially, excited Celia. She could hardly wait till John Pearl came in the evening to point it out to him.

> "When I would fain bring a Vision of my dear Love before mine eyes," said the writer, "I take out my lilac lutestring Gownd with the purple Flowers to look at, for in that he did see me for the last Time and found me Fair. In truth I shall ever love that Garment more than all others I have, and I would I might have it for my Winding-Sheet, if that could be. For he lifted the Hem of it to his Lips, as a Court Lover might do, albeit a sober Quaker and said he would see me in it always in his Memory. If I but knew the Spot his Lips had pressed how sweet would it be to me. Like Violets in fragrance."

"I am afraid our fair Lavanda was a sentimentalist," John had said, when Celia read this out to him, "but this is all to the good, so far as we are concerned. And no doubt the lilac lutestring gownd is the one you found in your closet."

They concluded that Lavanda's mother had cherished the gown after her child's untimely death. That Lavanda had died young was plainly enough indicated by the diary, which ended abruptly, and probably of 'a consumption,' since there were many passages telling of cures she tried for that disease. Here and there they came across passages referring to her sufferings from 'rheums,' 'hot sweatings' and 'feavers,' with remedies for these quoted from Dr. Culpeper.

> "Of late I have been so sorely afflicted with melancholic Humours and Swoonings that my Mother hath made me take a Cordial which Dr. Culpeper commendeth. It is made from Borrage, which he saith is an Herb of Jupiter and under Leo, so a great strengthener of Nature. The Flowers are made into a Conserve which is good for those who are weak from long Sickness and to comfort the Heart and Spirits of those that are in a Consumption or troubled with Swoonings or Passions of the Heart. My mother made this Conserve for me herself, with a Lohock to cleanse my Lungs of Flegm, putting herself to many Pains that the Herb might be well dried and fine enough to sift through a Tiffany searce.[47] But truely I felt little the better for these Remedies, though the Lohock did somewhat ease my Cough. It is mixed with Honey which is soft and soothing. But I could take only a little of it, as it made me to Vomit."

"Poor Lavanda, what terrible messes she had to swallow!" said Celia, when, after reading this aloud, she read another passage in which a remedy from the *English Physitian* was given, composed of green hyssop, salt, honey and cumin seed, and said to be good for "Griefs or Diseases of the Chest and Lungs." "No wonder she died young under such treatment. And of course they would keep her rooms with every window closed according to the theories of the day. Isn't it all wonderfully clear, John? The poor tubercular

---

[47] Lohock: a linctus, a syrup taken to relieve a cough. Searce: a fine sieve.

child fretting her heart out for her Quaker lover, swallowing all these dreadful concoctions, in stuffy air, and growing worse every day, with no consolation but that of pouring out her woes in this diary. The father and mother watching and praying, but never conceiving that the cure might be in their own hands, or that severing her from her lover might hasten her death. And then, when she died, preserving the gown she had worn, and, possibly, other things of hers—oh, isn't this tragic?"

John Pearl did not respond to this. His eye had been caught by words on the page opposite to that from which Celia had been reading as he sat beside her at the table.

"Do I see something there about the Treasure?" he said, craning his neck a little, and pointing to the line at the bottom of the page. Celia looked and, reading, turned it over.

> "Would that I knew where to hide my Treasure," Lavanda wrote. "I have promised my Love that no eye but mine shall see it. He fears its Destruction and for that reason hath entreated it to my Keeping, knowing that my Father's House will not be espied upon, as his own Father's House is at present, he being suspected of Rebellion against the King because of his Refusal to bear Arms and take the Oath of Allegiance. But I have no Hiding place in my Room that my Mother cannot see. I have placed it now at the bottom of the little Cradle that old Silas did make for my Poppet, where I also hide my Letters from R., but it might easily be discovered there and my Mother would be angered and burn them all together. I must think of a safer Place."

John Pearl and Celia turned to look at one another with wide open eyes.

"What do you make of that?" he exclaimed.

"That her diary is not the Treasure. Could her mother have found it—whatever it is—and destroyed it, as she suggests?"

"I think not, or why should she continue to manifest her presence and bewail leaving it here?"

"You feel sure she is still here? Anabel treats the idea with scorn."

He did not reply at once; he was thinking. When he did it was to say: "There are just two ways of regarding this matter: Miss Flack's way of declining to believe in anything she cannot account for on a materialistic basis; or to believe in the persistence of the spirit after death. Of course she would say that she believes in the resurrection of the dead and after life for the soul: but her resolute scepticism is really a negation of that. Once admit that spirit exists, independently of matter, and we must admit that it may fall under laws we do not yet understand. It has always seemed to me irrational to accept, as a fact, the survival of the soul after death, and then to deny that the soul is able to manifest itself to us in any way; that, being alive, it must nevertheless remain as dead to us as the flesh it once inhabited. To declare that it is immediately borne off to some unknown region, beyond time or space, is to assume knowledge of the unknowable; to assert that the spirit God breathed into man, when He made him a living soul, is limited by our conceptions of what is possible or impossible. And if one believes in Divine revelation, as I do, the Bible offers me confirmation of ghostly reappearances on earth. To tell the candid truth, Celia, I have far more sympathy with the agnostic who refuses to credit anything he does not consider proven, than I have with the so-called Christian who, because he has had no ghostly experience himself, scoffs at all the evidence of such experience in the countless generations that have gone before him."

Celia listened to this long speech in silence. She was thinking less of its philosophy than of its implications, and followed it only so far as it touched upon her own case. Her mind was putting two and two together.

"I wondered," she said slowly, "why we should still have strange things going on in my house—that light from the windows the other night, and the whisper I heard again. If the Treasure is still to be discovered——" she paused.

"You think the manifestations will cease when we find it. Perhaps they will. But we must remain as uncertain of that as we are of everything else in that unexplained and unexplored region of psychic phenomena. It would seem that the spirit of Lavanda hovers in your house and desires to have her Treasure found. It would also seem as if she possessed the power of manifesting herself to different kinds of people; or why should the idea of hidden treasure have penetrated to many minds and given the house its uncanny reputation. In any case, we have first to find the Treasure. That, at least, we know is not chimerical, since we read of it in the diary. And if you are psychic, as I think you are, why should you not be the medium through which the secret may be discovered? Note your dreams and intuitions, Celia."

She laughed. "The amusing part is that it was not I who was the medium of finding the casket," she said. "Anabel found it and fetched it out of the roof cupboard. But for her it would still be reposing in the dusty darkness. May I suggest that she is the psychic medium?"

They laughed together over the incongruous idea. Anyone less likely to be a psychic than Miss Flack it would be difficult to imagine.

"But the fact remains that, medium or no medium, she heard strange and unaccountable things," John said, "and so did your uncle, and who knows how many more? What does she herself say about it? I have never dared to ask her lest she should wither me with scorn."

"She is certainly less withering on the subject of ghosts than she was. And the night we saw the lights and found no one here she owned that she was unnerved—that there was something queer about this house," said Celia.

CHAPTER EIGHTEEN

ALTHOUGH John Pearl was spending nearly half his life in that 'other world' of which Celia had spoken, she was aware that his mind was often pre-occupied by his daughter. He let fall many hints of this when he and Celia were working together. Suddenly he would break off in a discussion to say: "It is strange how Lavanda's case resembles Faith's. Both suffer under the tyranny of ideas. Lavanda, child of her age, subject to the ideas of her parents, while Faith, a modern girl, is free to make her own choice. But is she any the happier for that? She is sundered from her lover by Ideas just as effectually as Lavanda was sundered by her parents. Only she had no solace but her diary, while Faith has her work.

Or: "Poor Lavanda! hoarding her love in secret, with no other interests in life to compete against it. What was there to live for?"

Celia knew he was pondering over Faith's problem continually, and his attention often wandered from their book in the midst of some discussion on words, or on its remodelling. But she kept her promise to Faith, and said nothing on the subject that they agreed should be taboo. Her object was to keep him in the world they shared together, that invisible and enchanting world of the imagination where "happy souls go wandering all free," and after Michael Staniforth had bid his last farewell and flown off; when Faith, with rather red eyes, had settled down to her routine of hard daily work; John Pearl was able to throw himself more completely into that paradise.

He came to Clew Lodge in the mornings now, and worked with Celia for three or four hours. She rose an hour earlier in order to dust and sweep before he arrived. Their method was for Celia to write a chapter which John took home to study, criticised, marked with a red pencil, brought back next day for her approval, and then carried home with him to type. They fought every step of the way together. His desire was to make the book a thing of beauty and distinction, to give it an atmosphere of the past and a flavour of eclecticism, after the manner of Pater and Shorthouse, at no matter what expense to drama. It might begin nowhere and end nowhere; have no crisis, no human passion and no story, so long as it was a medium for pure English prose and the colour of its period.

Celia, on the other hand, wanted an emotional romance, breathless suspense reaching out to a dramatic climax. It irked her to be continually pulled up for a word that was not, as he called it a 'disfiguration.' But she had to admit there was chaste beauty in his writing, in his economy of adjectives, search for '*le mot juste*' and balanced sentences. He shuddered when the same consonants appeared too many times in a phrase. He laughed at her vivid descriptions calling them 'twopence coloured.' But he let them go, more often than not, realising that she was his superior in imagination, in the sense of dramatic effect and insight into human character. Moreover, she leant upon Lavanda Selcroft and called her in as a witness to the defence.

After he left every day, she drew a long breath and felt tired. The excited tension of their animated discussions and effort of marshalling her ideas to his order exhausted her. She put all the spoilt sheets of MS. in her waste-paper-basket and went to browse in her garden, where the scent of flowers and song of birds restored her and gave her mental repose. The flowers rioted in autumn profusion, but the song of the birds had changed. August was well on its way before the book had reached its final, and most difficult, chapters.

"I'm told you and Mr. Pearl's writing a book together," said Mrs. Coles, when she was doing a day's charing at Clew Lodge. "I expect it's about finished by now, as he's bin a-coming so often."

"Who told you he comes often?" Celia asked, smiling.

"Oh, everyone in the village knows as his car's allus at your gate. They wondered what was up till Miss Faith told 'em you was writing a book. Is it all about Misty Vale, as they say?"

"Yes; Misty Vale three hundred years ago," said Celia.

"Lor!" There was disappointment in the woman's tone. "What do we know about three hundred years ago? Why didn't you make it now, and let us see us 'ow we are?"

Celia explained that doing so might bring her actions for libel; and that the things that happened long ago were more interesting and romantic. Didn't Mrs. Coles think so?

No. Mrs. Coles did not. Why should they be?

This question Celia did not know how to answer. Mrs. Coles, who was wringing out cloths, went on:

"Sometimes they has stories about olden times at the Pictures, in old-fashioned dress and all that, but nobody wants to see 'em—in this village, at all events. They look such sights. It seems unnatural."

This point of view had not struck Celia before. She realised, for the first time, that the uneducated and unprivileged have no roots in the past, and are not interested in what has gone before them. The present alone is theirs, with, perhaps, a glimpse of the future. They may have a vague sense of to-morrow but of yesterday they know, and care, nothing.

When the good soul had departed with her fresh pail of hot water to the room she was cleaning, Miss Flack appeared in the doorway, and Celia realised that she must have heard, from the garden, what Mrs. Coles had said. So she was not surprised when Anabel opened fire.

"You see how the village people talk."

"Talk!" echoed Celia, with amused innocence.

"About you and Mr. Pearl. He comes too often, Celia."

"Why?"

"It causes talk and it must make Mrs. Pearl uneasy. How would *you* like it, in her place?"

Celia felt she was losing her temper and dared not reply till she had filled a kettle and put it on the fire. Then she said pleasantly:

"A difficult question, Belle, because you see I am not Mrs. Pearl, nor am I in her place. Wasn't it Oscar Wilde who said: 'never do unto others as you would they should do unto you: tastes differ'?"[48]

"I call that blasphemy, whoever said it."

"Well, isn't there a grain of truth in it? Tastes do differ, and temperaments and feelings. I imagine that dear little Mrs. Pearl and I would not think or feel the same in the same situation. For I am excitable and emotional, and, yes, perhaps a little jealous and suspicious by nature; whereas she is placid and sweet-natured, unselfish and unsuspicious. She beams on John and me as if we were her two children, and I am positive—yes, quite positive, that it gives her nothing but pleasure to think he enjoys working on this book with me."

"You can't make me believe that she isn't human," retorted Anabel, with some heat, "and it isn't in human nature for one woman not to feel jealous of another if she knows her husband

---

48 This is actually from the play *Man and Superman* by George Bernard Shaw: 'Do not do unto others as you would that they should do unto you. Their tastes may not be the same.'

likes her, and prefers her company to—to——"

Celia interrupted her with a little peal of laughter. "My dear Belle, you got that out of novels," she said. "Real life is different. I don't mean that no woman is jealous—haven't I said that I am myself?—but *all* women are not, and no woman is when she is sure of her man."

"How can anyone be sure?"

"Mrs. Pearl is—dead sure. If anyone told her that her husband was unfaithful to her, she wouldn't believe it, because she knows better. She knows her man, and that he would die rather than give her a moment's anxiety."

Miss Flack sat down in a Windsor chair by the kitchen window and pondered. Celia wondered whether this meant obstinate negation or consideration of her arguments. She was therefore a little startled when Anabel said: "I daresay you won't believe that a man was in love with me once?"

"Why should I not believe it?"

"It must seem improbable to you. But I wasn't always so—what I am now. And a man I knew fell in love with me, or said he did. I was in love with him, too."

"What happened? Why didn't you marry him?"

"He was married already, to a very beautiful woman. But she had left him years before and he was glad to be rid of her, for she was a selfish, immoral creature. I didn't know till he told me. It was an awful shock. Of course I had nothing to do with him after that."

"Poor fellow!"

Miss Flack opened her little eyes to stare at Celia. "It served him right; a married man has no right to make love to a girl. It only shows what men are, and how little you can trust them," Anabel concluded primly.

Celia smiled. So Belle had given her this little piece of private history as a warning and a moral lesson.

"I never think of them like that," she said, "I mean as a separate order of creation, a mere sex. I think of men as human beings like ourselves, and just as different from each other as they are from us."

"That's absurd! 'Male and female created He them,' " declared Anabel emphatically.[49]

"Do you really think He made their souls male and female, as well as their bodies?" was Celia's retort, disregarded by Anabel, who went off with a parting shot for propriety.

"If Mr. Pearl would walk here, or put his car in the stable, it wouldn't be so noticeable," she said, leaving Celia amused but irritated. It annoyed her to hear John Pearl's conduct impeached.

And still his car continued to sit outside her gate nearly every morning throughout September, while they worked and wrangled, wrote and corrected and rewrote the pages of their seventeenth-century romance.

The continual strain and long hours spent indoors began to tell on Celia's health. The old nervous terrors began; she dared not sit alone in her parlour at night, and suggested to Anabel that they should spend their evenings together, as they had not done since John Pearl had ceased coming at night, and it had been found necessary for the collaborators to work together in the mornings. Anabel was, secretly, only too pleased to comply, for she too was feeling more nervous than she would admit in the strange old house, now that the nights were lengthening. While Celia was writing, Anabel reclined on the couch by the fire, reading or sewing till bed-time. Celia soon became so used to her presence that it

---

[49] Genesis 1:27 and 5:2 (KJV).

did not disturb the current of her thought.

At last, one day in late September, a certain crisis arrived, after she and John had spent four hours together over a chapter in their book dealing with necromancy, a subject that had a great fascination for them both. The scene they had painted, in which the spirit of a dead woman is evoked by an Eastern seer, was so vivid to them that Celia was haunted by it all day. They had described minutely all the conditions of necromantic evocation; the Oratory of the Magus in which the solemn ritual and adoration of the dead could be carried out, draped in silk the colour of the emerald, whose magical power was insisted upon; the white marble altar, bearing in its centre the five-pointed star of the pentagram, as an exorcism against malign spirits; the copper tripod and chafing-dish, in which to burn special woods and flowers, with the candelabrum, also of copper, holding a tall candle of the purest white wax. Then the ceremonial evocation; the burning of roses and violets, laurel wood and alder in the chafing-dish, and sprinkling of this, with other incense of spices from the censer upon the altar, culminating with the incantation to "the supreme Potency which manifests itself by Ever Active Intelligence and Absolute Wisdom:

"Glory be to the Father of Life universal in the splendour of the Infinite Altitude, and peace in the twilight of immeasurable depth to all spirits of good will." And, the evocation complete, they had pictured the raising of the dead, the slow, silvery mist gathering in the stifled air, gradually condensing to a column and taking human shape. Celia had imagined it all so clearly that it haunted her all the rest of the day, and she could not shake off the sights and sounds her own fancy had raised. For John Pearl had left the writing of the scene almost entirely to her; since it had been her idea to incorporate necromancy with the magic and witchcraft that played so large a part in their romance.

It had been a heavy breathless day, with black thunderclouds and occasional rumblings in the distance. Although all windows were open there seemed no air in the house, and the dead calm outside was ominous of electrical disturbance to come. Once or twice Celia felt an unaccountable shudder run through her, and when this happened she spoke to Anabel. At last she laid down her pen and gathered up her papers.

"I can't write any more to-night," she said. "My head seems bursting. There must be a storm brewing for us, and we had better get some sleep before it comes."

"I am quite ready. In fact I've been half asleep already," Anabel admitted. As she took off her glasses and set down her two stubby feet, clad in bedroom slippers, on the floor, she paused and ejaculated: "Hark! Listen!"

"Oh don't!" cried Celia, springing forward and clutching her arm. "What is it?"

"I thought I heard thunder. That's all. Why, Celia, you're quaking. Whatever is the matter with you?"

"My nerves have gone wrong again," Celia's laugh was shaky. "And so would yours be if you had been poring over the Evocation of the Dead all day."

Anabel frowned severely. "What silliness! If you pore over all that kind of stuff you must expect your nerves to go wrong. Surely you are not putting any of that nonsense in your book."

"Indeed we are. It is thrilling—in a book. Can't you imagine it, Belle, all the weird conditions, the incantation, the evocation of the Spirit, and then the dead woman slowly arising, in a column of mist from the floor—ugh!" She shivered.

Her intention had been mischievous, to shock Anabel and

perhaps make her shiver too. But she only succeeded in calling forth scorn.

"Idiotic! Dead men never come to life."

"What about Lazarus, and the daughter of Jairus?"

"I wish you would not always drag in the Scriptures," said Anabel sharply. "As if such miracles had anything to do with our life to-day. Come, let us go to bed. You'll be seeing things next."

Two hours later the storm broke over their heads, rousing them both from sleep with a crash that seemed, in their dream, like the Last Trump.[50] Miss Flack watched the lightning dance about her window, like a gigantic will-o'-the-wisp, and was ready for every detonation that shook the old house and threatened its chimneys: Celia, on the contrary, crouched under her sheet and one blanket, to shut out that blinding orange and blue light whose dazzling velocity gave her a vertigo: consequently, every violent explosion came as a sudden shock that seemed to turn her heart over. She was almost suffocated by its hurried beating and by the lack of air.

Strange tales of storm and tempest flooded her mind. Was it Milton who called the thunder 'heaven's artillery'?[51] And was it not always brought into action by the Powers of Evil? She thought of Thor, the thunderer, of Jove and his thunderbolts, of Witches' Sabbaths, or Lucifer disappearing in blue flame with a crash of thunder. And she began to wonder if there were any vestige of truth in the well-established tradition that supernatural appearances were usually accompanied by elemental strife: recalling Faust in

---

50 Referring to the last of the seven trumpets that will be sounded at the Last Judgement. Corinthians 15:52 (KJV): 'In a moment, in the twinkling of an eye, at the last trump'.

51 From Book II of *Paradise Lost* by John Milton.

his cell, the three witches in *Macbeth*, and other famous instances. There is something in the storm atmosphere suggestive of unnatural phenomena, making the supernatural seem possible. One feels so puny and helpless in it, so much the prey of invisible powers.

And then, as she lay thus thinking, she heard, plainly as ever, the piteous whisper:

"I had to leave it there. I had to leave it—my Treasure."

Suddenly Celia threw off her bedclothes and sat up, staring through the dimly-lighted room. Now was the time! She must not be a coward. If ever the revelation of the secret were to be made, it must be now.

A blinding flash made her blink and shake her head. She put up both hands to her eyes and then let them fall. In the flash she had seen Something by the window, a luminous column in the shadow of her big bedstead, thrown by the night-light at her side. It remained visible for a few moments after the lightning, as she gazed, and then slowly dissolved into mist. In those seconds it had seemed to take a woman's shape.

As the thunder rolled over the house again like a monstrous, earth-shaking Juggernaut, Celia shrank back once more beneath her bedclothes, faint and cold. Her skin which, a few minutes before had been feverishly hot, now turned icily damp; her scalp felt like a tight cap on her head. Through the open window a swift rush of air blew into the warm chamber, making all the curtain rings chime like a tiny peal of bells. The rain, which had been falling lightly for some time, now descended in a torrent, with a sound like a herd of strange beasts trampling over her garden. Celia drew a long breath, as if pressure on her heart and brain had been relaxed, and her mysterious terror ebbed slowly away. She began to think of her garden, which needed rain; of her hollyhocks and dahlias and blighted apple-trees, and yellowing lawns; for the month had been dry, and so had August. This would clean and refresh them though it would batter the borders and lay many things flat. As the hurricane gradually ceased and the storm went growling into the distance, a cock's crow reached her ears faintly, and she knew that Aurora was on her eastern way.[52] But before the first grey hint of dawn Celia was sound asleep.

[52] Aurora: the goddess of dawn in Roman mythology (Eos in Greek mythology), who rides across the sky ahead of the sun.

CHAPTER NINETEEN

WHEN Celia, next morning, told John Pearl what she had seen in the storm, he received her statement more guardedly than she anticipated. A glance at her face had told him that her nerves were under strain, and that she was not very well. It was only to be expected, he observed, that she would see an apparition after their chapter on necromancy and the book on occultism they had studied for it together. He asked her to note that the Appearance had been in the exact form described by the writer of that book, that of a luminous misty column, gradually assuming human shape, and suggested that her imagination might have been responsible for it. He proposed that they should take a day off their work and go to see his sons at Millborough, who had heard so much of Celia that she would receive a very hearty welcome. Ruth wanted to see her grandchildren, and he had promised to take her soon. It was a lovely day after the storm, so why not seize it? If she agreed he would telephone at once to Nick, his eldest son, and say they would be there to early dinner.

Celia consented eagerly. She had long wanted to know John Pearl's sons, and a drive in the country was always delightful to her. She ran upstairs to tell Anabel, who said, with her usual frankness, "And a very good thing too. You've been worrying over that blessed book long enough and stuffing your head up with nonsense about dead men coming to life, and so on, till you've lost all your complexion and nearly all your good looks. It would do you good to go away for a week, or more."

Celia gazed anxiously in the glass when she put on her hat.

Had she really lost her good looks? Yes, no doubt she had aged this last week or two. There were lines—her skin looked yellow, her eyes faded and a little red about the rims. She would put on a veil. No, she would not. The air caressing her face would not feel so delicious under a veil, and she did not care how she looked. It would be absurd to care—at her age. John Pearl had seen her as she was every day, and he did not notice her appearance. She rubbed both cheeks with her two hands, to give them a slight flush, and laughed at herself in the glass, knowing that she did care, how she looked: for that was part of her nature. If she lived to be a hundred, Celia thought, she would be anxious to have the kind of cap that suited her, or a charming grey wig. She wondered if she would ever bear to look at herself in the glass when age had withered her and destroyed her last vestige of beauty.

"You look better already," John Pearl said, when he came back to fetch her, noting a quick transformation, "I wish I had thought of this trip before."

"Did I not tell thee, John, days ago, that I thought Celia needed a change," said Ruth.

She was perched up in the little 'dicky' behind, which she pretended to like best, declaring that she wished to have all the air she could get.[53] Celia accepted this declaration for what it really meant: that Ruth always 'preferred' the things and places other people did not want; the back seat, the leg of a fowl, the uncomfortable chair. She was of the world's spoilers, so selfless as to cause selfishness in others.

The drive through the lovely Sussex country, now clothed in

---

53 Dicky seat: one that folded out at the rear of car, where the boot would usually be, separate from the two front seats and open to the elements.

gold and bronze and ruddy tints, put fresh life into Celia, and dispelled the vapours of the night before. When they reached the tarred roads and moved smoothly between high banks and hedges, the motion exhilarated her and stimulated her mind. She had forgotten that invigorating power of rapid movement to aid creative thought. Ideas rose swiftly and took shape in speech. John Pearl had never seen her more animated. He was less stimulated than she was because his attention was held to the steering-wheel, or recalled there if he veered from it; but he, too, felt the refreshment of spirit and the spring of ideas. They were not too absorbed in these ideas and plans for the final chapters of their book to note all the beauty that seemed to pass them on their way, flying swiftly by to join the world behind, and they would break off, now and again, to comment on the hedge fruit, reddening in September sunshine; the different ways of trees in their leaf colouring; the queer roots tangling about the rocky banks among strange flowers and grasses (reminding them of Arthur Rackham's most weird pictures), and all the other entrancing things one may see on a drive through the country.

When they arrived at Millborough John drove straight to the shop, and there Celia was introduced to his son Nicholas, a young man with a very pleasant face and bright eyes. He was not so tall as his father, and had a rather chubby face like his mother; but he had John's voice and laugh. His welcome was very cordial, and he seemed genuinely pleased to make her acquaintance. It was strange, he said, that all this summer they had not met before, but his visits to Misty Vale could not be frequent, as he was tied to the shop, and during August had joined his wife and two children at the sea for weekends. Celia gathered that he was a very busy, hardworking man, and much interested in his business, as he has need to be, with so much dependent upon him. His brother, he said, was away, buying for the firm. He would be sorry not to see Celia.

It was with some surprise that she found herself rather fascinated by the shop. She had thought, and said, that she never wished to enter a draper's shop again: but now that she was in one, old interests revived. She talked quite eagerly to Nicholas, as he took her round the different departments, and introduced her to his head show-woman, with whom she had a friendly chat on fashions and the vagaries of customers.

Celia felt a compassion for her that was certainly wasted, as she realised later; for the young woman had a post she liked, was well paid for it and comfortably housed. The assistants lived over the shop, cared for by an efficient housekeeper, and were happy together. That life which had been to Celia so irksome and fettering, to Miss Stiles was the agreeable fruit of success after years of steady work.

In Nicholas Pearl's private house a little way out of the town, Celia found two delightful children to amuse her, a boy of six and a girl of four. They fastened upon her at once, without a trace of shyness, and took her to see their rabbits before she was allowed to have lunch, which they called dinner. Their mother was one of those plain women who are able to charm by their intelligence and sympathy; the house, a new one, was furnished in excellent taste; the large garden delightful. But it was the children who captivated Celia. The boy, named after his grandfather, was very like him, she thought, with the same bright sparks in his eyes and whimsical mouth. The children were obviously devoted to their grandfather, whose manner with them was a curious blend of raillery, pretended gravity and childish eagerness. They seemed to regard him as one of themselves.

Celia duly admired the pretty, mole-coloured rabbits and a tabby cat with kittens. She told them about Lob-lie-by-the-fire, and was going to give the legend of his prototype, but the children knew all about Robin Goodfellow and the rest of the goblin family. They gave her plenty of information too, about the 'donkey man' in *A Midsummer Night's Dream* who shared, with Puck, their chief interest in the fairy play.

After lunch Johnny challenged his grandfather to a game of "Snakes and Ladders," and Phoebe, after watching them till she was bored, asked Celia if she liked dollies and would like to see hers. They went together to the nursery, and when Celia had been introduced to a rather battered little company of dolls, bunnies and Teddy bears, she told Phoebe about her own dolly, who was two hundred years old, and had lain all that time in a box under the roof. She described its quaint dress, its queer little yellow face and shining beady eyes, till Phoebe's own eyes grew rounder and rounder. She was fascinated by the description and demanded eagerly to see the old, old dolly.

"When may I come? Gramp will fetch me," she declared, 'Gramp' being the children's abbreviation for grandfather. And as soon as they returned to the sitting-room, the child ran to him.

"Gramp dear, when will you take me to see Celia's old old dolly in a box?" she cried. "I want to see her so badly. I've never seen a dolly censh'ries old. Wouldn't you like to see her, Johnny? She has a waxy face and beady eyes, like Golliwog."

"Who are you calling 'Celia,' you impudent rascal?" said her grandfather, with twinkling eyes. "Do you mean Miss Grey?"

"I didn't know she was called Miss Grey," was the prompt reply. "You called her 'Celia,' Gramp. I like 'Celia' best."

"So do I. Grey is so—grey," said little John, who had just put away his game reluctantly, and was now ready for a diversion. "It is an ugly colour," he said to Celia patronisingly, "I like green."

"Will you take us, Gramp?" reiterated Phoebe.

"Perhaps Celia doesn't want a horde of children in her house," he suggested gravely.

"I do indeed," said Celia.

"She does," said Johnny. "I am sure she likes children: don't you?" to Celia.

"Very much; and specially children like you," she replied. "You must certainly come and see Gulielma, and Phoebe must bring Rosamund and Daisy and Aurora to see her too."

"Was she named after William Penn's wife?" Johnny enquired. Celia replied that she was.

"Tell Miss Grey what you know about William Penn," said his mother, smiling, and the boy, always willing to talk, plunged into a graphic account of the great Quaker, ending with the Holy Experiment.[54] His eyes grew very round and large as he described the Red Indian chiefs: "Awful savage-looking men but really good inside, you know, specially when they knew William Penn did not want to hurt them or take their lands away," he concluded.

"Will you fetch us to see Celia's dolly, Gramp, or will Father take us?" persisted Phoebe, who, like most children, never lost sight of an object in view or gave in before a purpose was accomplished.

"What does Mother say?" asked Gramp.

"They shall come in the holidays."

A dismal howl went up from the children.

"Not till Christmas—oh, Mum!"

"Why not some Saturday afternoon," suggested Gramp.

---

54 An attempt by William Penn and the Religious Society of Friends to establish a Quaker colony for themselves and other persecuted religious minorities, where religious tolerance would be maintained and everyone could live in peace.

"Or on Sunday?" suggested Celia.

Mrs. Nicholas shook her head. "Their father likes a quiet Sunday," she said. "He needs a rest, and it is no rest to drive on the day when everyone is joy-riding about the roads. And he is not free on Saturdays, you know. But even if he were, it is too long a drive there and back for the children to take in an afternoon, and be back for their bedtime. However, we will see if it can be arranged."

They had to be content with that, and with the assurance from Celia that she would be prepared at any time, without further notice, to show them Gulielma.

"I would give her to Phoebe," she said on the homeward drive, "but she seems part of the house, somehow, and I don't think Lavanda would like her to leave it."

A thick mist was rising, making the trees look like strange monsters as they approached them, and softening the landscape's outlines into almost unearthly beauty. On the main road, meeting other automobiles incessantly, John had to drive with great care, the high banks and many curves making it the more dangerous. His horn was so continuously hooting that conversation faltered until they reached the by-road to Misty Vale, and he was able to relax his vigilance. After that they met no vehicle except a farm-cart bearing a load of wood, and a tradesman's van. They talked of Nicholas then, and the interesting children. Celia said she had no idea before that children could be so interesting, and he gave his opinion that there could be nothing more engrossing in the world than to watch the development of a child into a man or woman. Psychology was, in fact, his great subject, and Celia, knowing this, drew him on to expound his views, which were always so impregnated with his strong personality as to seem quite original. He purposely refrained from discussing their book, or the occultism of the last chapter they had written together, and Celia's thoughts were imperceptibly led into other channels.

As she sat by the fire telling Anabel all about her visit and how much she had enjoyed it, a sense of release from obsession stole over her, and the fears of last night seemed foolish. Practical matters, too, exercised their peculiar charm. She enjoyed talking with Belle about the necessity for some autumn cleaning next month, and preparations for the winter. Belle suggested that they might save coal by having some of the old trees in the orchard cut down for fuel, and that they themselves might chop it up if they bought a good strong chopper and saw. The trees she declared, had borne no fruit worth speaking of that year, and only took up room in the orchard. Celia was inclined to fight for them. She had an abiding love for trees, and hated to see one felled. Moreover, event he most gnarled and aged pear or apple-tree put on an exquisite garment of bloom in spring, and the thought of destroying beauty always hurt Celia. But Anabel pointed out, ruthlessly, that coal was becoming dearer and dearer; that Celia was already entrenching on capital for her hand-to-mouth expenses; and that the house, being almost void of sunshine as the days grew short, must be well warmed or it would be damp and mouldy. They must have fires in other rooms as well as the one they were in, she urged, or must buy oil stoves to set in them, which would be almost as much trouble and expense as wood fires.

Celia gave in. The commonsense of all this could not be evaded. She agreed that Coles should be engaged to come and cut down a few old trees, not only fruit trees, but an ancient ash-tree that had been struck with lightning and was only half alive. Miss Flack declared that ash was the best of all woods to burn, and quoted the old verse she had once read and learnt, in support of this statement:

"Poplar gives a bitter smoke,
Fills your eyes and makes you choke;
Apple wood will scent your room
With an incense-like perfume.
Oaken logs, if dry and old,
Keep away the winter's cold;
But ash wet, or ash dry
A king shall warm his slippers by."[55]

"There were other verses I've forgotten," she said, "but I remember one said that hawthorn baked the sweetest bread and elder brought death to your house. And every verse ended in praise of the ash. 'Ash green or ash brown is fit for a Queen with golden crown,' was one. So your old ash will be a godsend, Celia; keep us warm and save our pockets."

"It has magical properties, too," observed Celia, smiling. "The rowan-tree or mountain ash is a guard against witchcraft. Witches and other evil things will not go near it."

"It is about time, then," said Anabel, "that we had some in this house. For it certainly seems bewitched."

"What! Did you hear or see anything last night, in the storm?" exclaimed Celia, who had not told her of her own psychic experience.

"I am not going to say anything about it," declared Anabel, rising and shutting her mouth like a trap.

Nor could Celia draw from her another word on the subject.

---

55 'The Firewood Poem' by Lady Celia Congreve, often stated to have been first published in *The Times* in 1930, though versions of it appeared in print prior to that year (see the *Wiltshire Times and Trowbridge Advertiser*, 31 January 1925, p. 8).

CHAPTER TWENTY

OCTOBER, ripe and mellow, with chastened sunlight ripening apples, slid by only too quickly for the collaborators in *The Crystal Lamp*. Every morning a thick mist turned the trees into vague phantoms, and veiled their flaming colours in pearly grey. The sun rose late, to fall asleep early in a bed of purple cloud. The garden grew dank and heavy, with frosty dews bearing down the flowers and

> " . . . leaves, brown yellow, grey and red
> or white with the whiteness of what is dead.
> Like troops of ghosts"[56]

rustled gently from the trees and huddled together in drifts about the paths and beds. Birds chattered actively under the bushes, some making ready for flight, others on mysterious business of their own. If she strolled in her garden at dusk Celia was often startled by their sudden swirls near her from unseen hiding-places. Great leisurely toads sprawled almost under her feet, and iridescent blue-bottles basked idly on cabbage leaves.

The mornings were all too short for her. The book, now that it was nearing its completion, obsessed her wholly, and she rarely thought of anything else. With Miss Flack her manner had become distracted, and she often gave the wrong answer to questions. Not only was she absorbed in the working out of her plot, the drawing together of different threads in the story, but every time

---

[56] From 'The Sensitive Plant' by Percy Bysshe Shelley.

she opened Lavanda's diary (and she was very often drawn to it) she found therein something more to intrigue and perplex her. This, for instance, caused her hours of inward questioning:

> "My Mother found this Journal Yesterday," Lavanda wrote, "and took it from me. But I did beg so hard, with many Tears, that she gave it back to me. And now I must find an Hiding Place for it so that it may never fall into her Hands again. For if she read it and learn about the Treasure R. gave unto me for Secrecy, she will not rest until she find it. And that God forbid."

A little further on Celia read that she had thought of 'an Hiding Place' that none would ever discover, even when she was in the Tomb. And that her Mother would seek no more for it, since she, Lavanda, had told her that she had flung the diary down the well in the courtyard, adding: "God forgive me for thus lying to my Mother, which I never would have done had she not parted me from my only Love. And if she ever do find the Coffer beneath the Roof—which I pray not—she is not like to discover the Treasure itself, for that lyeth well hid where no one would think to discover it."

By now both Celia and John had realised that the Treasure still lay hidden; but if they had not these words would have convinced them. It was obvious that it was something quite apart from the diary, and that it had been entrusted to Lavanda by Richard Butler with earnest injunctions to secrecy. From that fact John Pearl had deduced that it was something of great interest and value to Friends. So, when Celia, after pondering the above passages, read them to him, he begged her to search the house from attic to cellar, with the outhouses and stables, offering to do so himself, if she would allow him. Of course Celia was only too pleased to do so, and eager to help in the search. For nearly a week they 'played hide-and-seek,' as she called it, in every conceivable corner, and it was a kind of game they enjoyed, for who does not love treasure-hunting?

They brought to light several interesting relics of olden times: a pomander box in the corner of a powder-closet; some quaint MS. songs; a tinder-box, with flint and steel, in one of the garrets; and, best of all, a spinet in the stable loft. Celia had never been up into the stable-loft; the ladder looked too worm-eaten and rickety. Coles had climbed up, looked into the loft and pronounced that there was nothing in it but some "old bits of chairs and things, dusty hay and sacking," so she had not troubled about it. Now John found the remains of a dilapidated spinet and was wildly excited. "Come up—come up!" he urged Celia. "I've found something. The ladder's quite strong." She went and found him hauling something out of the *débris*, in a cloud of dust.

The spinet had no stand, and if Celia had found it she would merely have taken it for a flat, queer-shaped box. It was badly damaged, hopelessly so, she thought, but John was not concerned with the instrument itself; he thought only of what might be inside it. The moment his eyes had caught sight of it in the *débris*, and recognised it for a spinet, he made up his mind that it held the Treasure. It was just the place Lavanda would, most likely, have hidden it, he thought, and he was prepared to find in tucked away in that part of the instrument upon which the lid did not open.

But he was doomed to disappointment. Nowhere above or below the jangling yellow keyboard, or behind the plucking 'jacks' was anything concealed. He looked at Celia and laughed ruefully.

"Too bad of Lavanda! She led me to expect it here," he said. "But no matter. It is a 'find,' Celia, if not a Treasure. I will take it to an expert for you and have it put in order. You shall have a spinet to play on, and perhaps it may invoke the spirit of Lavanda to further revelations."

Celia hesitated. "It is good of you, John, but, you see, I can't afford to pay for it. I must wait till the book makes its fortunes."

"It shall be my Christmas present," he said. "I was going to send you a few tonnes of coal, though it jarred my romantic soul to give you so prosaic a gift. Now you shall have a spinet instead, to match your wainscoted room and your own picturesque beauty. I can already see you sitting at the keyboard, in the gloaming, with the firelight falling on your bronze hair and green dress, softly singing 'I sowed the seeds of Love,' from the MS. we found yesterday."

Their search after that soon ended. And the Treasure remained undiscovered. John took the spinet away with him, and next day they began to take up their interrupted work on the book.

With the end of October the days became more dark and gloomy, Misty Vale being usually clothed in fog or drizzling rain. Miss Flack began to suffer from rheumatism, to which she was subject, and as her room could only be warmed by a rousing fire, which involved much coal and the carriage of it upstairs, Celia invited her to use the sitting-room as much as possible. They had chopped and sawn together quite a number of good ash and apple logs, and with a little coal Celia was able to keep her sitting-room warm, in spite of the fact that no sunlight reached it after 3 p.m., and that the fireplace threw most of its heat up the chimney, as old fireplaces are wont to do. Her beloved house, Celia had to own, was not cheerful in winter. Its passages were dark and chilly, its leaded windows gave but tempered light; for most of the lozenge panes were of discoloured or faintly tinted glass. Although it was so solidly built, its doors and windows too well fixed in their panes to be draughty, winds, especially the southwest, had an eerie way of moaning and wailing down the wide chimneys and through the keyholes. Sometimes they howled like demons; sometimes they cried like children; sometimes they screeched like banshees. And, more eerie still, they sometimes whispered. The aspens had shed their leaves. No longer was their soft rustling speech to be heard in the garden or through the open windows. This other whispering was more sinister. It seemed to tell of ugly secrets and hidden crimes in the old house. No. Clew Lodge was not too cheerful in winter.

And yet Celia loved it as dearly as ever. Your true lover is nothing daunted by faults in the beloved, and Celia had given her heart to the old house. It might be dark and dismal, full of strange secrets and invisible menaces; but it was her own house, her home, and it breathed that delicate aroma of a romantic past which affected her mind as the scent of sweetbriar affected her senses. No new house, bright, airy, warm and full of modern comforts, could ever be to her what this ancient dwelling-place was; could ever supply the same romance to her spirit. Indeed, she often told herself that even the ghostly phenomena of Clew Lodge were dear to her, and she would not be without them. But that, it must be confessed, was when there had been no uncanny manifestation for some time.

Perhaps the happiness that had arrived to her since she had come to live in it was one reason why the house had remained so dear. Had it not inspired her to new creative work, and brought her that ideal friendship with a man of which every woman dreams and expects to find in lover and husband? If she had never come to Clew Lodge she would never have met John Pearl, and he had made of her life a new thing, a fresh adventure. She could not now conceive of life without him. Their friendship transcended all material limitations; and while his strongest affection, his duty and devotion were all pledged to his wife and children, he nevertheless dwelt with her alone in that 'other world,' which they shared with such illimitable joy. For John Pearl, therefore, Celia was truly thankful, and as her house had brought them together she owed to it a debt of gratitude.

The book was at its final chapter, and she was eagerly awaiting John's arrival one morning when he did not appear at the usual time. She tried to write, but could not, and wandered about the room feverishly, growing more and more anxious as half-past eleven struck from her old clock in the hall; then twelve, then half-past twelve, but still John did not arrive. What could have happened? He had never been late before. She went to her garden gate, to gaze despairingly down the road, as if her presence there could draw the little car into sight. But it was too cold to keep watch long and she went in.

"John hasn't come," she cried, bursting in upon Anabel, who was washing some handkerchiefs in the back kitchen. "What can be the matter, Belle? Do you think his car has broken down?"

"More likely a burst pipe," said Belle, taking a clothes' pin out of her mouth. She was hanging the wet articles upon a line hung across the kitchen, where there was always a fire. "This thaw will burst all the pipes. It's a good thing you emptied your cistern."

"I'm sure a burst pipe wouldn't keep him away."

"If it isn't a pipe, it's a visitor," observed Anabel, calmly. "Somebody had dropped in, just as he was coming. Don't fluster yourself, Celia. You look quite feverish."

At that moment the jangling old bell of the front door rang, and Celia ran out at the welcome sound.

"What has kept you?" she asked. And then she noticed how grave he looked.

"Ill news. Poor little Faith! She has just heard from the Vicarage. Michael has crashed."

"Not killed!" Celia cried, with eyes full of horror.

"No, but seriously hurt. They don't know how it will go with him. Mr. Staniforth sent the telegram round to us. Faith is nearly frantic. She says her last letter to Michael was unkind, and she is breaking her heart over it, poor child!"

His lips quivered and he turned away.

"Oh, poor girl! I am so sorry—it is awful!"

Celia's own voice broke as she went into her sitting-room and he followed. Her heart ached for Faith's agony. To love a man and think of him suffering, perhaps dying, thousands of miles away, was bad enough without the 'unkind letter' to reproach one. Oh, why do we ever write unkind letters, she asked herself, since we never know when they may turn and torture us? But she could not say this aloud. She could not think of anything more to say in the face of this tragedy.

John Pearl sat down heavily, as if exhausted, for indeed he was. The sight of Faith's grief, the emotional strain had tired him. He looked his full age of fifty-five years, and Celia was deeply stirred with compassion for him, as well as for Faith, knowing how anything that hurt his child must hurt him.

His next words showed that he was not thinking only of the pain of his daughter.

"I can't bear to think of his father and mother," he said, in a low, choked voice, "their only son and only child."

"I know; it is cruel," Celia spoke huskily. Then she cleared her throat and added: "But a soldier's parents must always be prepared, mustn't they? Was he in action?"

"We don't know. Probably. The worst of it is—from our

point of view—Faith declares she must go out to him at once. And she will, too, if I know anything of her. She has always had her own way."

His mouth curved in a grim smile.

"What is the good of that?" asked Celia. "By the time she arrived in India he would either be better or—dead."

"She means to fly. I have telephoned about a passage. And if she goes, I go with her, of course."

A cold dread shivered through Celia and struck a chill to her heart. The thought of his going to India in an aeroplane appalled her, turned her faint and sick. She felt a sudden conviction that, if he did, he would ever come back alive. A spasm of fear overwhelmed her.

"Oh, no, no!" she cried. "John, you can't go—I can't let you go—I—Ruth—we——"

He clasped both her hands and held them tightly, looking into her eyes.

"Dearest of friends," he said gently, "I am sure you would not wish me to let our little Faith go so far alone; perhaps to find her lover dead and herself stranded among strangers. No, you could not wish that. She is my child. I set her in this chequered world and she has first right to my devotion. It is only my simple duty to shield her from its sorrows, so far as I can. Ruth feels the same. Anything we could do for Faith would not more than pay for the joy she has given us and our debt to God for her."

You shame me." Celia began to cry and could not stop for some minutes. "But you must forgive—you see—I don't know what it is—that feeling. I've never——"

He knew what she meant and answered her unspoken words.

"You have had the joy of creation without the pain," he said.

"One pays for having human children, Celia. Perhaps that is what makes them so infinitely precious. But I must not stay now. How have you got on since yesterday?"

"Quite well last night, but not a line this morning. I could not. And now it doesn't seem to matter."

"Now is but a point in time. To-morrow comes. I shall bring you all the news there is."

"Shall I come to see Faith?"

"Better not. Such griefs have to be met alone. Even her mother and I feel outside—intruders."

When he had gone Celia collapsed into a condition of hopeless depression. For the first time she realised how small a part she played in John's life compared with the part he played in hers. How little he cared, he thought, about the work they were doing together in comparison with the child his wife had borne him! She envied Ruth that child and her two sons. She even began to envy Leslie Hale's wife her two handsome children, that might have been her own. When Anabel came in to lunch, tired and hungry after a morning's work, she found her sitting dejectedly by the fire, with her hands dangling before her. Celia had told her John Pearl's news after he went. Anabel began at once to discuss it.

"Those horrible things," she said. "We were much better without them. They're impious, too. If God had meant us to go flying up in the air, He would have given us wings. Every day some promising young man is killed. Thank goodness I'm not a mother."

Celia smiled and felt a little cheered. There was, of course, that point of view, and she had often consoled herself with it, in forlorn moments.

"You might be a mother without having an airman for a son," she said.

"Then there would be something else to torment me. People who have children never have any peace of their lives. They are a continual anxiety. First measles and whooping-cough and mumps; then falling in love and getting into debt, and marrying the wrong people and so forth. You may be very thankful you never married, Celia. I know I am."

To which Celia replied that they had indeed much to be thankful for, and then went off into a peal of laughter which seemed to aerate her soul. She remembered that only the day before she had told herself no woman on earth could be happier than she was; and now, half an hour ago, she had felt a miserable derelict, even envying Dora Hale.

"The worst of it is," she replied to Anabel, "you can't tell what it is to be wife and mother till you've tried it, and so your choice has to be made in the dark.'

"That's what I say," remarked the little spinster promptly, "and that's why it's best to be on the safe side. Marriage is like going on a long voyage in a ship. If you are ever so sick you can't get out."

"What about divorce?"

"Divorce can't unmarry you, or prevent your having children," was the sapient reply.

CHAPTER TWENTY-ONE

JOHN Pearl called that evening to say that there was no further news from India, and that Faith was more calm, going about her duties as usual. Next morning he came again, bringing an account of the flying disaster in his newspaper, and the same afternoon he appeared once more with a cablegram from Michael himself, or, at least it bore his name.

"Not so bad as first reported—Michael," it ran, and the air was cleared by it, though still a mist of doubt and fear lingered. But all question of a flying voyage to India was shelved for the moment. For a week nothing further was heard. Then came a message from the War Office that Flight-Commander Staniforth was to be invalided home, and would leave on a certain ship at a certain date.

The tension of their nerves, suspense and sympathy, during that week made work on their book very difficult for John Pearl and Celia. The 'other world' seemed to be invaded by the troubles of this one, and its characters, before so positively real and vital, faded to shadows. But when they knew that Michael was well enough to travel and would soon be on his way home, the strain was relaxed. They were able to concentrate on the last chapters of their book.

Celia finished it one dull and drizzling day in mid November. She danced round the room and waited impatiently for John to come and read it. Having stared at it so long and made so many deletions and changes, she could not tell whether it was good or bad. But he would know.

She watched him read it, saw his mobile eyebrows rise and fall, meet and part, until he threw over the last sheet. She waited breathlessly for the verdict.

He glanced at her sideways; his mouth twitched.

"Terribly bad, isn't it?" he said.

Celia's smile faded out. Then she laughed.

"I was afraid you would think so.

"False one! you know better. You know it is very good. You are bursting with pride. But I must take it down a peg. There are words here I don't like"—he fumbled back over the sheets—"here is one."

They made corrections together. He folded the MS. and put it in his pocket.

"Are you glad or sorry it is finished?" he asked.

"Glad, of course—I danced a jig. Aren't you?"

"No. The end of a journey is never so happy as the setting forth and travelling—hopefully. I am always sorry to come to the end of things I enjoy."

"You will not feel like that when you see it in print. The sight of one's own dear book is the happiest of moments."

"I don't know about that. Print vulgarises. Like dressing up a wood-nymph in a skirt and jumper. It may well mean disillusion. But you don't agree."

"I am not sure that I don't—when one looks into it. But a book, all printed nicely and bound in a pretty cover gives, at least, a momentary joy."

"If it hasn't a hideous wrapper! Well, well, we must hope for the best. But it must not be our only child, Celia, or the last of our work together. I should miss that too much, and I hate being unemployed."

"So do I," Celia declared. "I should like to start on another to-morrow, before—any disappointments come, John. If no publisher will take our book, shall we ever have the heart to try again?"

He looked at her in surprise.

"Have the heart! Why, Celia, what does it matter whether the book is taken or not? Its rejection would only make us the more determined to conquer the benighted publishing world. And our next would be the masterpiece. Isn't the next always going to be the masterpiece? And nothing, no disappointment, can take from us either the joy we've had or the joy in our work to come. So set that wonderful imagination of yours to work at once, and we'll start again after Christmas."

When he had gone Celia ran upstairs to tell Anabel *The Crystal Lamp* was finished.

"I hope it has a happy ending," was her comment. "I can't stand books that end miserably."

"All true romances end happily," said Celia, "in real life, as in fiction. If they don't, they are not real romances."

"Well, I should think you are glad it's done," was Anabel's next observation. "It has been a lot of trouble, hasn't it? I hope you'll make something out of it."

"Oh, I have already," Celia cried. "I've made a lot out of it, Belle, more than you can possibly imagine."

"I suppose Mr. Pearl won't be coming so often now," said Anabel, with obvious satisfaction. At which Celia merely laughed.

Life seemed very flat and stale next day, and Celia was glad to see Faith in the afternoon. She had read in the paper that morning the name of Micheal's ship, starting from India, and wanted to talk of him to Celia.

"Of course he will not get the letters I have sent," she said, when, divested of bonnet and cloak, she sat with her feet on the fender, "but to have him home again—oh, Celia! God is too good to me. And if——" she paused.

"If he does not have to go out again, you will marry him."

"Yes. But I wasn't going to say that. If he is pronounced unfit, he will have to leave the service. You see, we don't know how much he is injured. He may be—oh dear—I hope he is not crippled for life. And yet—that he may not be fit for that kind of work again. His nerves may be shattered—or—Celia, don't look so shocked at me. Is it very wicked to hope that this accident has made it impossible for Michael to go on killing his fellow-creatures any more?"

Celia found herself unable to pronounce a judgment on this vital question. She could only shake her head and press Faith's hand.

"Suppose," she said, after a short pause, "that Michael does not have to quit the Air Force, what then? Will you not marry him?"

Faith looked away. Her lips trembled.

"I don't know—I can't tell you," she faltered. "It would be worse than ever. But I suppose . . . I don't think I could ever hurt Michael again. I shall never forget that hour when the telegram came."

"It must have been awful," Celia murmured.

"Isn't life a queer puzzle?" Faith went on. "We talk about free-will and yet can't command our own hearts—they command us. An emotion can sweep away all opinions, convictions, aspirations, resolutions. But what is the use of thinking and puzzling? Action is the only refuge. To be always *doing* something. I wonder idle people ever keep sane. I couldn't."

"Because your mind is active. I expect idle bodies are chiefly inhabited by idle souls. Your inhabitant is terribly alive, you know: so is mine."

Faith smiled. "I've never thought of my soul as an 'inhabitant' of my body," she said.

"Well, but isn't it? And a very mysterious inhabitant, too, 'in this clay carcase crippled.'[57] Take heart, Faith, and don't brood on problems, or meet troubles half-way. You are young, and life is all before you."

"So is death! And a nurse has to take all risks. There isn't a cottage I go into that may not be the home of concealed 'mysterious inhabitants' ready to pounce on my 'clay carcase,' Celia—germs of typhoid, diphtheria, scarlet fever and the like," declared Faith, as she rose and kissed her. "I must go now. Thanks for letting me talk off some of my trouble. I can't do so to Mother and Father: it hurts them too much. Remember me and Michael in your prayers, friend Celia."

"I will, indeed," Celia promised earnestly. To herself she thought: "Our next novel shall have Faith for heroine. I shall delight in describing her ash-blond hair, her grey-blue eyes, her apple-blossom tints, her dear little hard hands, her straight, gallant figure, her brave heart ready to face disease and death and any terrors but those of her own soul."

She could never think of Faith without a swerve of the mind to Lavanda, and the difference that lay between the lot of an eighteenth-century and a twentieth-century girl. And this sent her now to the diary, to read again poor Lavanda's outpourings of the heart. But she lighted first on a page early in the book that amused her and made her forget, for the moment, the diarist's sorrows:

> "I went with my Father and Mother yesterday to dine at the Medlicott's Mansion. I did have my Hair dressed the day

[57] From *The Rubáiyáat of Omar Khayyám*, translated by Edward Fitzgerald.

before and had to sit up with Pillows all Night which was vastly uncomfortable. But the Dinner did please me, not so much because of the dainty Dishes provided, but the Novelties. They had great Pies full of live birds and toads which did hop and fly about the Table when they were cut and made us all to shreek. One Frog hopt upon my Plate and I nearly fainted with Fright. But it was very diverting."

Further description of this banquet followed at length, the most appalling array of dishes, roast and boiled, fried and stewed, steeped in wine and oil, with sweets of every possible description. No wonder that poor Lavanda had to be given a 'vomiting mixture' that night, and her father had to be bled next day. But as the pages went on week by week and month by month, such feasts and descriptions of food became rarer and rarer. Celia could see the poor child immured in her room and given strange concoctions, cordials, electuaries, possets, as she grew worse and worse. Yet her spirit never failed, nor her love. Almost at the end she wrote, in handwriting perceptibly fainter:

"I have had a letter from R—at last. It was brought to me by Tabitha, from the Place we wot of. Tabitha hath been very good to me these months and I know she will never betray my Secret. But I cannot go to the Place now, being no more allowed to leave my Room, as indeed I have no Wish to do, for Walking tires me and my Limbs fail. I had a Bloody Flux yesterday and Doctor Lang came to see me. Yet did he not do me so much good as R—'s Letter, which assured me of his constant Love and Devotion. I believe could I have a Letter every Day and see my Dear Love I should soon be quite well again. But I dare not speak of him. Last time I did so speak my

> Mother was very angry and called him a 'vile schismatic.' If only I had been born a Quaker, or he a Churchman, that we might come together to be Wed!"

A few pages further on the last words were scrawled:

> "I can write no more. I can but put this in the coffer Tabitha hath found for me, with my dear Gulielma in her strange Attire. She will guard my Treasure and I have no fear that it will ever be found by my Parents. For Tabitha is True and Loyal to the Core of her Heart and she will never betray my Secret."

Celia thought of Faith's words about idle people and insanity. Poor Lavanda, forced to be idle, too sick to be active, could only brood on her unhappy love affair until she died. And died convinced that opposition to her love had killed her. Could she have been wed to her Richard, she would have been well.

Celia had her doubts about that, but of one thing she felt assured: that if the poor girl had been wedded to her Richard, she would not still be whispering in the night about her Treasure. She would have had greater treasures to love and cherish.

November trailed into December, with thick mists and heavy rains. Birds were silent, all save Robin Redbreast, who perched on Celia's fork when she dug a weed-haunted bed or border. She could afford to have help in her garden but once a week now, so it was necessary to do what she could herself. Weeds had spread everywhere, and grass sprawled over her stone paths, making them green and slippery to walk upon. An army of obscene black slugs stole forth from their lairs at night and devoured all the green things they liked. On the lighter and warmer nights Celia went out, with boiling water and salt in tin cans, a trowel and a torch, to wage war against the pests. It was unpleasant work, but she made herself do it, shuddering violently every time she doomed a marauder to a brine bath; and sometimes Anabel went with her to help.

"I suppose," said Celia one night, "these horrible creatures have as much right to life as I have; but I can't let them demolish all my young sprouts. After all, to a certain extent, might is right, and the race is to the swift, the battle to the strong. It seems a law of life."

"And why not?" demanded matter-of-fact Anabel, sharply. "You wouldn't have the race won by the slow and the battle by the weak, would you?"

As the rain season was followed by hard frosts, hail and snow, the slug family retired to their fastnesses, much reduced in numbers, and Celia had no call to venture out in her garden at night. Nor could she continue to weed and dig. The ground had set like iron. Her house grew colder and colder: the hall and passages were freezing, and there was no way of warming them save by an oil 'Perfection' stove, in which she invested.[58] There was a big old-fashioned fireplace, it is true, with an open hearth and great wide chimney; but that only made the hall, and the whole house colder, since she could not afford to have a fire there, and the icy wind blew down that chimney with a hollow roar when it was in a certain direction. She contemplated buying a screen to set before it, or having boards nailed across, but that would have involved expense. On quiet days the cold indoors was not so penetrating, but a north-easterly gale made its atmosphere arctic. The journey up to bed at night then became a real penance, and Celia was often kept awake by the cold, in spite of an oil-stove in her room.

---

[58] An oil lamp stove.

Christmas approached as the days grew darker and shorter. Celia missed John Pearl's daily visit, and threw herself into plotting a new book with feverish energy. She could no longer write at her table, even when it was drawn close to the fire, for her fingers became numb and she could scarcely hold a pen. She drew her wicker-chair close to the hearth and wrote in comfort, on a board laid across her knees. She and Anabel took all the exercise they could, in long walks and in chopping wood. Nothing happened to disturb their peace of mind. Anabel heard no more 'rats' over her head, and the whispering voice had ceased its plaint. When the wind moaned and cried about the house Celia sometimes fancied she heard an eerie wail that it could not quite account for; but she accused her own imagination and was not perturbed. Anabel spent her evenings in the sitting-room downstairs. She and Celia knew each other so well now that they did not feel obliged to talk and, when they did, could avoid subjects of disagreement. Anabel's room was cruelly cold, its small fireplace giving but little heat, and she found the carrying of coal and wood upstairs irksome. Although neither she nor Celia minded being alone, or were bored with their own society, they were both glad to have company in the uncanny old house, where each of them had experienced sensations of dread and fear. They did not refer to these, but remembrance lay at the back of their minds and made companionship desirable.

Faith ran in to see them often. Her delicate bloom had come back, and she looked happier than she had done for months, almost since Celia had known her. Michael's ship was reported at different ports. She always came to tell Celia, who did not take a daily paper, and the thought that it was bringing nearer and nearer every day the lover she had so nearly lost gave new life to the girl. Her beauty fascinated Celia, who could not take her eyes off Faith, as she sat, glowing in the firelight, looking like some fairy thing in homespun, with the flaxen tendrils of hair escaping from her close brown bonnet, eyes shining like stars and a laughing mouth. She could laugh now, poor Faith, in the hope of seeing Michael soon, and finding him less injured than her first fears had prophesied.

There were evening visits from John Pearl, always stimulating to Celia. Anabel listened to the enthusiastic planning and put in a dry sentence occasionally that had always the effect of making both of them hilarious. John called Anabel 'the antidote' or sometimes 'the extinguisher.' But with all her wet squirts she had not been able to put out *The Crystal Lamp*, now shining its brightest in a publisher's "dark and dismal den, dazzling its denizens." He loved to chaff Anabel, who had learnt to know him so well now that, it may be suspected, many of her sharp speeches were designed to provoke his repartee. They were all three merry together.

On a murky night, ten days before Christmas, he entered the house with a face so full of boyish glee that Celia knew instantly what had happened. And when he said solemnly, drawing his mouth down, "Bad news, bad news," she only laughed.

"I know better," she cried, as they went into the sitting-room. "What is it, John? Tell me quickly. Is it accepted?"

"Alas!" He laid his hat on the table and went to the fire to warm his hands. "Be prepared for the worst, Celia, and never despair."

She saw his eyes shining behind his glasses.

"You are a fraud," she said; "you know they haven't returned our book."

"No, that's true. They want to publish it, Celia, but they offer only a ridiculous royalty." He laughed and threw off his pretence. "Ridiculous, I mean, considering the inestimable worth of our masterpiece, for which no price would be too high for any discerning publisher to pay. But these pusillanimous worms only offer us ten per cent. on the first thousand. Can we humble ourselves to accept, friend Celia, or treat them with scorn and contumely?"

"We will embrace them with all our arms," cried Celia, dancing a few light steps, "the dear delightful creatures! I really think I must go up to town to-morrow and hug them."

"They mightn't like it," suggested Anabel.

"Only very gently, very tenderly," said Celia, "like a mother, in fact. How many of them are there, John? Not more than two, I hope."

"It's a company; but I daresay if you embrace the managing director it would be enough," he replied. "Here is the offer. It isn't really so bad after all, as they will pay quite a nice little sum in advance, and the royalty rises quickly. I will leave it with you to digest, and call for it in the morning. I promised to go back at once. News has come that Michael's ship will be in to-morrow, and Faith has gone to the Vicarage. She wants to go and meet him with the Vicar to-morrow, if she can possibly get off. We have a good deal to talk over at home. But I could not wait till the morning before telling you of this letter. It came by the last post."

When he had gone Celia threw herself at Anabel's feet and hugged her.

"Oh, I am the happiest woman on earth!" she cried.

"I don't see what there is to be so happy about," said Miss Flack, wonderingly.

CHAPTER TWENTY-TWO

MICHAEL Staniforth came home next day. Faith did not go up to town to meet him, as she could not procure anyone to take some of her cases in the village. But she saw him at the Vicarage that night, and so did her father. The sight was terrible indeed, and, for a time, put all thought of his book out of John Pearl's mind.

For Michael was very seriously injured, and appeared to him as a physical wreck. His right arm had been preserved, almost by a miracle, but its muscles had been so drawn and strained that it seemed doubtful whether he would ever be able to use it again. His face was dreadfully cut and disfigured, one eye being covered by a shade and, possibly blinded; though he said that was, as yet, uncertain. He had two ribs broken and other wounds. He had suffered from concussion and been unconscious for forty-eight hours, he told them, and he looked as if all his blood had been drained from him. When he arrived, with his father and a trained nurse from London, he was put straight to bed. John and Faith saw him only for ten minutes there, and left in a state of deep depression. Faith cried herself to sleep that night.

But next day the doctor said he was very much better; he had slept well, had no alarming temperature, and altogether justified the medical decision to allow him to be sent home and not to a military hospital, as it was at first feared. There was nothing, he declared, from which Michael might not recover in time, unless it was the use of his right arm and the sight of one eye. Loss of strength and nervous shock would keep him invalided for many weeks, even months; but his cuts were healing healthily, and his ribs would soon be sound. Faith took this news round to Celia that afternoon.

"If this ghastly accident is an answer to prayer," she went on, "I hope no prayer of mine will ever be answered again. I prayed, you know, that something would happen to turn Michael from the profession of slaying, and it has. He will never fight, or fly, again, they say. But oh, Celia, if he could but be as he was when he left England, I would gladly give him up to another who would make him happy. You don't believe me, but I would. It tortures me to see him lying there helpless and suffering. It tears my heart."

She broke down and sobbed. But Celia noted that, even in her self-reproachful misery, Faith had not altered in her decision not to marry a soldier. That if Michael had returned home safe and sound, she would still have refused him. And, being the woman she was, Celia could not comprehend this; could, indeed, hardly believe it. She could only rejoice that an obstacle had been removed between two lovers.

Faith's incomprehensible attitude, however, raised a question upon which she afterwards pondered. Suppose all the best women in the world refused to marry soldiers, what would happen? Would it put an end to war, or only make immorality easier and the lighter women mothers of the next generation? She recalled some lines of Coventry Patmore's:

> "Ah, wilful woman! She who may
> On her sweet self set her own price
> Knowing he cannot choose but pay" . . .[59]

---

[59] Based on 'Unthrift' by Coventry Patmore, where the line is 'Ah, wasteful woman, she who may…'

but that was surely fantastic, since it took for granted the solidarity of women when there are no two who think, or feel, exactly alike. They may follow a herd leader, or a fashion, it is true, but never expect them to combine in any revolt: least of all a revolt against man and their own instincts.

As soon as Michael was able to leave his bed, which happened a few days before Christmas, he had a long talk with Faith about the future. It began with his expressing a wish to break off their engagement. He was still very weak and, as soon as he had begun to move, very depressed. He had thought it all over, he said, and he was not going to tie Faith down for life to a miserable wreck of a man who might probably never be able to get a living for her. What did that matter, Faith had demanded, since she could get her own living, and his, too, if necessary? Michael had been shocked and disgusted at such a proposal. Did she think he was the kind of man who would be kept by his wife? To which Faith had retorted that she saw no reason why it was worse for a man to be kept by his wife than it was for a woman to be kept by her husband. And before he could protest again such a—to him—monstrous distortion of accepted ideas, she went on to say that it was not a question of being 'kept,' but of love. If you loved anyone, she declared, you were ready to share with him, or her, everything you had in the world; and to refuse simply meant that you did not love enough to give up your independence. Upon this Michael tried to make out a case for man's natural independence and woman's natural dependence, in which he was thoroughly worsted by Faith, who told him he was living in a former century and not the twentieth, or he would know that such ideas had been exploded about the time that steam gave place to electricity. They wrangled on till she saw he was flagging, and then she said: "Michael dear, we won't argue any more till after

Christmas. Of course you're going to get quite well and earn your living, like any other man. I won't promise to give up my profession, but I may have to if—any little Michaels come along. So there."

She laid her flushing, lovely face against his and he was conquered.

The Pearls were to have their cottage full for Christmas-tide, as both the sons were coming with their wives and children. David, the second son, had only one child, a baby nearing two, who would sleep with him and his wife in one room; the other available being occupied by Nicholas with his wife and small John, Phoebe was to sleep in Faith's room. There were great preparations to be made, and Mrs. Coles was called in to help the daily maid who served the Pearls. John was busy turning the laundry into a nursery; making a guard for the old open fireplace; hanging a swing from the ceiling, putting down matting and storing the room with old toys from past days, including a bald-headed and tailless rocking-horse, a pen for baby Ruth, and various arrangements for games. Leaves had to be put in the dining-table, cots and little beds put up in bedrooms; while Ruth made stacks of mince-pies and jellies, laid in stores of foods suitable and unsuitable for children.

They invited Celia and Miss Flack to tea and to spend the evening afterwards. The Christmas dinner was to be, of course, an early one, on account of the children. Faith was going to tea at the Vicarage, but would return home early. Anabel Flack was more excited at the thought of this little festivity than Celia expected her to be. She had not been to a Christmas party, she declared, for twenty years, and Celia had to help in choosing a new frock for the occasion, one ready-made from the Pearls' shop at Millborough. It was to be very sombre, as much as possible like every other dress she had worn for the last thirty years, but a little more fashionable and a trifle shorter in the skirt. Celia persuaded her also to indulge in silk stockings and court shoes with heels higher than those she habitually wore. For her own attire she fished out an evening gown she had bought at a sale two years before and remodelled it. It was a shot blue and green taffetas, whose shimmering effect had attracted her.

When she accepted the Pearls' invitation Celia had made a condition that they were all to be her guests on Boxing Day, and she felt a keen delight in this, her first effort at entertaining. She must have a small Christmas tree, and she planned a new and original game for the three little ones—an "adventure party." They were to travel on her old couch, supplemented by chairs, without any light but that from the fire (the lamp was to be taken outside) and were to go, in this coach, through the Steppes of Russia, pursued by wolves. Phoebe was to drive the horses (a large clothes-horse, covered by a rug), while Johnny kept off the wolves with a toy pistol, which Celia bought at the Stores. She, with Grannie and baby Ruth, and any more who could find room on the coach, were to be travellers and the rest were to be wolves, prowling about in the corners and growling horribly. But one was to appear suddenly through the door, declaring herself to be a Good Fairy, and she would instantly change all the wolves into friendly goblins, who would bring out good things from hidden places and lay a feast on the floor in front of the fire, where they would all sit and have tea, picnic fashion. For Celia had not a table large enough for ten guests to sit round.

Anabel entered into the spirit of her game, though she thought it rather silly for grown-up folk to pretend to be wolves and fairies. She bought a number of small toys for the Christmas tree and sweets for the feast. They were very merry over it.

On the morning of Christmas Eve a huge packing-case arrived

at Clew Lodge, and Celia found, to her unbounded delight, that it contained the restored spinet, now a very lovely relic of old times. It was not, to tell the truth, a remarkably good one, being almost undecorated and of no particular make; but its date, 1712, and its sweet tinkling tone, enchanted Celia, and she resolved to play it as soon as she could get her fingers into exercise again. It was so many years since she had touched a piano. She despatched a rapturous note to John by Mrs. Coles, who was helping to prepare for her party, and went dancing and singing about her work all the rest of the day, like a girl.

"I'll tell you what," said Anabel, as they sat at tea and Celia could not eat. "You are going the right way to knock yourself up and are thoroughly tired out. You ought to remember your age, and not carry on as if you were a young girl."

"How can I remember my ridiculous age," Celia retorted, "when I feel like eighteen, and should like to dance all night. I am going to suggest we dance *Sir Roger de Coverley* at my party, to the spinet. Just think of dancing Sir Roger to the spinet!"[60]

"You don't suppose those Quakers dance, do you?" said Anabel, "and besides, there won't be time. They will have to go soon after tea; it will be the baby's bedtime."

She added a minute later: "And you won't be feeling eighteen by then, my dear. You'll be worn out, and so shall I. We shall be thankful to sit quiet by the fire and go to bed early. You look tired to death now."

"And so I am," Celia confessed. "But it is a kind of tiredness I like, Anabel: a happy tiredness."

---

[60] One of the most popular country dances, usually performed at the end of an evening, hence its alternative name the Finishing Dance.

She felt the same 'happy tiredness' the next night after the Pearls' Christmas party, when she had romped with the children and played games with their parents till eleven o'clock. In the morning she had gone with Anabel to the early service at the Church, a fairly long walk to the end of the village and back, and prepared their dinner afterwards. It was an old-fashioned Christmastide, of the kind we associate with coaching days, heavy snow and robin redbreasts. Thus the walk, enchanting in its exquisite purity and frosty air on the way there, became a tiring one on the way back; when the sun had half melted the snow so that it clogged their shoes. But John Pearl fetched them after dinner in his car, and they were thankful to be carried; especially as snow had begun to fall again, and the wind had risen to a keen, northerly blast.

"It is my first Christmas at Clew Lodge," said Celia as they were at tea, "and here I am leaving it to a cold, dark loneliness. You know I have always thought of it as the Forsaken House," she turned to Mrs. Nicholas at her side, "but I never meant to forsake it myself."

"Still, it is only for such a few hours," said Mrs. Nicholas, "you will so soon be back in it."

"It will give its old ghosts a chance to enjoy themselves," said John Pearl, smiling. "I expect they have all their weird lights on, and are scrambling about the attics like a lot of rats—eh, Miss Anabel?"

The elder children, who had been eating chocolate biscuits and chattering over the coloured paper in which they were wrapped, paused to listen at the word 'ghosts.'

"John!" Ruth exclaimed, with a warning frown. But it was too late.

"Have you any ghosts in your house, Celia?" young John asked, with wide eyes.

"No, darling, not now," she said.

"Gramp was only joking, John," said his father, and the subject ended.

But when the children had gone to bed John's sons and their wives asked about the ghosts at Clew Lodge, and recounted to Celia what they had heard a long time back. Was there any truth in the stories? Was Clew Lodge really haunted?"

When Celia had told them of her experiences, in which they were greatly interested, their father quoted Longfellow:

> "All houses wherein men have lived and died
>   Are haunted houses. Through the open door
> The harmless phantoms on their errands glide
>   With feet that make no sound upon the floor."
>
> "The spirit world around this world of sense
>   Floats like an atmosphere, and everywhere
> Wafts through these earthly mists and vapours dense
>   A vital breath of more ethereal air."[61]

"Ugh!" Mrs. David shrugged her shoulders, "How uncanny! I'm glad I don't live in an old house."

"It is rather a lovely idea, I think," observed Celia, "to think of such a vital breath of spirit going through and about a house."

But she felt, nevertheless, a sudden dread of returning to Clew Lodge, with its 'harmless phantoms,' and she knew that Anabel felt it too. They were relieved when the subject was changed and, to clear the air of haunting mystery, John Pearl played *The Harmonious Blacksmith* on his harpsichord, ringing the anvil on its resonant tones,

---

[61] The poem 'Haunted Houses' by Henry Wadsworth Longfellow, previously mentioned on p. 64.

that seem so oddly to combine harp, bell and organ.[62] After that they sang carols until they woke one of the children overhead, and Celia said it was time to go.

John insisted on taking them home in his car, although both his sons offered to do so. The snow had been falling for some hours, and lay very thick in drifts here and there. A young moon had retired for the night, the wind had fallen, and he found it difficult to steer between the hedges. He drove very slowly and, even thus, found himself more than once perilously near to a crash into the rocky bank by the roadside. At last, when they had risen slightly and were nearing Clew Lodge, he stopped altogether. His head-lights showed nothing but a bank of snow, which had drifted almost to the hedges, and a sudden thickening of the fog hid them and the trees from view.

"I don't quite know where we are," he said to Celia, who sat beside him. "There seems to have been a heavy drift of snow just here. I had better get out and feel my way. We cannot be far from your house."

"Oh, do be careful," cried Celia. "Don't get buried in the snow."

"No fear." He stepped cautiously, and presently called out: "I thought so. We were heading for the bank at the turn. Now I know where to steer."

As he came back to the car, a faint light glimmered through the thick white cloud about them, from a point high up to the right of them. Celia gave a little gasp as John turned to see whence it came. She and Anabel rose in the car to look.

"There it is again!" exclaimed Anabel, in a tone of grievance,

---

62 The popular name for George Frederic Handel's *Air and Variations*, the final movement from Suite No. 5, written for the harpsichord.

as if she held her companions responsible for the haunting of Clew Lodge. She gave a little click of annoyance with her lips.

"A friendly light to help us on our way," said John Pearl, getting into his car again and starting the engine. "Surely sweet Lavanda is coming to our assistance. God rest her soul!"

They both noted Anabel's silence behind them. It indicated that her scepticism had worn thin. Otherwise she would have explained, as before, that there were burglars in Clew Lodge.

When they reached the gate they saw the light flicker and go out, as it had done before.

"Oh dear!" said Anabel, shivering, as Celia inserted her key in the door. "It is really awful, you know, Mr. Pearl, going into this house late at night. I am all goose flesh."

"I think it is good fun," he said, laughing; "you would have to pay for such a thrill at the theatre, you now, friend. I feel like a boy playing at pirates."

"I don't," said Celia, who had lighted the candle that stood ready and now led the way to the sitting-room, where a miawl met her, and softness rubbed against her legs. She had left food for Lob, and a window open at the back, but he wanted his belated supper. "I feel horribly cold and trembly," she added.

The house was impregnated with an icy, damp mist. Celia seized her bellows and began to blow into the embers of the fire they had banked up before leaving that afternoon. It was not quite out, and a few dry sticks, with a log, revived its dying cinders. They gathered round it to warm their cold hands and, as soon as it was well going, Celia put a kettle on it.

"Light your pipe, John, and sit down, while I make you a hot drink," she said. "This is the psychological moment to tap Mrs. Cole's elder wine. We used to drink it after skating when I was a girl."

"It is a pleasant enough poison," John said, "and I will certainly sup it; though what its effect will be on turkey and plum pudding I shudder to think of. But I will not light up, Celia, as I must not stay many minutes. Ruth will give me up for lost in the snow if I do not appear soon."

"I am wondering how you will ever turn the car," she said.

"I shall not try. She shall sit in the snow till daylight, as a punishment for her sins. That is, if you can give me some rugs and rags to cover her up a bit. But I shall never get her turned and home in this fog without coming to grief. I shall walk."

The hall rug and some blankets were tucked round Phyllida and she was left to her fate. John swallowed his elder wine, laced with nutmeg and other spices, and went off soon after midnight had rung from the Church steeple. He took with him Celia's hand torch and a stick with which to feel his way and avoid stepping into drifts. Celia had gone out with him to hold the light while he wrapped up the car. She returned to the house shivering violently.

"I vote," said Anabel, as she entered, "that we make up a rousing fire and sleep here. You can have the couch and I the armchair, which is very comfortable. We can fetch down our blankets and eiderdowns."

Celia agreed without a moment's hesitation. They went upstairs with a candle each, to bring down pillows and blankets. And, with a big fire roaring up the chimney, the sense of comfort was able to dispel the uncanny presence of things unseen that menaced them both and oppressed their spirits. They soon became drowsy, and no sound in the silent house disturbed them. If there were spirits invisible in the warm firelit room, they watched kindly and did not trouble the sleepers. Beneath its heavy white cloak of snow the old house slept peacefully.

CHAPTER TWENTY-THREE

THE sun rose on a bright frosty morning. John Pearl came at ten o'clock with his sons to fetch the car, and when they got her started—a work of time and effort—they ran her backwards and forwards between the Thatched Cottage and Clew Lodge to make a safe track for later in the day, and the evening's darkness.

Celia, full of excitement over her party, amused herself by hiding things for the children to find in her sitting-room, kitchen and hall. In the hall she lighted a great fire, and had already garnished it with holly and bay from the garden. The cakes and other good things for tea had also to be hidden where the wolf-goblins could find them. And all through her morning's joyous work Celia found herself repeating over and over again the absurd little jingle of a fairy tale, probably suggested by her Christmas tree, which was hidden in her back kitchen, ready to be brought out after tea. The couplet fitted itself to a tune in her mind, and she hummed it continually:

> "Shiver and shake, dear little tree,
> Gold and silver shower on me" . . .[63]

until she began to ask herself why it should haunt her, whether the 'gold and silver' had any connection with the Treasure that was never long out of her mind. And as the day wore on and the rhyme persisted, she began to experience a sensation of strange inner excitement. It was as if something were going to happen.

---

[63] From *Cinderella* by Jacob and Wilhelm Grimm.

She said so to Anabel, as they were sitting for a quiet half-hour after dinner.

"I believe something is going to happen to-day," she declared.

"Something always happens every day," said Anabel drily.

"I mean something . . . unusual. I have a queer belief that this day is going to put a mark on my life."

"You're always having queer feelings," was Anabel's reply; quite good-natured but sceptical. Celia said no more, but her head went on singing:

"Shiver and shake, dear little tree,
Gold and silver shower on me."

At three o'clock all the Pearls descended upon Clew Lodge, two car-loads. The cars were parked in her stables, which had been swept and garnished by Coles that morning for their reception. When all the outer garments had been shed upstairs in Anabel's room, where a fire was burning, the Adventure Party started off on its perilous drive through the wolf-haunted Steppes of Russia. The room was lighted only by one candle. The wolves were extremely fierce; the pistol was fired at them as quickly as fresh caps could be adjusted. Their howls of dismay and withdrawals caused the children shrieks of delight. Small Ruth was frightened at first, but revived on being told that the wolves were really Daddy and Mummie and Uncle Nick. Everything went off as Celia had planned it, and by half-past four the friendly goblins had laid a sumptuous tea in front of the fire, where they all squatted round to enjoy it. The lamp was brought in and two more candles lighted to add to the brightness. These and the lamp were banished again after tea, when the Christmas tree was brought in, illuminated with its tiny candle flames. It filled the dark, wainscoated room with an atmosphere of its own, an atmosphere of Anglo-Saxon origins and memories of a day long past. Celia recalled her old delight in *Carl Krinken's Christmas Stocking*, in Andersen's and Grimm's *Fairy Tales*. The little rhyme came floating back into her mind. She sang it to the children::

"Shiver and shake, dear little tree,
Gold and silver shower on me."

and they caught it up gleefully.

In the dark shadows of the room strange things seemed to lurk. Celia, watching the flicker of topaz flame on the childish faces, hearing their little excited cries and ripples of laughter, thought strangely of life surrounded by death; thought of Lavanda, a child in that wainscoated chamber, perhaps dancing round a Christmas tree—she was mentally vague as to the date of its introduction into English homes—or plucking plums from a dish of snapdragon.[64] And then Lavanda, in a chair by the fire, wan with love-sickness and disease, watching the flames leap up the chimney from the Yule log and waiting for the grisly skeleton with the scythe. Celia could see her there; could almost see the spectre in the shadows. The room seemed full of some mysterious element she could not fathom. In the midst of all the fun she had so happily organised her nerves were shaken by an unseen force, a strange inner excitement. Again she felt, as she had said to Anabel, "something was going to happen."

The vision of Lavanda, that seemed to steal out of the shadows, brought to her mind the promise she had made weeks before, of which the child, Phoebe, had, several times, reminded her. So when

64 A party game in which fruit and nuts—typically raisins, almonds, figs and plums—were snatched from a bowl of flaming brandy.

the tree had been completely dismantled and the children had tired out their elders in a wild romping game, she brought out the little wooden trunk and disclosed Gulielma.

Its queer waxen face and black staring eyes gave them all a shock; the same shock it had given Celia and Anabel when they first saw it. A little shudder ran through them.

"I think it's horrid. It's like a witch," said Johnny, drawing back from the table on which the box was laid. Baby Ruth, in her mother's arms, turned away and began to whimper.

"It is indeed like a mummy," said Mrs. Nicholas.

"May I hold it?" asked Phoebe, in an awed tone.

As Celia took the doll out of its ragged silk and paper wrappings a sudden thrill seemed to dart along her nerves. She had not touched it before. It was John Pearl who had taken it out of the box, to find the diary beneath, and laid it back again. She put it into Phoebe's arms, and the child carried it to the fireside, where she sat down to nurse it with an odd expression on her little face; a mixture of repulsion and interest. Celia noted it, noted also that Phoebe had imagination, like her grandfather. She was trying to find in the two-century-old doll a story of her own.

"But we want to see the diary as well, if we may," said Nick, and Celia brought it forth to show them.

They were eagerly scrutinising it, as it went from hand to hand, with many ejaculations of interest, when a sharp cry from Phoebe arrested them. She jumped up and ran to Celia with the doll, whose outer garments she had taken off.

"Look! Look!" she exclaimed, "Gulielma hasn't got any undies—only stiff paper wrapper round and round. Look!"

She put the doll into Celia's arms as she spoke, and again Celia felt that same thrill of premonition. lds round its body were of manuscript. She turned to John Pearl with dilated eyes.

"Oh, John! What is it?" she cried. And into her mind came words she had read somewhere in Lavanda's diary: "My poor little Gulielma in her strange attire." She had thought vaguely, "why *strange*?" The dress, though strange to the twentieth century, was surely not strange to the eighteenth. Was this, then, the treasure Lavanda had concealed? And why was it a treasure? Her unspoken question was answered by John Pearl, who was unfolding the manuscript from the body of the doll, which he held close to the lamp and examined.

"We've found it at last," he said quietly, looking at her over the top of his glasses. "The Treasure is here, Celia, and, unless I am much, much mistaken, a priceless one."

He looked round upon his family with a shining light of joy and triumph in his grey eyes.

"What do you say to an original document by William Penn?" he asked them, with a laugh of sheer delight.

"Father! You don't mean it! How can you tell?" they cried, almost together.

"I've seen his script. I know it well. I am certain it is his. We have only to find the signature. And if I am right——"

"Then Celia's fortune is made," ejaculated David. "Congratulations, friend Celia."

They all turned to her. She had sunk into a chair, very white and still.

"I knew something was going to happen to-day," she murmured and, closing her eyes, lost consciousness.

When she came round they were all standing by her, with faces of deep concern, while Anabel had a wine-glass of brandy and water in her hand.

"She's been doing too much. I told her she would knock herself up," said that lady, severely. "I am always having to remind her she's not eighteen. Here! drink this up, Celia, and for goodness' sake keep quiet. I'll put the things away."

"Miss Flack is a jewel," said John Pearl, "and we can leave friend Celia in her capable hands. I will put the doll, with the diary, in the locked drawer, and come round to examine the papers to-morrow. Now, children—away at once."

When they had gone, Celia, still lying back in her chair, began faintly: "Didn't I tell you, Belle, that something was going to——"

"Yes, you did, and that's enough of it," snapped Anabel before she could finish. "You're going to bed now, this minute, and I'm bringing you up a cup of hot milk and bovril. I've no patience with you people who live on your nerves and never know when you've done enough. You may thank your lucky stars you are not dead. I never saw anyone look more like it than you did. This is the second time you've given me a fright, and I can tell you my own nerves won't stand it."

Meekly Celia crawled upstairs on her friend's arm, for her heart was jumping strangely, and had a queer tendency to stick in her throat. The capacity for excitement, for feeling pleasure, anticipation or curiosity, seemed to have departed from her. Nothing was left but a feeble desire to examine those papers John Pearl had locked away, too feeble to produce any effort. Her mind had hardly reacted to his triumphant announcement: it was not functioning as usual. After her Bovril and milk she fell asleep peacefully, just hearing, as she entered dreamland, a whispered word 'Treasure,' and something about a little green tree showering down gold and silver.

CHAPTER TWENTY-FOUR

TWO months later, when all proofs of *The Crystal Lamp* had been corrected, and the New Year had brought with it amazing hopes and promises, Celia could look back upon that period with wonderment and thankfulness that she was still alive. For after the night of her party she had remained for weeks in a perilous state of nervous prostration, under a doctor who commanded a complete rest from all worry or excitement. She had overtaxed her heart and strength those last months of the year, he said, supported by a nervous system that could carry on with apparent ease, under certain conditions, for a long time; then flag, suddenly and completely, without warning. Miss Flack had taken charge of everything, and put up a bed in Celia's room, while Faith went in every day, morning and evening.

The papers that had been found wrapping the doll remained in their locked drawer, and, if Celia spoke of them, Anabel promptly changed the subject. It was not until a very definite change for the better in Celia's pulse and temperature had taken place, that she was allowed to see John Pearl and talk about their discovery.

Sitting in a low chair by her fire, in a worn blue dressing-gown, with her thick russet hair tied by a ribbon behind and falling loosely about her face, she looked almost girlish. Her greenish-grey eyes were shining with pleasure, and there was a pink glow in her cheeks. John could see that it was necessary to go warily, not to excite her, and his manner was, therefore, even quieter and cooler than usual. He had told her about the proofs that were coming in and that he was going through; had brought the second set for her to read at leisure, and suggested that a week hence they should go over them together. He had stayed but half an hour, and carried away with him the papers they had found.

Next day he came to see her again, and this time did not find it so easy to keep from exciting her. For he was powerfully excited himself. He had found William Penn's signature to the papers and what was, he declared, even more important and valuable, a letter to his wife which he, John, believed had never been seen since the time it was written; or, at least, since the time that Richard Butler had found it and put it into the hands of Lavanda Selcroft.

The manuscript was of a pamphlet printed in the year 1675, which John Pearl had seen, but was sure that the original had never before been found. Its title-page was as follows:

> "Saul smitten to the Ground: Being a Brief but *Faithful Narrative* of the Dying Remorse of a late Living Enemy (To the People called Quakers and their Faith and Worship) Matthew Hide; Attested by Eye and Ear-Witnesses, whereof his Widdow is one. *Published in Honour to God, For a Warning to Gainsayers and a Confirmation to the Honest-hearted.* With an *Appendix* both to *Foes ad Friends* on this occasion, by William Penn."

How this manuscript, with the short but tenderly affectionate letter to his wife, had come into the possession of Richard Butler, was never likely to be discovered. One could only surmise the papers had been found in William Penn's house at Warminghurst, afterwards destroyed by fire (or so it was supposed), since it was known that the house had been sold in 1702 to a Butler, in whose family it had been till 1789. Celia must see the site of this house, with its ancient barn remaining and quiet little church close by, as soon as she was well enough to drive so far, John said, as he left her, warned by the eager flame in her eyes.

For it had sent up her temperature, this dangerously exciting news, with all its implications, and accelerated her heart-beats. Anabel Flack was angry when she saw Celia after he had gone, and he was not permitted to see her again for several days. But she had given him permission to take the papers up to London for examination by experts (after insuring them, which he was careful to do), and by the time Celia came downstairs and took up the threads of life, news was flashing round the world of a wonderful discovery, and there were paragraphs in all the papers about an autograph manuscript and a letter by William Penn found in a hunted manor house, and through the medium of spiritual phenomena. It was far too good a story for journalism to disregard.

The publishers of *The Crystal Lamp* knew their business well enough to make this strange discovery of the Pen MSS. and an eighteenth-century diary a matter for skilful advertisement. Paragraphs began to appear in which the authors of a new romance were given as the discoverers of these important documents, and the book was rushed through the press as quickly as possible: which is to say, as quickly as John Pearl and Celia could—and would—correct two sets of proofs. For he refused to be hurried or to let the book be printed before Celia was well enough to go through the paged proofs with him. But before the book was ready there came an offer from Philadelphia for the Penn MSS., and Celia was faced by the necessity of making a decision whether to accept or refuse a hundred thousand dollars. This necessity fretted her so terribly that she could think of nothing else, day or night, and was in danger of a serious relapse.

But John Pearl settled the question for her decisively. She must not, he declared, allow the letter to leave England, or to lie anywhere but in the Quaker stronghold. With the Society of Friends she might make her own terms. The MS. pamphlet might go to Pennsylvania.

It ended in her accepting £50,000 for it, and in giving the Letter to the Society of Friends. She had English offers for it. They poured in upon her till she was dazed, and for some weeks the temptation of selling it tormented her. She argued with herself that she could do so much with the money: that the Letter would remain in England, would be treasured as it ought to be and shown when required. But eventually her soul conquered. She thought with distaste of the rich men who coveted it simply for its fame; who cared less for William Penn and the Quakers than they cared who won the Derby, and who would, probably, sell it to the highest bidder in America. Better let the Town Museum of Philadelphia enshrine it than that. She refused all these offers, and her spirit went free from that moment.

The offer made her from the Society of Friends was absurdly small after the others. She considered it but a very few days, and then she presented the Letter, through John Pearl, to the Society. This made her supremely content, but she did not feel so after accepting the Philadelphia offer. She was overcome with qualms of self-disgust at her own mercenary weakness.

"I cannot bear to think of the manuscript going to America," she said to John Pearl, when the matter was concluded. "It makes me feel like Judas and the thirty pieces of silver. And I am afraid of Lavanda. It is ridiculous, I know, but I feel that she will haunt me more than ever. And I can echo her lament. I shall be crying in my sleep, not 'I had to leave my Treasure,' but 'I sold my Treasure for filthy lucre.' " She smiled ruefully. John smiled, too, as he laid his hand over hers.

"My dear, we all have to leave our treasures on earth, sooner or later," he said.

"I know. The time cannot be far distant when I must leave my dear home—and you, John, whose friendship is my dearest treasure," she murmured under her breath, and without looking at him.

"No, not that. You will never lose that. Whatever happens we are one, Celia. Friendship like ours cannot be broken. It is one of the treasures that neither moth nor rust can corrupt, nor death destroy."

They were silent a few moments. She raised her eyes, full of tears, to his.

"I believe that too," she faltered.

"Of course you do." He pressed the hand he held and left it. "And so, knowing that treasures of the spirit are incorruptible and bounded by no time or space, why regret that you have sold an earthly treasure to those who know how to value it. We love that link of written words by a long-dead hand, but it is perishable, just as the dollars you receive will be. No one can take the imperishable memory of that great man from us, and we have here, in the sacred ground about us, traditions to keep that memory a vital—a living thing. If, over there, they have the tradition, the witness to his Holy Experiment, we have, in this country, the meeting-house in which he worshipped; in Buckinghamshire another such meeting-house and his mortal remains. I like to think that the Treasure has gone to our brothers in the New World, Celia, where it will be revered, as all Friends must revere it."

"I read in all the papers a reproach . . . " she began.

"Do you really care what outsiders say, Celia?"

"And as for the 'filthy lucre,' " he went on, smiling, "it will not be selfishly spent—I know that. Do you remember our conversation about the fortune that might come to us, and how you would use it?"

"A bathroom and gardener," she said self-scornfully.

"A hostel for pilgrims, eventually—or was it a convalescent home? I forget all the schemes. But there are excellent ways of spending money, friend Celia, let me tell you, once you have it. And spiritual content follows money well spent. What is the old proverb, 'A fortune well-spent brings a life of content,' is it? If not, that is how I would put it. If you expend your fortune on Misty Vale, surely the benign spirit of William Penn will smile upon you."

"And," he continued, "the gentle soul of Lavanda will be appeased."

The weeks ambled on till that heavenly morning in the month of daffodils and primroses, when a large and heavy parcel arrived for Celia from the publishers, and she knew that their precious book had come. Her fingers trembled with eagerness as she untied the knotted string and unfolded the many wrappers. It lay there, the darling thing in its coloured wrapper, picturing a Crystal Lamp with a shadowy background, its cover of delphinium blue, its wide margins and small clear print; for the publishers had given it an attractive setting. She adored it silently for a few minutes, and then ran upstairs so quickly that her heart beat too fast, and she had to lean against the door of Anabel's room to breathe, as she gasped out:

"It's come—our book! I am going to tell John."

As she tried to walk slowly, against the spring of her dancing spirit, along the road, she felt as if April were rejoicing with her. The larks above seemed to be singing of her book; their song trembled in the air as her excitement trembled in her heart. Squirrels lolloped across the road in their funny, hunching gait, and took flying leaps from branch to branch of the budding trees, all in a delicate filigree of green. Violets under the hedges sent, here and there, a whiff to greet her, and the banks were starred with primroses. Celia thought of the year before, when she had first entered her Forsaken House, and how wonderfully that year had sped. Was the old house happy now, as she was: were its haunting spirits laid? She felt that it must be content now that it was no longer forlorn and forsaken, now that it was loved, as a sentient thing is loved; now that the children had romped in its sad deserted rooms, and flowers were again springing everywhere, unchoked by weeds, in its old garden. It rejoiced her heart to think that; to know that now she might have her daily gardener to tend the precious green children of the earth, to prune the trees and rose-bushes, to grow every kind of delicious vegetable and fruit. To know, moreover, that she could afford to fill her house with friends whenever she wished, and with others needing rest and change from the hard necessities of life. Already her mind was dwelling on one or two women she had known in her London days, wearied and worn with shop or office work, yet unable to pay for seaside or country lodgings without drawing from scanty savings set by for rainy days.

She found John Pearl digging in his garden, clad in a grey flannel shirt and very dirty old trousers, with his thick white hair standing up all over his head. Anyone less like the author of a seventeenth-century romance it would be hard to find. Ruth was with her, and she called "John!"

"Hail!" He looked round a saw Celia. She waved her small parcel over her head.

"Joy, joy, wassail!" she cried. "The child has arrived, clad in silver and gold—and trailing clouds of glory! Wash your hands quickly."

"Are you pleased with it, Mother?" he asked, as the three of them walked to the house together.

"I haven't seen it yet," said Ruth, smiling.

"I didn't mean you—obtrusive woman—I meant Celia. If she isn't the book's mother, who is?"

"I suppose you think you are the father," said his wife, smiling.

"Of course I do."

They were all in laughing mood. John examined his book, with clean hands, and pronounced it all right.

"The jacket might have been a shade less obvious and more ethereal," he said, "otherwise they have done us very well, I think, Celia. Doesn't it look attractive? Don't you want to read it?"

"Yes, indeed. It looks just the kind of book I shall like," she said, entering into his spirit. "I foresee the time when we shall spend half our time chuckling over it by the fire on winter nights."

"We may even pretend to ourselves that we wrote it!" He laughed. "Are you going to present me with an autographed copy, Celia?"

"Preposterous man! Half the copies are yours, of course."

"I say—suppose we buy up the whole edition and scatter copies in all the libraries. Then the publishers would have to get out another and put 'second edition,' or 'tenth thousand,' or some agreeable legend like that, on it. Wouldn't it be fun?"

"Not at all. If it doesn't sell on its own merits I don't want it to sell at all."

"Virtuous female. Do you think books ever sell on their own merits? I've heard it doubted. But what does it matter to us? We have it printed and bound, and that ought to be enough for any reasonable being. What do you say, Ruth?"

"I think you are both very foolish children," said his wife, "and talking a lot of nonsense."

"That is because you are not the happy parent of a book," remarked John, looking owlishly wise at her. "You've only had flesh and blood children—and only three of them. We may have forty thousand, scattered all over the world. Think of that, woman, and hide your diminished head. You can't compete with Celia—in numbers, anyway."

Faith came in presently and joined the chorus of delight. The book, she declared, was perfect. Anyone who did not wish to read it, on sight, could have no taste and no sense. She was in very good spirits these days. Michael had found a post in London, and they had fixed their wedding day. It is true the post was in the Admiralty, which was, in Faith's eyes, nearly as bas as the Army, but, at least, it was not active service. He would never wear uniform again. She asked Celia for a signed copy of the book as a wedding present, and Celia promised her one especially bound, with her autograph in gold on the cover.

"But your father will have three copies," she said. "I could not carry more than one to-day."

"I want but one, with your name written in it, Partner," he said. "You must keep the rest, and I am writing for a dozen copies to give to my friends and relations. 'Behold!' I shall say, 'your old friend, John Pearl, in a new rôle as novelist.' They will never know that I merely typed it and corrected a few of your worst errors, but will give me credit for the major part—being a man—whilst thou, friend Celia, art naught but a woman."

He wore the air of a schoolboy who has been given a football.

When their first cheque arrived there was more rejoicing. By that time, Celia, with a bank account swollen by the American cheque, was feeling a very rich woman, and the English one seemed small enough beside it. But the news sent with it was worth more. For, said the publishers, orders for *The Crystal Lamp* were coming in at the rate of five hundred a week, and a second impression was in the press. Their skilful advertising of the book, as by the owner of the now world-famous Penn manuscripts and eighteenth-century diary found in a haunted house, had created curiosity and interest. Celia was inundated by letters from photographers anxious for a sitting, and by editors demanding her portrait 'with personal notes.' Numbers of people from London called at Clew Lodge, begging to see over it and view the diary; till Celia, complacent at first, had to affix a notice to her gate denying admittance except on important business.

She had several very tempting offers for Lavanda's journal, but declined them all. It should go, she decided, to the British Museum at her death, but she must keep her one precious Treasure while she lived. For, although she had a feeling that William Penn belonged to the Quakers and she had no right to keep his MSS. from them, with the diary it was different. Lavanda was hers: she had spoken to her; she had lived and died in her house, her dear forsaken house. To sell Lavanda's diary would be like selling Lavanda herself. Celia could not do it.

In July Faith and Michael were married. And they made their vows at The Blue Idol. The Vicar was not pleased, of course. It was but natural that he should wish his son's wedding to be solemnised according to the rites of the English Church. But a bride can hardly be gainsaid in such a matter. Faith did not wish to be married in a 'steeple house,' or by elaborate ceremony, and she was as stubborn over this as she had been in her pacifism. To stand behind the table where William Penn had stood, where he had been moved to speak those thoughts that filled his great mind and winged his soul into every quarter of the civilised world, there to take Michael for her husband, seemed to Faith a privilege few may enjoy, and the ideal spot upon which to consecrate her love.

As she stood there in her white frock and hat, as daintily tinted as a Faïence shepherdess, with her Michael by her side and their parents before them, friends all round, and sweet airs blowing in at The Blue Idol windows, Faith spoke her wedding vow with more firmness than Michael had done before her, as he was obviously nervous and constrained. Her sweet voice rang out clearly.

"I take this, my friend, Michael Ambrose Staniforth, to be my husband, promising, by divine assistance, to be unto him a loving and faithful wife until it may please the Lord, by death, to separate us."

So simple as that it was. The preliminaries beforehand had been less simple, and the civil side was completed when the Registrar of the local Meeting came forward with the certificate of marriage for them to sign. It was signed, also, by the Vicar and John Pearl.

In the short meeting for worship that followed, it was the Vicar who broke silence with a few words of blessing, and a reference to the mystical union of the bride and bridegroom. After another short silence Faith and Michel went out, and the Registrar gave all Friends present the opportunity of signing the certificate if they wished to do so. The wedding was over.

The village folk felt injured. A wedding is a public event, and the good folk who knew and loved Faith, who knew and loved, also, their Vicar, considered themselves deprived of a little pageant that was their right. The Blue Idol was too far from Misty Vale for many to attend, although Faith had chartered a charabanc for her friends and some of her oldest patients. But there was a wedding feast in the Vicarage garden that evening, given by the fathers of the bride and bridegroom, which went far to console the villagers. As Mrs. Moore said to her customers at the Stores afterwards: "It was a right-down banquet, though they did call it a tea, and we didn't miss much in the ceremony, I'm told. Them Quaker weddings are very plain and slow affairs, no bridesmaids and nothing much worth seeing."

There were speeches at the feast. One speech made Faith frown by its expressions of pathetic regret that the bridegroom could no longer serve his King and Country. But this passed unremarked and unchallenged. The young couple went off in a car to the station at Millborough, and the rest of the daylight was spent merrily in the old Vicarage garden, where tennis, croquet and all sports dear to the village men and maids were kept in full swing till nightfall. Celia had played till she was tired, and was thankful when John Pearl offered to drive her and Anabel home.

They did not speak much on the way. She knew he was feeling the loss of Faith, and his thoughts were all with her. But so were Celia's. It was not until they came to Clew Lodge that her own joys and privileges took possession of her again ad she felt once more the charm of home.

CHAPTER TWENTY-FIVE

WHEN Leslie Hale's wife died some years later, he went to call on Celia. She gave him a kindly welcome, not without misgivings, and for a long while he talked of himself and his loneliness. Celia was very sympathetic until her patience gave out, when she asked:

"But what about your children, Leslie? Are they no comfort to you?"

"Oh, well," he hesitated. "Of course they are, in a way. They are good children, but they're growing up fast, you know, Celia, and will, I expect, soon be leaving me."

"Why should they? You say Wilfred comes home every night and Ethel has left school, so that you have her."

"Ethel has a boy hovering round. I expect she will soon be engaged and married," he said gloomily, "and Wilfred is always out somewhere on his motor-bike. They're not like a *wife*, Celia."

"Of course not."

She thought: "What a silly speech—and how like Leslie to make it!"

"Of course I was very fond of poor Dora," he went on. "She was a good wife to me, and I miss her very much. But you know, Celia, she was not my first love."

"Few men marry their first love," said Celia, airily; "it is the exception rather than the rule, Leslie."

"I have only really loved one woman," he declared, looking at her very hard, "and you know who that is, Celia."

Celia could find no word to say, so she held her peace. She

was conscious of a great longing for Anabel to come in.

"I want *you*," he breathed. "Only you, Celia darling. When—I mean, after a decent interval—will you marry me?"

"No, Leslie."

She spoke firmly. There should be no possibility of his mistaking her.

"Why not?"

"Because I do not wish to be married."

"You are waiting for Mr. Pearl?"

Anger flamed into her eyes. She made an effort to control it.

"That is a thing you should not say, Leslie," she said; "it is unwarranted and insulting. I hope John Pearl will long have his dear little wife with him."

"Do you mean to say, then," Leslie demanded, "that you prefer to spend the rest of your life with that little old maid to living with me?"

"Yes, Leslie, I mean just that," she said quietly. "We are happy together, two old maids. Too old to marry and change our ways; too happy to wish for any change."

"Of course you are rich now," he said bitterly, as if he regretted her independent position.

"That is true. And I have always been too rich to marry for money—or a home," she said.

All her sympathy and compassion for Leslie had vanished. She felt only anger. But her mood changed when he put his head in his hands and wept.

"I am very sorry, Leslie," she faltered, "really sorry that I can't return the love you have given me. Believe me, I have valued it. But have never concealed from you that you are not the man I want to marry. Have I ever, Leslie?"

"No. You have not," he confessed, raising his head and getting up. "It has been all on my side, I know. Oh, why *can't* you love me, Celia?"

She looked straight into his eyes.

"Because you are not my man," she said. And after a pause, she added: "I love my house more than I love you, Leslie."

It was cruel perhaps, but the truth is sometimes a cure and she felt it necessary now. He went away without another word.

When he had gone she drew a long breath of relief and went out into her garden. In the courtyard, where her nasturtium bed had not yet been caught by the late autumn frost she stood looking at the pent roofs in their grey slabs, the climbing ivy and woodbine whose leaves were dropping, and the queer old chimneys where no longer jackdaws chattered. How dear it was to her, her once forsaken house; how much dearer than Leslie Hale, for all his devotion! She had felt a pang at saying farewell to him; it was like a farewell to Romance, for she knew that he had gone out of her life for ever. But it was not so poignant as a farewell to Clew Lodge would have been. Leave it for the sake of Leslie Hale—never! Nor for any other man, she wished to believe; but of that she could not be so sure. The old house had a human rival. And yet, she told herself, he was no rival. He was bound up with it in her thoughts, in her heart. Her only longing now was that, in the years that were left to them, she and John Pearl might write more books together, and their relation remain as it was—a close, imperishable friendship, founded on sympathy, understanding and love: love of the same heavenly things—of beauty, nature, art, humankind and the God of them all.

. . . . .

Sometimes in years to come she seemed to hear the soft lamenting whisper by her pillow:

"I had to leave it—my Treasure . . . "

and her heart echoed Lavanda's plaint. She knew that she too, would have to leave her earthly treasure, her dear, once forsaken house that she had rescued and cared for; that had responded so perfectly to the love she had bestowed upon it. But never again would it be deserted and forlorn, since she was leaving it, with an endowment, to Faith, who would cherish it and devote it to the service of others.

And whatever flight her spirit finally made, Celia hoped she might not quite leave behind her the things and friends she loved: that she could sometimes hover near them to cheer or comfort. Although she desired earnestly that the part of herself she left behind in her books might persist after her earthly life was ended, she desired still more that her memory might remain green in the hearts of those dear to her.

www.ingramcontent.com/pod-product-compliance
Lightning Source LLC
Chambersburg PA
CBHW020933310726
48980CB00007B/750/J

* 9 7 8 1 9 1 7 1 1 3 0 2 1 *